The Garrote

Carmel McAlistair Mysteries, Book Two

Liz Graham

OneEar Press

Copyright

To Iona, the painstaking editor, Kathryn and Bev, my Beta readers——I couldn't do this without you guys. And thanks also to Allan, who can explain computerese in plain English!

My heartfelt thanks to WANL (Writers' Association of Newfoundland and Labrador) for their work and for introducing me to Joanne Soper-Cook, whose help was invaluable, and also to the Writers' Federation of Nova Scotia for short-listing this manuscript in the Atlantic Writing Competition-Unpublished Manuscript Division. That was such a boost!

Chapter 1

The Mississippi Preacher Man. It was a childish nickname, and she couldn't remember who she'd first heard use it. Probably Phonse.

"The Lord of Misrule is upon us!" The man, known more respectfully as Reverend Wilson, raised his soft southern voice and searched the small crowd gathered before him as he stood on a wooden bench at the War Memorial in Portugal Cove. His brown homespun robe flapped in Newfoundland's North Atlantic December wind. Some of the people––those of his faithful congregation––stood straight and met his eye with concern. They too were dressed simply, with the women in plain cotton skirts and the men in dark suits from another age. Others in the crowd shuffled, embarrassed for him perhaps, but wanting to see the show to its end. Didn't often get entertainment like this so far out of the city.

"I am a weak man. I have sinned, yet I did atone for my deeds. I have been exiled to this wilderness to do God's work amongst the heathen, the ignorant and the poor." Some of the native Covers caught this reference to themselves with an air of mild offense, but he carried on: "As God sent trials to Job, so is He testing me. Even as I foreswore all worldly goods, so did God give them back to me tenfold. Yet did He lay a burden upon me beyond belief––beyond what He would ask of any man." He brought his fist down through the air as if smiting the evil therein. "What has been sanctioned by God has been torn asunder, to reveal a cesspool of filth so unimaginable, so unnatural, and the root of all this evil is the love of money. Yes, money, my friends! Do I look like a rich man?" He was thundering now. "I ask again, do I look like a wealthy man? No, you say, no, Reverend Wilson. You are a simple man."

The faithful nodded. The unfaithful locals held their peace, keeping their cynicism to themselves for now.

"No more, I say! No more will I carry this burden of wealth and the unspeakable slime that accompanies it. The love of money is the root of all evil. I have tried to be a good man. God knows I have tried, yet it was this very goodness that allowed this state of affairs."

"You are a good man, Reverend Wilson!" cried out a tall man. He sounded alarmed. "We all believe in you!"

"Now the Abbot of Unreason has shaken my life, my very home, and I have seen the light! All that God gave me will go where it belongs, where it should have gone, to be used for his work. I shall cut off my own ear to stop Satan from whispering his evil and spreading his poison." He stopped and looked around at the small congregation as if seeing them for the first time, his shoulders drooping in defeat as he searched for understanding and forgiveness. He brought his eyes up over the crowd, up to where the mountains met the endless sky. "Thy will be done," he whispered, and then clambered down from the bench to be surrounded by his people.

Carmel McAlistair watched the small group make its way up Cemetery Lane to their church. Reverend Wilson walked like a man carrying a heavy burden. He looked broken, but not insane despite his rantings. She hefted her grocery bags in her hands and turned toward her home.

Whatever the Reverend's personal troubles, he was a good orator. She'd never heard him speak before, as he and his congregation tended to keep to themselves, unsullied by the worldliness around them. This public denouncement was unusual. She'd seen him around Portugal Cove, of course.

Reverend Wilson was hard to miss in the monk's habit he always wore. His congregation, likewise, were distinctive by their dress and they never really mixed with their neighbours. Affectionately nicknamed the Mississippi Preacher Man (because he was from somewhere in the southern United States), Wilson had arrived in Portugal Cove some years ago with his people, bought the old deconsecrated Anglican church and the land behind it, and started a communal carpentry business. They called themselves the "Flock of the Innocent," and quietly went about their business of doing good.

Like the Yukon, Alaska, and other extreme lands, the island of Newfoundland attracted odd characters. The vast wildernesses within its thousands of kilometres of cold coastline could make room for large personalities; there was space here even for those who'd been rejected by mainstream society. Artists, entrepreneurs, pirates, and––now––evangelistic preachers from the southern US. Perhaps they had space to breathe in these sparsely populated regions, away from the madding crowds.

Carmel turned down the steep lane to North Point Road leading to the outskirts of her small town. Just where the mountain erupted from the ocean-washed rocks, the pavement ended and the gravel began. This was the only indication that she was about to enter St. Jude Without, the tiny, strange community that she had made her home.

Reverend Wilson's house was the last one in Portugal Cove on this road. She'd never wondered at the placement before, or questioned why he lived so far removed from his church a mile away. Pausing to catch her breath, she looked curiously up his driveway. It was a grand house, with its pillars and portcullis in front, hidden behind a solid row of salt-eaten cedars lining the road. Not the typical Newfoundland saltbox, it was more reminiscent of Scarlett O'Hara's residence––on a smaller scale, of course. Come to think of it, it was a pretty wealthy house for a man who affected a monk's habit as his daily dress. It rather marred his image of simplicity.

A silver Land Rover purred by her easily, catching a puddle with precision and drenching her with cold mud churned up by the speed of its wheels. Carmel jumped out of the way too late and yelled, but the car had already turned up the driveway and was pulling up in front of the grand doorway of Wilson's house. The driver's door opened and a slim man dressed in black went around the vehicle to let the passenger alight. She was a vision of loveliness——soft blond curls now blowing in the wind, and a long sable coat clutched tightly around her against the December cold. A querulous voice reached down the driveway. This was the good Reverend's wife, and she didn't appear to be very happy at all.

Chapter 2

D ue to a series of unfortunate incidents, Carmel found
herself once again making her way back along the long
winding road. It was the second time that day. The first had
been a walk for pleasure in the morning right after she'd
landed back from the airport, when she'd overheard Reverend
Wilson, a trip to the bakery for fresh croissants and to the
grocery store for fruit and milk. It had been a crisp, clear day
after the previous night's rain, and had been a great way to
blow the dirt of international travel off her. This second time
was an enforced hike, and not pleasurable at all.

She had arrived back in Canada earlier that morning——as a
travel writer she sometimes had to travel. The airline had lost
her luggage somewhere between Newfoundland and St. Kitts,
where she'd spent the last month, so she'd driven back to the
airport at 7:30 at night on the off chance that her bags might
have shown up on the evening flight.

It was dark out by that time, of course, so close to the winter
solstice. She should have heeded the warning, should have
recognized the bad auspices of the journey and turned back
for home after being almost driven off the road. It was the
silver Land Rover again.

Just as she'd reached the Mississippi Preacher Man's house,
the vehicle had torn out of the driveway, careening wildly
onto North Point Road and narrowly missing her own car.
Carmel had been forced to turn away, into the weeds and

rocks on the side of the road and up against a rusted wire fence surrounding grassland long turned fallow. She'd hopped out of the car with a cry of annoyance and watched the larger vehicle fishtail down along into Portugal Cove, almost scraping the wooden siding of the houses abutting the road, those built when the thoroughfare had been a mere footpath. The auto was soon out of sight, but she could hear the car horns blaring down by the ferry terminal and imagined the uproar caused as the luxury vehicle wove its way across the ferry lineup.

He must be drunk! she thought, trying to picture why the ponderous, worried man she'd seen that afternoon would be driving so madly. Or in a heck of a rush to get to church.

She turned back to assess the damage. The fence would no longer be serving its purpose of keeping animals in or out, even if there was no longer a reason to do so, and her car had a new set of deep scratches—almost gouges—along the right bumper from meeting the rusted wire.

"Well, damn it all!" she said aloud. After a time, the car was ready to start again, though she didn't like the coughing sounds it was making. She made her way carefully back to the main road and from there to the airport.

No luck on that, though as her luggage had not arrived, so she turned around to drive back down the long hill toward her home. Just by Windsor Lake, however, the car had sputtered, coughed, and finally given up. She could have sworn she'd filled up the gas tank before she'd left the country a month ago. In fact, she knew she had, but it was obviously empty now. To make things worse, no one—not one of her new friends in St. Jude Without—was answering their phones to come give her a lift. And unlike downtown St. John's, there were no cabs to be hailed on this lonely stretch of road. Carmel had no choice but to walk the long winding hill down toward Portugal Cove, and then along the ocean road to her home in St. Jude Without in the dark.

She paused as she reached the end of Portugal Cove, watching a single seagull rise up into the night, a ghost bird against the cold depth of the stars, white feathers lit by the mercury street lights below it. On it flew to the north, purposefully, its seagull mind intent on the next meal.

Her own mind returned to the Mississippi Preacher Man's words. The Lord of Misrule. Wilson had it right—today was the 17th of December, the beginning of Saturnalia and the reign of the Lord of Misrule, according to the old pagan calendars. For a week, the world would turn topsy-turvy, a time of annoyance and buffoonery when drunkenness ruled. A tradition more ancient than Christianity, the celebration had been abolished by bishops, popes, and kings alike over the years to no avail. It lurked on in the collective memory through the centuries.

On a dark night like this, it was easy to believe that the old habits died hard. Carmel, exhausted now, struggled up to the last corner leading to the forgotten cove of St. Jude Without. There was no sign marking the small community, nothing to tell travellers that they'd stepped across the border, nothing, that is, except the absence of street lights and the end of pavement. Her heavy purse weighed down her shoulder, and she stopped to flex her hands and fingers, numb with cold. She shivered and pulled the lapels of her light jacket closer over her chest. Little good it did now, as she had no body heat left to conserve. The hot sun of the Caribbean that her skin had soaked up mere days ago had long since dissipated, and her tan was no protection against the icy air. The sneeze she'd been suppressing escaped, and she wiped her nose uncaring on her sleeve. What a rotten homecoming this was turning out to be.

"Stupid car. Stupid airline," Carmel McAlastair cursed aloud between chattering teeth. But once she wound her way past that last corner snaking around the foot of the mountain which loomed over the small village, she forgot all the stupid elements that had led to that moment.

Before her lay Snellen's Field, a no man's land dividing the 21st-century civilization of Portugal Cove and her destination of St. Jude Without. Against the darkest black backdrop of mountain and sea, the field was lit up like a scene from Dante's Inferno. A blaze of pine pitch torches ringing the field revealed a heaving mass of human-like bodies, mummers intent on beating each other senseless with their bare hands. Screams and blood-curdling yells drifted up above the spot where she had stopped––dumbstruck––on the road.

This was Saturnalia come to life, straight from the imagination of Hieronymus Bosch. Who were these demons? There was no apparent sense to this battle. She could see no faces: all identities were hidden with masks and brin bags and pillowcases. The bodies too were likewise disguised in baggy dresses, robes––all stuffed with cushions to disguise and protect. An empty bottle was tossed out of the fray with the sound of smashing glass and a flare-up of a torch, along with a renewed vigour from that end of the melee. It was like a medieval fantasy game come off the screen, and everywhere she rested her eyes was a snapshot of horror. She watched as one hapless soul was felled by a good thumping on his head, only to grab the legs of his foe out from under him. She saw a mummer leap and tackle another dressed similarly, and then both disappeared under five bodies materializing from the crowd.

It was the night of Cain's revenge on Adam's sins, each soul dressed to hide its true identity, intent to pay back past grudges and insults, to inflict hurt and hatred on neighbours and uncles and strangers alike. It was the Mummer's Affray of St. Jude Without.

Ah, wait—was that a familiar head of greying curls behind a mask of Venetian feathers, receiving a right hook from a burly "woman" wearing her bra outside her dress and scarf tightly tied around her head? And surely the skull on the back of that leather jacket belonged to one of the bikers who frequented her neighbourhood bar? The white of an anonymous mask flashed briefly in the torchlight and even Richard Nixon had joined the free-for-all, throwing himself over a scrum of bodies already wriggling on the ground.

Surely that wasn't the Mississippi Preacher Man at the edge of the crowd. Did he really think he could stop this carnal madness when countless others of his ilk had tried unsuccessfully for centuries past? Carmel watched as the Reverend's hooded monkish figure turned toward another similarly dressed, the fires catching a glint of golden curls as the cowl fell back momentarily. In a strange choreography, Reverend Wilson reached out for the other, who slipped away and danced behind him, white hands reaching up as if to pull the Reverend's hood down and reveal his identity, but Wilson––if it was he––leaned backward toward the other, back and back until they both disappeared beneath the unruly mob.

"What are they at now?" she asked, shaking her head at her neighbours and fellow residents of the cove. "I've been gone for a month, and all hell has broken loose."

But suddenly, as if on a predetermined signal, the mob dissipated. Grabbing pitch torches to help make their way over the rocky field, bodies streamed left, right, and up to the road where she stood. Instinctively backing up against a boulder by the mountainside, Carmel held her breath and stood unmoving to avoid detection. But she needn't have worried, for the heat of the affray was over now and all grudges had been spent. The mummers nursed their wounds and laughed as they climbed over the rocks. Those who'd been foes were now friends again, all agreeing that it had been a good bash, no doubt, and—any rum left in that flask? Costumes discarded, faces unmasked, Catholic and Protestant were arm in arm as they wove their unsteady ways back to where they'd come from––St. Jude Without and Portugal Cove and beyond. They were ready now for the coming of the Christ child and the season of enforced peace and goodwill.

Chapter 3

The next morning, Carmel lay in bed long after her eyes had opened, reluctant to move out of her nest. The tip of her nose signaled the ice in the air, attesting to the fact that her ancient heating system had not kicked in over night. But she finally had to give in to her bladder.

The house had been dark and cold when she'd let herself in the previous night, frozen to the bone. She'd advertised at the university for a roommate before she'd left the country. It would have been nice to have someone in the house, but nothing had come of it. Phonse, the gorgeous fisherman whom she'd once had a wild crush on (until she'd gotten to know him), had promised he'd have the house up and running for her return, but it looked like that had fallen through. She wasn't surprised, for responsibility was not Phonse's second name. Thank God they hadn't had a cold snap in late November, a not-unexpected occurrence out here in the middle of the North Atlantic, for then she might have been greeted with burst pipes and water damage. As it was, there'd been no hot water for her longed-for soak in the tub and no food in the pantry save a dusty can of soup.

Swaddled in her quilt, Carmel looked blearily at the bathroom mirror. Her lustrous brown curls which had been oh-so-well behaved on the glorious, hospitable island of St. Kitts—was it just two days ago?——were flattened yet frizzed around her head. How was that possible? At forty-three, she could still be quite a stunner, just not at this moment. Her wide mouth turned down as she noticed a sleep wrinkle running down the side of her face, and she rubbed at her face in an attempt to get the circulation going, to no avail. She sniffed and blew her nose. A cold, on top of everything.

Back downstairs, she lit a fire in the old fireplace in the freezing living room, not an easy thing to do when her hands were shivering. At least the power works, Carmel thought ungratefully as she filled the coffee pot, still wrapped in her quilt. She turned the radio on for the comfort of hearing a voice. No mention of the strange battle enacted on Snellen's Field last night, which didn't really surprise her. Her adopted community of St. Jude Without, just north of Portugal Cove, tended to fall below the radar of the populace and media at large except when something really outrageous happened there. The residents were happy with that status quo. They didn't want the eyes of the world to see what they were up to.

The fire was blazing nicely by the time the coffee was brewed, and she settled in the ancient armchair beside it, wiggling her butt around to best avoid the loose spring.

When you think about all the islands in the world I've lived on and visited, and all the friends I have scattered around the globe, she wondered, sitting alone in the icy house, what on earth am I doing here?

She'd been traveling her whole life it seemed, living on the fringes, and hopping from island to island in her search for a home, for somewhere to belong. Then she'd met the love of her life, Ruscan Milosevic, an enigmatic Ukrainian, and thought she'd finally settled down with him for good on the island of Taiwan. But Ruscan had disappeared on an overnight flight to Hong Kong, no trace of him remaining. His erstwhile Chinese business associates had advised her not to look for him, and then coldly closed the door on her desperate entreaties. Heartbroken and not a little scared, she'd been forced to flee with what little she could salvage, and had returned here, to the island of her birth, to recuperate.

Carmel, who'd honed her writing skills over decades of traveling, was ever the optimist even in the face of heartbreak. She had discovered that she was able to eke out a living writing travel articles about little known secrets of islands, encouraging intrepid voyagers to go off the beaten track to see the marvels of the world. With a good internet connection, she could do this from anywhere. On her arrival back in Newfoundland, she'd been determined to find a house with a view of the sea––in her price range, of course, which was no mean feat. But Fate, or something like it, was on her side, and the rental of this old cottage in St. Jude Without had popped up––and here she was. Frank Ryan, the owner, who'd beaten a hasty retreat to Florida after the death of his wife, had offered to sell it to her after vetting her with the other residents of the cove. She had accepted his offer, for the strange little community of St. Jude Without had cast its spell on her.

The stone and timber cottage itself was over 200 years old and had been built by Jeremiah Ryan, one of the original settlers of the cove. He had been a pirate down Bermuda way––one of the last––and had retired with his wealth to live peacefully and raise a large family of Ryans. However, the new priest had recognized him, and ratted him out. Poor Jeremiah had been attacked by a mob whipped into a religious frenzy, and hanged right outside the window of his cottage on an ancient white pine. The stump of this tree was still rotting there by the twisty lilacs, a testament to the long memories of his descendants. His body had been tarred and hung out on Signal Hill in St. John's, to serve as a warning to any others who broke the law.

She glanced up at the bookshelf by the fireplace, noting that the red leather Book of Pirates of New Founde Land was still in its place. Before she'd left for St. Kitts, Phonse had been playing jokes on her with the tome, leaving it out

every once in a while and pretending it was the actions of the
ghost of Jeremiah. Carmel's nerves had been so stretched that
she even imagined she saw the ghostly feather in the pirate's
wide-brimmed hat haunting her. Recovered now after her
month-long idyll in the Caribbean, she was able to laugh at
the memory. Well, she would if she didn't feel so miserable.

The front door thumped like a large body was thrown
against it, followed by loud cursing and a few kicks against the
solid wood. She recognized the voice. The door was locked,
of course, and she had no intention of leaving her nest to let
him in. He had a key which he could use; at least he'd had one
when she'd left for her travels. She would leave him to figure
out the complexities of keys himself. It wasn't as if he would be
bearing thoughtful gifts of anything approaching sustenance.
She sniffed.

"What're you locking your door for, missus?" Phonse
hollered thorough the door. She heard him thump his way
back down the steps. Half a minute later, he noisily burst
through the unlocked back door, pausing only to pour a coffee
and poke about in the kitchen before beginning his search for
her.

"Are you okay?" he demanded, standing in the doorway
of the parlour. "Why didn't you open the door? What's up
with locking the door, anyway?" He took a sip from the mug,
winced and looked at her accusingly. "You don't have any
cream. I can hardly drink this."

Carmel looked up at him silently. How had she ever let
herself get carried away in that enormous crush when she'd
first met him? Yes, he was good-looking, astonishingly so, with
his shaggy head of blond curls, slightly greying at age 45. His
life on the water had left him with a permanent tan against
which his blue eyes shone with the clarity of clean living and
moral turpitude. Appearances could be so deceiving. Beneath
the gorgeous exterior lurked a true narcissist, a Peter Pan

man-boy, a smuggler, an alcoholic, and a liar, who still lived at home with his mother, the horrid Vee Ryan.

"I saw the smoke from your chimney," he informed her. "You're back early. You were supposed to be in tomorrow morning."

"I think I got my own flight times right," she said. "Perhaps *you* were mistaken in the date?"

He slapped his arms together. "It's freezing in here," he replied, changing the subject. "Turn up the heat."

"It appears not to be working," her voice reflected the ice in the air.

Phonse paused. "Oh," he said, thinking hard. "I could probably fix that."

"Like you fixed my roof," she reminded him. Sometimes holding a grudge was very satisfying. She hadn't checked, but was willing to bet that the plywood patch hadn't been removed and replaced with proper shingles during her time away.

He gazed at her indulgently. "You're not still sore over that, are you? You have to let it go, or you'll never have any inner peace." Phonse smiled and strode over to her chair. "Welcome back. Give me a big hug, you."

Finding herself enveloped in his bear hug, her body remembered why she'd almost succumbed to him in the fall. The man was a seething mass of testosterone, his touch electric, his smell heavenly. She allowed herself to relax, just a little, and smiled ruefully. "It's good to be back, I guess."

"Whoa, lady," he said, his face cringing as he turned away and abruptly dropped her back into the armchair. "You might want to brush your teeth."

Typical. It was then she noticed a shiner forming on his left eye. "What was going on last night in Snellen's Field? It looked like all hell broke loose."

"That was the Mummer's Affray," he told her, tentatively poking his finger to the blackened eye. "It's a tradition around here."

Did she really want to know the details? "I saw you get that punch. You were wearing a Venetian mask, right?"

"You recognized me?" He seemed surprised at this. "Yeah, the one with the feathers. Bridget gave it to me. Mom wouldn't let me have a pillowcase this year." A thought hit him. "How'd you recognize me? That mask was really gay. You know, with all those feathers and things? I figured nobody would know it was me."

"A mask can't be gay." She didn't bother to hide the irritation in her voice, although she kept her mouth self-consciously closed as much as was possible. She remembered the collection of colourful masks at Bridget's house, each a fantasy of feathers, glitter, and silks. Ha. "But, yeah, if you put it like that, I think it was a woman's mask."

Phonse frowned, and placed his empty mug on the wooden mantel. He cleared his throat. "I'll have a look at that furnace," he said in a voice pitched deeper than his norm. "It can be tricky, takes real know-how to get it right."

He disappeared into the ancient cellar. He could have it—she wasn't going down there anytime soon, not if she could help it. Carmel had been deposited with the Good Sisters at a very tender age by her physician mother, whose calling in life had been to help heal the poor of faraway countries. The nuns for the most part had been wonderful women, except for Sister Mary Oliphant, who had locked her under the convent stairs as punishment for her childish misdeeds and fed her imagination on the terrors which lurked in the dark, like the black darbies––ghouls who ate naughty children. From that, she had developed a life-long fear, phobia––call it what you like––an absolute blanket of claustrophobia descended on her any time she was required to enter a small dark space. Like her home's ancient cellar probably was, but she didn't have the nerve to test it.

Within minutes, the old furnace had kicked in and was humming loudly. The radiators began clanging and knocking as the hot water met with cold air within. Carmel put another log on the fire, and slipped out of her quilt to run upstairs to get changed out of her flannel pj's and possibly clean up a little in the freezing water from the bathroom tap.

By the time she returned back down the twisty stairs, Phonse had finished letting air out of the radiators and the atmosphere was almost toasty. She had changed into her thick red sweater with the loose turtleneck collar and her old jeans. After her extended summer of a month down south, it was actually a comforting novelty to be dressed in cozy winter clothes. *The jeans are a little tighter than I remember,* she thought as she tugged at the waistband; fortunately, the sweater was baggy enough to cover up her muffin top.

She found him peering into her fridge. "You got nothing to eat here," Phonse said.

Carmel twisted her hair up in a scrunchie, as there was really no sense trying to tame that mess yet. She shook her head. "I've been away for a month," she reminded him. "I'm starved, too."

"Let me take you out for breakfast," he said, surprising her with the generous offer. It wasn't like Phonse to think about another person's needs.

A full hot breakfast with good coffee, steaming sausages, hot home fries, and raspberry jam on toast. Suddenly there was nothing else in the world that could satisfy her, and she had to have it, right then. It might help this cold on its way, too. "Alright!" she said, hauling her boots out of the closet and pulling them on before he changed his mind. "Let's go."

This was another lovely thing about the colder months. Boots. She had a collection of at least ten pairs, to cover every possible occasion, and she loved the way they showed off her long legs. Life was always better when you could wear boots.

Her car wasn't parked outside. Oh, right, she realized, it was still up on the shores of Windsor Lake, without a drop of gas in it.

"That reminds me. My car ran out of gas last night. I'm sure I filled it up before I left the country."

"Hmmm," Phonse said in a too-puzzled voice. "That's odd."

She looked at him suspiciously, and his eyes were shifting away from her. "You have something to do with this? What? What did you do to my car?" It was pathetic—he was so easy to read.

He cocked his head as if thinking hard. "I might have borrowed some gas while you were gone," he told her. "A couple of times." He nodded. "That's probably it."

By now she felt her stomach was digesting itself, so hungry was she. "You emptied my tank? And you didn't think to fill it up again?" she asked, her voice rising.

"Hey, no problem. We'll take my truck." He was smiling in a manner meant to placate her. They left her house and walked to the top of the rutted lane which descended down onto the point. In the distance she could see Phonse's filthy white truck parked next to the bungalow. His mother was removing his white T-shirts from the clothes line as the low clouds threatened rain.

"I'm not going down there," she said, shaking her head. The last time she'd seen Vee, the woman had accused her of causing mayhem and murder in the cove, and Carmel still wasn't over that insult. She folded her arms. "I'll wait for you up here."

Phonse shrugged, and sauntered off down the lane.

"And hurry," she called behind him. "I'm starving."

He continued down the meandering path without turning around.

She was too hungry to stand still, and didn't trust him to return in a timely manner. And if Mrs. Ryan knew Carmel was waiting for him at the top of the lane, the hag would find some reason to delay him. "I'm going to walk on," she called out louder. "Pick me up on the way."

This time, he lifted his hand in acknowledgement.

Arms still folded against the rising wind, she walked south down the road she'd struggled along the previous night. It was officially called North Point Road Extension, but locally known as "the road," as it was the only one in the community, and the only means of exit out of St. Jude Without.

She passed the old church, now a bar run by Sid for his biker cohorts and local drinkers. No motorcycles stood outside, and the place looked to be locked up tight. She looked back, but Phonse was still walking on the lane, not having reached his home yet.

Her eye was caught by movement down on the point, and she stopped to watch a moment. Two ponies grazing in the grassy meadow were an addition to the cove since she'd been gone. The Newfoundland Pony had literally been a dying breed since Confederation and automobiles, but people were beginning to keep them again––not for their work contribution, for that was no longer necessary––but as pets.

As the road turned to take the curve around the mountain, she paused to examine Snellen's Field below, the site of the horrific hellish scene she'd happened upon the previous night. All was quiet now, and only the detritus of the battle remained in the sodden chill of the morning. Carmel walked down the rocky path for a closer look.

Two pine pitch torches––now burned out––leaned toward each other at a crazy angle, and scatterings of costumes remained. She kicked at a Venetian mask lying cracked in the mud, its feathers bedraggled and bright colours muted.

She surveyed the carnage left by last night's battle of idiots. A bright red scarf fluttered in the breeze a short distance away, caught on a larger mass of clothing by a large boulder. Drawing near, she could pick out a shiny black shoe––expensive looking––at the base of a mound of cast-off costumes.

"Who would be so drunk as to not notice losing their shoe?" she asked aloud, disgusted at the whole lot of them. But on closer examination, she saw that the shoe was still attached to a brown silk sock, and that the owner had lost something surely more dear to him than a mere shoe.

"Oh my God," she muttered, running over to the body. For a body it was indeed––a plumpish man costumed in a long brown monk's habit, the cowl still covering his head. Quickly, she grasped a wrist to ascertain if a pulse still thrived, but the arm was limp and cold. No sign of life whatsoever. She drew back the hood and almost cried in horror. From the deep purple face, bloodshot eyes bulged, the watery green irises staring up at her. She recognized the owner.

Carmel looked wildly around for help, just in time to see Phonse's truck speed by her on the road above. "Wait!" She stood up and waved her arms. But she could hear heavy bass blaring inside the cab as it passed—wump! wump! wump! He was clearly not paying attention. "Darn!" she said, at a loss as to what to do next. She'd been too hungry to bring her purse and subsequently her cellphone with her when she'd dashed out of the house. All she had was a credit card she'd stuffed into her back pocket, on the not-unlikely chance that Phonse didn't really mean it when he said he was treating her to breakfast. Snellen's Field was situated halfway between the two communities, so she had a dilemma—should she return home to call the police or head to the next town? Carmel climbed to the road to make her decision.

And there was an unlikely saviour rushing toward her, or rather, backing up toward her. The gallant Phonse with his trusty white charger had evidently seen her and was reversing. She quickly jumped back down onto the path to avoid a collision.

"I almost missed you!" he called out over the music. "Saw you in the mirror. What were you doing down there in the field?"

Carmel opened the door of the cab. "Got a phone?" she asked. "There's a body down there."

"Wha?" he asked, putting his hand to his ear.

"A body!" she yelled at him over the music. "In the field!"

"A body? A dead body? Oh no!" He looked panic-stricken. "What do we do? Oh my God!" He made as if to climb out of the truck. "I'll check it out!"

"No!" she screamed as she lunged forward and grabbed his jacket. "Don't mess with the scene. And turn that stupid music off."

Shocked into submission, he flicked the dial down.

"That's so much better," she said, letting go of his arm. "We need to call 9-1-1. Give me your phone."

"Who is it?" he asked as he fumbled in his pocket. "How did they die? When did it happen?"

"I don't know all that," she replied as he handed her the phone and she punched in the numbers. "It's Reverend Wilson."

"Who?"

"The Mississippi Preacher Man."

Phonse looked relieved. "Oh well, then. Not one of us."

Chapter 4

C armel spoke to the emergency operator, tersely giving the details of all she knew. "Better move the truck out of the way," she said to Phonse after hanging up. "They'll probably send the police with the ambulance, and they'll need the parking space here."

While waiting for him to return from reparking his truck, she huddled against the large boulder overlooking the field and stared out at the tickle to the ferry chugging its way to Bell Island. Funny word that, tickle. She'd only ever heard it used here on the island. It denoted a narrow stretch of salt water that contained treacherous tides and rocks. Such a rare word, this usage wasn't even found in the Oxford Dictionary, yet it was a useful description of much of the island's coastlines.

The growling from her belly reminded her that breakfast had to be put on hold for now. She closed her eyes and remembered the last hot meal she'd eaten, a plate of stewed goat in the sunshine at a stand near the airport in St. Kitts. She shivered. The clouds were lowering and there was a fine mist in the air. The moisture was beading on the fabric of her jacket.

The Mississippi Preacher Man was lying dead in the field below. The man had never socialized with local people, not as far as she knew, so what had he been doing in the field with those other idiots? More to the point, how did he manage to die on that battlefield without anyone noticing? There had been no blood. Perhaps he'd been having a middle-aged crisis and had a heart attack with all the excitement.

Carmel became uncomfortably aware that she had perhaps watched his death the previous evening, but she brushed that thought aside. She'd seen him fall––yes––disappearing into the crowd. Had he been trampled to death?

"You started to tell me about this traditional warfare," she said to Phonse when he had returned and was leaning against the rock with her again. Anything to take her mind off her growling stomach and the uncomfortable memory of last night. "Down on the field. What was that all about?"

He lit a cigarette then offered the pack to her. She looked at it, sighed, and reached out. All the month she'd been in the south, she hadn't bothered with the filthy things. Well, she was home again now— besides, it might cut the hunger pains a little.

"You know about mummers going door to door at Christmas," he said. "Well, what people don't realize is that mummering is actually an ancient tradition, and pretty violent. It was an excuse to disguise yourself and create havoc, act out old grudges against your neighbours, things like that. What you saw last night was a historical re-enactment. A bit of living history, keeping our past alive," he added proudly. "We've been doing it for 30 years now."

Carmel admitted to being a little puzzled. "But that sort of violence, that was why mummering was made illegal," she objected. "Because people got hurt."

"Yeah, but we don't use weapons or anything," he said, a little annoyed that she was missing the point. "It's historical, a commemoration of our history."

"But it was a horrible part of our history," she insisted as she turned to face him. "People were killed. They were set upon by other people who disguised themselves like cowards and murdered in cold blood. What's to celebrate in that?"

He huffed and turned away. "It's fun, alright? Just a bit of a laugh," he said. "We're not assassinating each other, for God's sake!"

He stopped and turned back to look at her, then both sets of eyes slowly turned down to the field where the preacher lay in his brown robe. A seagull had settled on the ground nearby, also eying the large mass.

"You don't think ...?" Carmel asked.

"No, the Mummer's Affray isn't like that. No one gets hurt, well, not really bad. It's just meant for, you know, have a few drinks, a bit of a rumble ..." Phonse shook his head in disbelief. "We've been doing it for years, and this is the first time someone has died."

She flung the half-smoked cigarette to the ground. "The Mummer's Affray. You helped start that up, didn't you?" she said, knowing with growing certainty she was right. It was just the thing to appeal to this man who would never grow up. "You and Sid."

He grinned in recollection. "Yeah, we'd been doing local history in school. 'The Mummer's Song' came out and mummering was starting to be popular again—but all nice and soft for the tourists. We wanted to show the ... well, the more accurate historical side."

"Plus have a few drink and a few laughs," she reminded him.

He nodded, looking quite proud. "That too. It's grown a lot over the years."

Chapter 5

O f course it was Inspector Darrow who unfolded himself from the white police car. He had been in charge of the investigation of the horrible events the past August, and had helped rescue her from her ordeal when she'd been drugged and locked in a root cellar—her worst nightmare come to life. She shivered, remembering.

They had a rapport, Carmel and the Scottish Darrow; she'd felt it on their first meeting. Conversation had flowed easily between the two and she felt there could be something more between them, given the chance. However, between her schedule and his, that chance never arose. The last time she'd seen him before leaving for the Caribbean was at an art gallery opening on the east end of Water Street. They'd bumped into each other, and had spent a lovely hour discussing the exhibit, and then another hour at the pizza place up the hill. She had been secretly hoping he would be at the airport to welcome her home yesterday but, when he was nowhere to be seen, she'd pretended she wasn't disappointed. There was, after all, nothing between them.

Carmel ran over to greet him. It was a relief to have him here.

"Welcome back," he said, his arm lingering around her shoulder. "You're early though. I was expecting you tomorrow."

Oh. That was two people who had not been expecting her back yet. As much as she hated to admit it, she must have probably written the wrong date on her FaceBook post. Phonse was right, after all.

"What have you got yourself mixed up in now?" he asked her, his attention drawn down to Snellen's Field where the police were already busy laying out yellow barrier tape and photographing the scene. The fine mist was turning to drizzle.

"It's Reverend Wilson," Carmel replied. "The American guy, you know, the one in the monk's robe."

Phonse was standing with his arms crossed and frowning as he looked at the two. "He lives just around the corner there, last house on North Point Road," he interjected. "On the Portugal Cove side."

"Who found him?" Darrow asked.

"Me," Carmel said. "I was just down looking at the mess from last night, and I saw his shoe ... Oh God, his face! He must have had a heart attack or something."

"Did you go near the body?"

"I felt his pulse, and lifted back his hood. That's all."

"I don't see that you did any harm," Darrow said, looking disparagingly at the mess in the field below. "It's time to put an end to this business, this illegal hooliganism. We've been looking to for years and, sadly, we now have an excuse."

"It's harmless enough," Phonse muttered as he shoved his hands into the pockets of his leather jacket. "Just a bit of fun for the boys."

"It's not harmless when a man gets killed," Darrow said sternly. The two men had to be of a similar age, but it was if Darrow was addressing a youngster. "Now, you two don't need to remain here. I'll come by to take your statements later."

The tickle at the back of her throat became a spasm which turned into a cough and a sneeze. Phonse uncharacteristically put his arm around her and led her back to the truck.

He drove her to the small mini-strip mall in Portugal Cove, but her appetite was gone now. She picked up a few necessary groceries rather than going for the previously anticipated breakfast, for she just wanted to return to her home. But first she bullied Phonse into buying gas for her car, and he drove her up the long winding hill to the lake where the car sat abandoned by the roadside.

She stood in the rain and watched while he poured the contents of the orange jug into her car's gas tank, standing well out of the way of the spray flung up by passing vehicles.

"Sorry about this," he said in a subdued tone, not looking up. An apology from Phonse—it must be the first ever she'd received from him.

Chapter 6

The house was cozy now, and the water in the tub hot. Having scrubbed the grime off, she restarted the fire just for the comfort of its crackle and smell this time, and to let her hair dry. She was looking forward to curling up with a hot cup of tea. Her head cold was quickly moving to her throat and deeper. A sandwich and a book, listen to the rain dripping off the trees, and forget the mauzy old day outside and that cold wet body in the field.

But Bridget, the tempestuous flower child from across the road, had other ideas for her.

"You're back early then," the woman in her late thirties stated as she stood in the doorway of Carmel's living room, her long red hair misted with the rain. Bridget was dressed in jeans, a departure from her long Indian cotton gowns which had been her costume the previous summer when the two had first met. Heavy wool socks folded over the top of her lace-up work boots, and the thick lumberjack coat looked solid enough for the late fall weather of December. Carmel could actually pick out her body shape now, with surprisingly slim legs and hips which had been hidden under those long colourful dresses a few months ago.

Carmel rolled her eyes. Okay, so she'd gotten the return date wrong in her Facebook posting. Couldn't people let it go? "Change of flights," she lied, knowing Bridget was unfamiliar enough with flights and international travel that she would accept it.

The other woman shrugged, indifferent. "What's going on down in Snellen's Field?" she asked as if Carmel hadn't been away for a month. Bridget slumped on the worn sofa, its springs sighing as she crossed her legs, not minding her boots on the faded red fabric. "Saw the cops. Something to do with the Affray?"

"Glad to see you again too," Carmel said dryly. Her friend grinned back and jumped back up to give her a hug.

"Okay," she said. "I deserve that. Now, is there enough tea in the pot? I brought some banana bread."

They both settled down in front of the roaring fire. Carmel attempted to tell the other woman about her travels over the past month, but, as was often the case, folks at home were never really interested in hearing of the wonders abroad. The talk came back to what was really important: the here and now of the police presence in the no man's land between the two communities.

"The Mississippi Preacher Man?" Bridget asked, incredulous. "What in God's name was he doing out there in Snellen's Field last night?"

Carmel shrugged. "Joining in the Affray, perhaps? Seemed pretty popular, a big crowd was down there."

"He wouldn't be there," Bridget said decisively. "He doesn't socialize with local people at all." She looked down at her plate. "I can't believe it. Well, maybe he deserved what he got."

"Well, he obviously was socializing last night, if that's what you call dressing in a costume for the pure reason of anonymously beating people up. He already had the costume, but I don't see him getting off on the fight." Her adopted community of St. Jude Without had strange social customs. "And why would you call him down for not wanting to become part of the cove's social life? Usually people here just want to be left alone from outsiders."

Bridget opened her mouth to reply, but just as quickly shut it again. She frowned as she reached for a slice of thickly buttered banana bread.

Carmel eyed her friend biting into the bread, a drip of butter melting down her chin. She could see it was freshly made, and the chocolate chips were still warm and gooey. After the first time she'd tasted Bridget's special chocolate chip banana bread, she couldn't go back to the plain stuff.

"Mmph," Bridget said, holding out the plate. "Help yourself," she added, around her mouthful. "I used bittersweet chocolate this time. You'll like it."

Carmel found she did, despite her scratchy throat.

Bridget filled her in on the preacher's story. Somehow she knew all the gossip. "He was one of those televangelists down in Mississippi, this is going back some years. A big name, was never on TV up here, but I've seen some YouTube videos. Lots of glitz, people falling all around him, that sort of thing." She chewed thoughtfully. "But you know what? Even though he was surrounded by the usual glam, I think part of his appeal was that he came across as being honest; he could come through the camera at you like he really believed what he was saying."

"I heard him talking at the War Memorial yesterday—he was upset about something—but I know what you mean."

"Preaching in public? That's not like him." Bridget reached for another slice. She had an amazing appetite for food yet remained slim. "Anyway, he quit the TV thing—there was some talk of his misusing the funds. I was speaking with one of his congregation, Sandra, you know the one who sells jam at the craft fair? She told me all about it. Like I said, he felt really bad. To atone, he moved the whole church up here."

"I saw his wife yesterday too," Carmel said, remembering. "She doesn't seem to buy into the whole sackcloth and ashes shtick. Her coat was sable, if I'm not mistaken."

"Vivienne? That poor woman." Bridget shook her head. "Sandra says she comes from a really wealthy family, I mean rich-rich. But her father was also really involved in Wilson's church, very evangelical. She went to finishing school in Switzerland, and stayed there for a few years by the sound of it, basically being a ski-bum. But when her father found out what she was up to, he cut the purse-strings and she had to come back to the States."

"What was she up to?" Carmel held a tissue to her nose as she tried unsuccessfully to stifle a sneeze.

"Lesbian love affair, apparently. Didn't sit well with Daddy-Bigbucks. He sent her to some place where they 'cured' her and put the fear of God in her. She ended up marrying her own pastor––Wilson. That was before he had his change of heart, while he was still putting on the glitz. Sandra said when she first moved up here, she dressed like the rest of the women. But I guess she got bored with that after a while, and that's when they bought the house down the road. The rest of the congregation don't much like her."

Carmel thought about it. "Quite a big life change, going from the Swiss Alps to what must have seemed the armpit of nowhere."

"I feel sorry for her. Her daddy practically forced her to marry Wilson, and she hadn't been brought up to live that sort of selfless life. It was natural for her to revert, don't you think?"

"I can see that, yes."

"And when her father died, he left all his money to Wilson. Totally bypassed his own daughter. So she's been stuck up here because she can't afford to leave."

"She could leave if she wanted to, though, couldn't she? I mean, he wasn't keeping her against her will."

"Think about it," Bridget said. "What's she going to do? She hasn't been trained to do anything but be a rich man's wife. And it was her own father's money she'd be leaving."

Carmel thought about it for a moment. It was an odd story. "She couldn't have wanted to leave that badly," she pointed out. "Money's not everything. And Wilson seemed like a very good man—okay, maybe not ideal for her, but he was good in itself. Surely he wouldn't have stopped her. And she seems to have everything she needs."

Bridget was silent. It looked like she had more to say, but was uncharacteristically holding it back. "Do you want to hear what I've been doing this fall?"

"Okay, so tell me," Carmel said, letting it go. "What have you been doing this fall?"

"I have become politically active," Bridget told her in all seriousness, a smear of chocolate at the corner of her mouth. "Do you know the rates of domestic violence in this province?"

"I hadn't thought about it, no." It hadn't occurred to Carmel that she should think about it. Oh no, this sounded like the beginning of a lecture on political correctness. From Bridget of all people?

"Did you know that over the past few years violence against women has increased here, while it has been decreasing everywhere else in the country?" Bridget continued. "The Family Violence Court was closed to save a bit of money in the budget, yet at the same time spousal violence has been escalating?" She was leaning forward in her fervor, and shaking a finger at Carmel.

What's brought this on? Carmel wondered to herself. The Bridget she'd known was passionate, yes, but about her home, her family, and her community. She'd never pegged Bridget for one to be involved in anything outside of her own closed little world.

Turned out that Bridget, a potter with a studio in her basement, had had a booth at the Fall Craft Fair. The Craft Association also gave space to community service groups, and the Anti-Violence Hotline and Shelter group had been located next to Bridget. She'd gotten to talking with the women and men involved in that good group during the down times, and––next thing you know––she was their strongest supporter.

"We really need people to help answer the phones," Bridget continued, casting a meaningful look at her friend. "Maybe do filing, fundraise... anything that helps."

Uh oh, unless she moved quickly, looked like she was going to be roped into this phone line business. "Hey, I'm just back in the country," Carmel said, holding her hands out in defense. "Give me a chance to catch my breath and enjoy Christmas first, will you?"

"Some families won't be enjoying a Christmas this year," Bridget replied, gazing out the window.

"Why don't women just call the police if they're being abused?" Carmel asked, trying to keep the irritation out of her voice. "Or walk out the door?" It was a reasonable question, for the police were there to serve and protect. It wasn't her problem.

Bridget stirred herself and sighed. "It's not usually that cut and dried," she replied. "Women are scared for their lives, they may be financially dependent on the person abusing them; they're embarrassed to find themselves in this predicament—there's a million reasons why they would seek shelter rather than get the police involved."

"Besides," she continued, "what good are the police when it comes to family violence? Do they really care?" She sniffed, and ended on a bitter note. "They claim that their hands are tied."

Before she could develop this new spate, she was interrupted by a knock on the door. A heavy knock. No one in the cove ever knocked at doors, they just walked on in as if assured of their welcome.

It was Inspector Darrow, accompanied by Constable Evelyn Wright. This meant it was an official visit—which could only mean bad news about the body in the field. Carmel opened the door and brought them to the living room. Darrow cleared his throat.

"I know, I know," Bridget said, standing up. "Police business. I'll move on."

"Before you go," Darrow said, "I'd like to speak with you also, Ms. Ryan, as you're here. About last night."

She shook her hennaed head. "Nothing to tell here," she said. "I was in town all evening till midnight, helping out at the shelter. I haven't been involved in the Affray for years now."

Carmel looked askance at her friend, trying to picture the small woman taking part in that crazy drunken melee.

"You know that the deceased has been identified as the man known as Reverend Wilson, of North Point Road," Darrow continued in a sombre manner.

Both women nodded.

"His death was not natural," Darrow told them. "The man was murdered."

Not another one! She couldn't help it—that was the first thought that came to her head. Not four months ago Darrow had sat in this very spot and spoken the very same words. So much for Carmel's quiet peaceful hermit's existence that she had sought this past summer. It apparently was never to be––not in this cove.

"Surely an accident," she began. "It was such a crazy scene, easy enough for someone to get too enthusiastic in thumping ..."

Darrow shook his head as he interrupted. "No one gets garroted by accident," he said. "And I'm certain no one accidentally brought a length of electric cord to the Affray. As you may or may not know, that gathering has very few rules, however, one of them is that no weapons are permitted. This was intentional murder."

How horrible. She shivered as she remembered the man's bulbous green eyes staring up at her in death—it was an image hard to erase from her mind's eye. She knew nothing of Wilson, except that he was a preacher for the quiet fundamentalist group whose church was hidden in the trees up a back road in the hills. The adherents were easy to pick out in a crowd. The group didn't eschew modernity; they weren't like the Amish or anything, but they kept to themselves, a tight-knit community. All the children--and there were many--were homeschooled. They also tended to be communal in their work, together owning successful businesses like the carpentry shop, a farm, and a construction company.

Carmel re-told the story of what she'd seen the previous night, describing the atmosphere of the burning pine pitch torches, the inhuman yelps and war cries, the masked figures in their eerie war dance, the drunkenness and finally, the camaraderie she'd witnessed at the end as all had poured back into their respective communities and homes. In the light of day, it still sounded as strange as it had been when she'd experienced it.

"And ..." This was the hard part. She desperately wanted to be assured that she hadn't witnessed Wilson's murder, but first she had to tell what she'd seen. "I ... I think I may have witnessed his murder."

She looked up to see Darrow's warm brown eyes on her, concern furrowing his brow.

"It was toward the end," she said, and swallowed hard. "I know now that it was Wilson, it had to have been. He was dressed in that robe, like a monk, but his hood was up, as if he didn't want to be recognized or seen being in that crowd. He wasn't fighting. He was ... searching the crowd, standing at the edge looking in."

She closed her eyes and let the memory wash over her. "And then, there was another just like him. Same robe, with the hood up. It was almost like they were dancing, for that moment, one was reaching out to the other, following ..." She opened her eyes. "They were practically identical, at least looking down on them from my viewpoint. At the end, one of the figures danced behind the other and she reached up her hands behind him, and then they both disappeared into the crowd. They sort of ... fell into the affray ..."

"You said she," Darrow was quick to point out. "Why did you identify the other as female?"

Carmel visualized the brief scene. "Just for a moment, her hood slipped back, and the light from the torch caught her hair. Blonde curls," she remembered. "Not a man's head of hair. It had to have been a woman, the way she moved——very lightly, as if she were dancing around him."

A dance of death. Carmel was sickened at the memory and the banana bread sat heavily in her stomach. To think she'd watched the murder and had done nothing to stop it. She had watched a man die. A chill ran up her spine which had nothing to do with her cold, and she huddled into herself for warmth.

"I watched him die," she repeated aloud, this time in a dull voice.

"Did you see the electrical cord?" Darrow pressed on. "It was white."

Was it her imagination, or had she seen the white cord whipping through the air and around Wilson's neck as the other danced behind him? She shook her head. "There was a flash of white ... I don't know. I can picture it, but I didn't notice it then."

"Do you know anyone who matches your description of this other person?" Darrow asked. "Anyone associated with Wilson?"

Phonse had blond curls, though they were quickly turning grey. Carmel shook her head. That was ridiculous. Phonse was a good six inches taller than the preacher, and besides he'd been wearing a Venetian mask. There was also a dim memory of him in one of Vee's old cast-off dresses, too.

"I don't know," Carmel began, and looked to Bridget for help.

The redhead's face had paled. "His wife," she said softly. "Vivienne has curly blond hair."

Darrow looked at her sharply. "That would fit the bill."

"But..." Bridget looked confused. "What time was he murdered?"

"If, in fact, Carmel witnessed the murder," Darrow began, "that would have been approximately nine o'clock?"

Carmel nodded. "Thereabouts," she replied. "I got back in the house about 9:30, I guess."

Bridget's face broke into a smile of relief. "Then it couldn't possibly have been Vivienne," she said. "She was with me from eight p.m. till about eleven."

"But you said you were volunteering at the shelter," Carmel said.

"Yes," Bridget replied with certainty. "And Vivienne was there with me. She was looking for advice on how to leave her husband."

Darrow raised an eyebrow.

"It's a confidential matter," Bridget said, looking down at her lap.

"This is a murder inquiry," Darrow responded after a beat. "Nothing is confidential anymore. Particularly concerning the victim's wife and their relationship."

Bridget thought about it, and then slowly nodded. "I'm sure you'd take me over to the station and make me tell anyway," she said. A lifelong resident of St. Jude Without, Bridget had little liking for the police. "So to save time and energy ... Well, he was abusing her. Had been for years, she says. She was finally getting up the nerve to leave him."

"What kind of abuse did that entail?" Darrow asked softly.

Bridget shrugged. "Emotional. He held her passport and wouldn't let her leave the country. And he was starting to get physical too, she said. The odd slap here and there. That's why she came to us—she was starting to fear for her safety."

This news was greeted with startled silence as the listeners took it in. Could Vivienne, the preacher's wife, have a motive to kill her husband? Yet she was in the city at the time he was murdered. She couldn't have been in two places at once.

Carmel nodded slowly. "Yes, that's who it looked like. Vivienne," she said. "But, what was he doing there, in the first place? How did the preacher get mixed up in the Affray?" He surely hadn't been there to convert the wicked from their ways—no one with a grain of sense would think any of the souls in St. Jude Without wanted to be saved last night.

"We'll find that out," Darrow replied with certainty, then thought for a moment. "Do you remember seeing Wilson's body there at the end of the melee?"

"No," she began, shaking her head. "I was focusing on the crowd coming up over the rise—I didn't know if they were going to attack me. I was scared, to tell you the truth." She pictured the scene again. No, she hadn't been looking into the field itself, although she had noticed that there was still the odd body half passed out, and groaning. She'd been mesmerized by the swarm of laughing figures spilling in all directions, gloriously alive after their pretend battle, ready to begin the Christmas celebration in earnest now. She had watched as the group split at the top of the hill, some going to Portugal Cove and the others trailing down the road to the community of St. Jude Without, the group diminishing as they passed the houses and the lane to the point, before she had gotten up the nerve to continue her cold journey back home. She had not glanced back at the field.

"While you were watching the battle," Darrow began. She could hear the parenthesis around the last word. He was not looking kindly upon this cove tradition. "Did you recognize anyone you knew?"

She thought back. "Well, they were all pretty well disguised with masks and pillowcases and brin bags around their heads," she began. "There were a lot of people dressed like traditional mummers, you know, with the baggy dresses, or sheets, bras worn outside their clothing, scarves over their faces, that sort of thing." She could have been describing a scene in any outport kitchen over the long dark evenings of the Christmas season. "But there were also regular masks, like you wear at Hallowe'en or ..." Or at a costume ball in Venice. She sighed and looked up at him. The police inspector was watching her intently.

"I saw Phonse, of course," she said, looking apologetically at Bridget, who was Phonse's cousin and confidante. "He was wearing one of Bridget's fancy masks—I recognized his hair in the firelight." She gave a little laugh. "I saw him get punched in the eye by one of the mummers—that's how he got the shiner. I think that put him out of action till the end, because I didn't see him again after he disappeared under the crowd." She fell silent, thinking hard. "And ... I don't know which one it was, not Sid ... But one of the bikers was there. I recognized the logo on the back of his leather jacket."

The group of bikers who hung out with Sid at his bar were a scary-looking crowd, with their beer bellies, tattoos, and hairy faces, and appeared to be the real thing, not wealthy middle-aged yuppies who could finally afford their teenage-dream 'hawgs.' This group was not, however, connected with any of the large gangs or Mafioso groups that she knew of. This eclectic smattering of anti-socials was a law unto itself and had adopted a simple grinning skull with a large feathered hat as their mark, embroidered onto the back of their jackets. Yes, she'd seen one of them at the Affray, but she didn't think it was Sid, the owner of the bar in the old church. While all the others were shaggy of locks and overgrown in their beards, his hair was close shorn, almost militarily so, and he had the most wonderful handlebar moustache she'd ever seen.

"Anyone else?" Darrow was patient.

"It was all such a blur," Carmel confessed, shaking her head. "I remember those two, because I know them. All the rest ..." She spread her hands wide in a symbol of defeat.

"Well, if anything else comes to mind, call me," he said as he and his constable prepared to go. He hung back a moment as she walked them to the front door. "You do still have my number, don't you?" he asked softly.

She nodded.

"Well," he said, clearing his throat, "anything at all, call me." He nodded and closed the door behind him.

Returning to her armchair, she slowly sank into it.

"He was not a good man, you know," Bridget said. "Despite appearances."

Carmel looked up at her friend. This was rich, coming from the descendant of pirates and smugglers, the woman who hung around with bikers and others who lived just below the radar of the law. "Darrow?"

"Vivienne's husband."

"How bad could he have really been? Wilson was a minister, a leader for his very peaceful group."

Bridget nodded. "Yeah, but sometimes appearances can be deceiving ..." She stopped herself, then shrugged. "I can only tell you he was a nasty man. That I do know.'

Chapter 7

The murder was all over the evening news. Carmel had gotten into the habit of scouring the news for any hint of Ruscan after his abrupt disappearance on that overnight flight from Taiwan to Hong Kong last year. She had never picked up a hint of him on the international segments, but couldn't stop herself from trying even when she'd long given up hope of ever seeing him again. Well, almost never. There was that one time last fall when she was recuperating, she might have seen him on a clip from the Ukraine, but it could have been the Valium they'd given her at the hospital. Since moving back to her homeland, she also watched the news for its entertainment value, for sometimes the government's antics were stranger than fiction. Cabinet ministers resigned when they got caught with their hands in the till, or because they got a better offer from the private sector, or just because they'd reached the minimum years required to retire with a full pension. You couldn't make this stuff up, right?

Wilson's death featured on both channels, with pleas for anyone who'd participated in last night's event to present themselves to police. Not likely any of them would––not willingly––Carmel bet. Gerald Smythe, the top reporter for one local station, was taking great glee in giving the details of the Affray as if he'd just discovered it, and had stumbled upon a strange hitherto unknown tribe of savages in the wilds of the province's hinterland.

This short man had his reasons to resent the cove and its inhabitants. After his near-death experience at the hands of a former resident of the cove last August, he made sure to stay away from the place itself. He contented himself with strolling around Snellen's Field, pointing out the detritus still lying there which hadn't interested the police, and generally mocking the residents of Carmel's adopted community.

Smythe's reporting style was over-the-top commentary, more in the manner of tabloid sensationalism than true journalism. Other reporters from competing stations could complain as much as they liked, but no one could say he wasn't a popular figure. Smythe hooked in viewers not by presenting facts, but by appealing to the baser nature of society's lowest common denominator.

"Now, how many guesses as to who owns this?" he asked as he held up a muddied 48DD bra. He paused as if for a punchline drum roll and grinned his cheeky little boy grin. Oops, he'd done it again.

Smythe dropped the bra and the jokes, turning to the camera with a frown on his face. "Seriously now, folks," he said. His close-set features squinted together on his large head, making him look like an unlikable cartoon character. The wind flapped at his brown and mustard polka dot bow tie, yet his stiffly coiffured hair didn't so much as breath in the breeze.

"Seriously, for months now, the good citizens of this province have been hearing reports of sensational lawlessness that is happening right here, in the community of St. Jude Without," he intoned as the camera panned to take in a larger view of the cove behind him in the background. The exaggerated reports were mostly of his own making, of course, but that was beside the point. As he spoke, the screen showed flashbacks of his footage from last summer. "How much longer are the authorities going to allow this ... this barbarity, this ghetto of illegal activities to continue?" Up came shots of the potholed road, motorcycles parked outside the old church with its wind-eaten sign and then her own house, paint long ago peeled away by the salt air on the upstairs clapboard siding and rotted boards on her veranda. She hadn't realized it looked that bad. "St. Jude Without is a blot on the moral landscape."

"Incest, smuggling, prostitution, drug use ... this station helped bring these issues to the public attention four months ago," he continued. "But what has been done?" Smythe shook his head sadly as he gazed off into the distance.

"And now murder," he said, turning to look directly into the camera lens. "Yes, you heard me right. The devastating murder of a peaceful man, a minister of God, set upon by a band of ruffians, not a quarter mile from his home. The remnants of their costumes you see strewn on the ground. This is how the savages disguised themselves, I'm told, hiding under mummers' outfits like their ancestors did years ago. Is this the eighteenth century, for heaven's sake?" he thundered, thoroughly enjoying his soapbox now. "In the name of all that is good and Christian, how long will this insanity continue?"

He paused to visibly collect himself. "I'm calling out to all right-minded citizens," he said sternly. "Let's get this place cleaned up, for once and for all."

Chapter 8

C armel was glad to be back sitting on her wobbly stool in the bar that evening. The old church next door to her house had been bought by Sid's father to use as storage when it was deconsecrated 30 years ago, and after his father had passed away, Sid realized his lifelong dream of quitting the Coast Guard and opening a bar. He had changed little on the inside of the wooden building for the conversion—aside from stringing up some lights around the chancel to mark the bar area, and replacing the altar with a counter made of such thinly sliced granite that the light underneath shone through. It had originally been created for the poshest restaurant in the city but had cracked before installation, so Sid had picked it up cheap. Cobwebs hung from the faded green painted ceiling, the walls had taken on the soft grey of old white paint. Outside, the small rosette window in the bell tower glowed when the bar was open for business. The only addition to the decor since she'd last been here was a poster stuck up on the inside door announcing the phone number for the sexual assault and shelter helpline that Bridget had been going on about.

The beer strike that had crippled the island and had caused riots on George Street was long over, she was glad to see, although it had never affected Sid's business too much. He had found an alternate supply from the French islands to the south, but the less said about that, the better. Out of habit, she had brought her large Christmas mug with her, for Sid's services did not include the provision of clean drinking ware to hold the beer. And beer was the only drink on offer in this pub.

She looked around the large room at the familiar faces. There was Phonse as usual with his drinking buddies at the pool table, discussing the Mummer's Affray and the body found this morning. Clyde Farrell, the farmer, sat in his usual corner pew with his large black dog by his side, talking to no one. Sid manned the bar, his hooded eyes not missing anything, while Credence Clearwater Revival played on the sound system. It was feeling like home.

But there were new faces in the crowd, too. The four bikers now had an junior member accompanying them. A young man, hardly more than a boy, his heavy leather jacket engulfing his narrow shoulders, had not yet earned the right to wear the skull and feathered hat on his back as the others had. He hung on to every word spoken in the group like a puppy looking for affection, and his braying laugh rose irritatingly over the music and soft murmur of conversation.

A gentler new face was over by the pool table, joining in the banter like an old friend of the players. He was a much older gentleman with a head of white hair like a frizzy halo, heavy-set and wearing a clerical collar that was peeking out from his large fisherman's knit sweater. She heard one of the beer drinkers call him 'Father.' A priest, then, and Catholic, no doubt, for St. Jude Without had been a solidly Roman community, the sole church attesting to this.

Women were few in this drinking establishment, not that their presence was forbidden as might have been the case even 20 years ago, but St. Jude Without was an old-fashioned kind of cove where habits were slow to change. Stalwart female members of the community such as Vee Ryan would never be found inside the bar, even these days.

Yet here was an exception striding up the centre aisle, a tall woman with an athletic build, her thick blond hair bouncing with every step. Generous of proportion and smile, she called out to each member of Sid's congregation with a cheery word. Her eyes lit on Carmel and her smile deepened.

"Hi, there! You must be Carmel, our new volunteer for the shelter," the woman said. "I recognize you from Bridget's description. Welcome back from the Caribbean."

She took Carmel's hand in both her own and squeezed gently. "I'm Sharran," the woman said before letting go. "Bridget told you? No, I see not."

Carmel thought she had avoided being roped into Bridget's latest project, but obviously Sharran had not been informed.

"I don't know about that ..." she began, searching her mind for an out, feeling a tad guilty at her own selfishness.

"No matter," Sharran said. Forgiveness shone from her and she brushed aside Carmel's discomfort. "If you find yourself with some spare time over the winter, you can come on along and we'll get you trained up."

The tall woman winked over her shoulder at Sid, who passed her a beer with a flourish.

"Thanks, sweetheart," she said to him. Carmel intercepted the look between the two. Sid's usually dark and hooded eyes had softened, almost smiled.

"Let me think about it before I commit to anything," she began again.

Sharran laughed a loud guffaw. "Don't be embarrassed," she said. "I can come on like a bulldozer sometimes. Don't let me bully you into anything."

Sharran proceeded to tell Carmel about herself and her work. A freelance United Church minister, Sharran spent her time involved in numerous causes, all for the betterment of society's downtrodden. The latest was the Anti-Violence Shelter and Hotline that Bridget was so fired up about. Despite Carmel's reluctance to get involved, Sharran's enthusiasm was infectious and Carmel found herself asking pointed questions about the hours one would be expected to volunteer, and what a volunteer could expect to be confronted with over a shift. They had soon arranged to have Carmel drop into the Shelter to have a look around, after the Christmas season was over.

"Just a look," Sharran insisted with a smile. "I'm not holding you to anything."

Bridget drifted over from the pool table and talk between the three women turned to the murder, naturally.

"Did anyone know him?" Carmel asked. "I've seen him and his wife a few times, getting in their car, but they didn't seem to play a big part in the general community."

Sharran nodded. "I knew him from the Interdenominational Council meetings. And his wife, Vivienne. I've run across her."

"How is Vivienne doing?" Bridget asked. "I take it you've dropped in on her?"

"That's my job," the tall blond nodded ruefully. "I did go to her house today, but Franz, the butler, told me she wasn't home."

"Butler?" Carmel almost snorted her beer through her nose. "Oh, excuse me for that." She wiped her face with her sleeve. "But—they have a butler?" She couldn't imagine anyone in Portugal Cove wealthy enough, or socially upscale enough, to have the services of a manservant, let alone the minister of a small fundamentalist flock. Well, okay, the Helicopter King in his lush estate down in Beachy Cove probably had a whole slew of retainers, but the rest of the community was fairly middle-class in their leanings.

"Yeah," Sharran answered, and hesitated. "I don't quite know what the story is behind that, but they appear to be pretty wealthy. I think there might have been money from Vivienne's family, but don't quote me on that."

"I imagine her problems are all solved now," Bridget said.

A worried look crossed Sharran's kind face. "I wouldn't be too sure about that," she answered. "I mean, the shock of losing him so suddenly, of her changing circumstances ... I really think she will need more support than ever now. I know she was home because she never goes anywhere without Franz."

Carmel was about to ask what they were talking about when another sneeze which had been building in the back of her nose let loose without warning. She grabbed the crumpled tissues in her jeans pocket and blew.

"That doesn't sound good," Sharran said.

"Oh, just a cold," Carmel said, grateful for her sympathy. "You know how it is with travelling, crowded plane, viruses everywhere. Lack of sleep and food, too, your defenses get down."

"Do you have a doctor?" the minister asked, full of concern. "You might just want to get it checked out."

Carmel looked at her blearily. "No, I'm never sick. I haven't gotten round to looking for a physician since I moved back. How do you go about that anyway?"

"The clinic in Portugal Cove has a new doctor," Sharran said. "You might want to go register there before her slate fills up."

Carmel nodded. Health was so easy to ignore when you had it. "I'll think about it."

"And here's Father Wish," Sharran greeted the snowy-haired cleric who had made his way over to the group. "How's it going, buddy?"

"It goes, Sharran, it goes much as it ever did," he said. He turned to Carmel. "Don't believe I've had the pleasure."

Carmel found herself smiling at the man, tickled by his name. With his white beard, curls, and solid body, he looked like a Santa figure.

"Father Aloysius," he said shaking her hand. "So you're Carmel, the one who has Frank Ryan's place next door?"

"That's me."

"Always happy to meet a new member of the congregation," he said.

"Oh, yes, well, I've been meaning to get to the church," Carmel said, thinking of the fine white building overlooking the bay in the town next door. She had very much lapsed in her Catholicism over the years. "I've been, you know, travelling ..."

Sharran threw back her head and laughed. "Wish isn't here drumming up business, Carmel."

His eyes crinkled at her under his bushy white brows. "No, no, but you'd be more than welcome to join us for Mass anytime. I actually meant Sid's congregation––the bar of St. Jude Without." He paused, looking about him, enjoying the thoughts he was about to expound. "It is a fitting use for a tired old church building, wouldn't you say? It still serves as the community gathering hall; in fact, I believe attendance is more regular now than it was in my day. Sid dispenses goodwill from his altar and all are welcomed inside its doors. Yes, sometimes the soul needs to attend Sid's Mass and celebrate the joy of the physical body. We need to remember that God created ale to soothe the spirit, too. I have good memories of this building."

"Were you the priest of this church?"

He nodded. "I baptized at least 50 percent of the folk here tonight," he said. "I know each family in the cove still, their sorrows and joys." He paused to look about him, his eyes resting on the young biker Carmel had noticed earlier. The music had changed to AC/DC, the old standard 'Highway to Hell,' and the youth was up dancing now to this, playing air guitar and screaming an unmelodic tune in time with the music. He was high, no doubt, the drugs in his system making him oblivious to those around him.

"I recognize his face," Father Wish said. "But he's not from here, is he?"

Sharran stated that the young man was from town, meaning the city. "He's been hanging out with the bikers for a while."

"I remember him now," he said, a look of sadness passing across his face. "That's a troubled young man. He was an altar boy at his home parish once, but lost his way somewhere along the line. It's good of these gents to take him under their wing."

Carmel had never considered the bikers in a paternal light. She looked over at them now as the largest, the one with the bushiest beard and most proud beer belly, got up and walked over to the youth. He picked up the skinny youngster by the scruff of his neck, gave him a soft clout across the head, and returned him to his chair at the outskirts of their table. The others took a moment to glare at him before resuming their discussion.

Chapter 9

S he woke herself up coughing the next morning, so it was time to do more than just think about seeing a doctor. Having had no reason to find one since moving back to the province, she decided to try the walk-in clinic that Sharran had suggested, the one on Portugal Cove Road on the way to the city. Her head felt thick as she struggled through the telephone book to make an appointment. She was lucky: they had an opening in a half hour's time because of a cancellation. Other than that, she would have to wait until next week.

Her old blue car coughed a little, too, as she coaxed it to life. Turning the last curve out of St. Jude Without around the mountain, she saw yet again the silver Land Rover pulling out of the driveway to the Wilson's house. The driver was much more sedate this time—he had carefully slowed down to look in both directions before pulling out onto the road. Even from this distance she could make out Vivienne's profile in the passenger window.

Carmel drove slowly behind the vehicle, unable to forget the memory of that unmistakeable blonde hair peeking out of the cowl in the torchlight. Her virus-addled brain played the moment over and over, the blond woman reaching up to her husband. How could she have been in two places at once? Carmel had herself witnessed Vivienne's vehicle driving toward the city at 7:30 that night, and Bridget would not have lied about Vivienne being in her presence all evening. Well, she might, but not in the middle of a murder investigation. No way.

Perhaps the answer was that Carmel had not, in fact, witnessed Wilson's death. That was a possibility she hadn't thought of. Perhaps Vivienne had slipped back down to Snellen's Field long after the Affray was over. It was surely unlikely that Wilson would be at the scene not once but twice in an evening, but not impossible. This cheered her up until she coughed a violent spasm, ending with a sneeze, reminding her where she was headed, and why.

But then a thought swam up through the muzziness of her brain—what if Vivienne Wilson was leaving town, headed for the airport to catch an international flight, and getting away with murder? She could see the silver SUV up ahead on the road toward the city. Toward the airport, too. Oh no, she thought, I have to tell Darrow. She waited for a break in traffic, then turned into the clinic parking lot. Darrow's phone went straight to his voice mail. She'd try again when she got inside out of the rain.

Carmel didn't have time to make the call when she got inside the clinic, for she was immediately ushered into an examining room. Perhaps the receptionist didn't want her spreading her germs around too much. She sat huddled on the padded table in the examination room, her tissues clutched in her hand as she waited for the next attack of sneezes. If only her head didn't feel like it was stuffed full of cotton wool.

The door opened and a woman in a white coat breezed in. "Right then," she said, turning to her new patient and peering authoritatively over her reading glasses. "And it is you. How have you been for the past 20 years?" The bright eyes behind the designer spectacles were familiar.

"Rhonda Clerkwell? Oh my God." This was a woman she had shared much of her undergraduate years with——long seminars in medieval history, and time goofing off in the student bar, but they had lost contact soon after Carmel had set off on her world travels. They'd never been really close, friends through circumstance as many university relationships were, yet they shared good memories. She jumped off the table to give her a hug, but the doctor backed away.

"Germs," she said, holding her hand out to stop Carmel from advancing.

"You're a doctor now?" she asked Rhonda as she leaned back against the table, but, somehow, she wasn't really surprised. With Rhonda's strong intellect and drive, she could have become anything she wanted, done anything she wanted to do. With her family money behind her, the world was her oyster. Truth be told, Carmel had always been a little intimidated by the other woman's strong style—Rhonda had always been perfectly turned out in expensive outfits, hair always just so, and never seen without makeup. Carmel herself had been a typical arts student—jeans and sweatshirts, hair in a ponytail, and had never owned a pair of heels until she graduated.

"Hmm, so it would appear," Rhonda said, as she pretended to examine her nametag. She flashed her brilliant smile to show she was joking. "The history degree was fun, but not as lucrative as this gig."

She hadn't changed except to grow more polished and more expensively turned out. "Now, we really must catch up," the physician said. "I want to hear everything. But not on billable hours. Here's my private cell number. I suggest we meet over dinner and drinks soon. I'm free tonight." She certainly hasn't lost her efficiency over the years, Carmel thought as she took the business card.

"Okay," Carmel replied, getting off the examining table and putting the small card in her purse. She turned to the doctor, who was making quick notes on her chart. "The way I'm feeling right now, I don't think tonight will happen ..."

"Take these pills," Rhonda said, passing her over an envelope. "You'll be feeling fine, believe me. Mind you, no more than one every six hours. I took two together once, that was the night I met my second husband. We got married in Jamaica twelve hours later. You want to be careful with these babies." She looked up over her half-glasses, her highlighted and glossy hair swept neatly and professionally back with a diamante buckle. "We'll meet at Oceanica. That's handy for both of us. I'll make arrangements for 7 p.m."

"Ah," Carmel replied, stalling for time as her mind tried to push past the muddle within. Oceanica was on the main road in Portugal Cove, an unlikely spot for a fine-dining restaurant, one might think, but the sunsets would be fabulous there in the summer, as it overlooked the water. As a travel writer, she knew that Oceanica was listed as one of the top ten places to dine in the whole country, let alone the province, and that this exquisite dining experience came with a hefty price tag which was out of reach for a lowly freelancer like herself. A meal with wine there might be equal to half her monthly mortgage payment. Her mind tried to race through the sludge of her illness. Perhaps she could use it as a tax write-off, or convince them she was a food critic and get a free meal.

Rhonda clearly recognized the dilemma playing on her face. "Don't be ridiculous. I make a doctor's wage. You probably still don't by the look of you. The meal's on me," she said with a smile. "Consider it a Christmas present."

The physician quickly pooh-poohed the idea that Carmel had anything but a non-Ebola type virus. "If it doesn't pass in a week, that will mean it's gone bacterial and we'll address that as necessary. Eat well, stay hydrated, and get fresh air into your lungs." She waved her out of the examining room and on her way.

The cold drizzle had begun again as Carmel got in her car. No, Rhonda hadn't changed at all over the years. Coming from old St. John's money, she always knew what she wanted and had the confidence to reach her goals. She had been just as generous in their student years.

Blowing her nose, Carmel was suddenly aware of feeling restless. It felt like the tablet Rhonda had given her might be working already. Seeing her old friend again had cheered her up, and that made her feel better physically, too. There were all sorts of errands she could run in the city, restocking her fridge from the big box grocery store, or just forcing herself to take a walk around the lake to get the fresh air Rhonda insisted she needed. She took a quick look in the rear-view mirror. Her nose wasn't too red; she looked passable.

"Right, then," she told herself in imitation of the confident Rhonda. "Off we go to the city."

Chapter 10

Her mind still wasn't as clear as she believed it to be, though, and on her way to Quidi Vidi Lake she ended up being forced to take a wrong turn due to a new-to-her one-way road system in place. She found herself in a part of the centre city which she only half recognized. Tall townhouses stood in solid rows where once small bungalows had squatted amongst large gardens, cutting off her view of the landmarks which would help her sense of direction.

She negotiated yet another difficult intersection by a huge grocery store that never used to exist, and then found herself across from the Royal Newfoundland Constabulary's headquarters. Even this fine institution had changed beyond recognition in the years she'd lived away. The building sat in the approximate location where the keepers of the laws had sat for centuries, on Fort Townshend overlooking the old city, but was a different building entirely now. She recognized the old university campus building, now taken over for police training. A huge art gallery proudly stood where once the old fire station had squatted, and the RNC building was now a glass and brick building.

"Darrow!" Carmel exclaimed as she remembered. She had meant to contact him but that intention had been forgotten after reconnecting with Rhonda. Well, she was right here now, so it seemed a good idea to run on in to his office. She didn't stop to gather her thoughts to see if the muddle-headed idea she'd had previously was actually worthy of a visit. She only knew she wanted to see Darrow, to feel his presence, even to be a part of the investigation again, though she knew as a civilian she could never be a part of it officially. She thought back to last August, at the events which had all taken place almost at her doorstep. Inspector Darrow and she had quickly developed a rapport, and it had not seemed strange for him to drop into her house for a quick chat, bouncing theories and ideas off each other. Despite the horror surrounding those events, she had enjoyed the contact with him. And she knew he had too—she could almost feel the sadness lifting off his soul at times, yet they had never spoken of this, of anything between them. And now that she was back home again, she realized that she had missed it.

The inside of the large police station was nothing like she had pictured, nothing at all like the New York precincts of the movies. This was not a welcoming place. The outside door led directly to a small dark room with locked doors and metal grills over three windows. Even the large windows on the outside wall were tinted a dark brown and prevented the daylight from coming in. Only one wicket at the far end was open to business, a glassed-in affair like a ticket booth. She had no choice but to join the lineup if she wanted to get farther into the building.

As Carmel waited to speak with the uniformed cop at the wicket, the thought crossed her mind that she might be making a fool of herself. What exactly had she planned to say to Darrow? She cast back in her mind. She was going to inform him that she may not have witnessed the murder after all, that perhaps both Vivienne and Wilson came back to Snellen's Field after the Affray was over. Seriously? She started to feel embarrassed as her mind cleared a little. No doubt Darrow and his team had already thought of that and dismissed it out of hand. She had also wanted to tell him that Vivienne might be leaving the country. As if the RNC didn't have the resources or brainpower to think of something like that. She slapped her forehead.

"I'm an idiot," she said aloud, then looked up to see that she was next in line for service. The officer gave her a look of polite inquiry.

"I'm, uh, I made a mistake," she told him as she felt her cheeks flushing. "I'll just ... go. I don't know what I was thinking. Sorry."

"Carmel?" She heard the soft Scots accent behind her. Too late! She wondered how to explain this as she turned to face him. Briefcase under his arm, he had one hand on a locked door, a swipe card in the other, having just entered the building, and beckoned her to follow with a flick of his head.

Darrow opened the door and ushered her inside to a much brighter space, with fluorescent lights overhead and outside windows visible through the glassed-in cubicle offices. "This is a surprise," he said as he led her through the maze of hallways. His brown eyes smiled at her warmly, crinkling at the crow's feet developing around the edges. Stopping at a door marked with his name and rank, he held it open, inviting her to enter first. He had good manners, Darrow did.

She sat in the seat in front of the large desk, the visitor's chair, a standard wooden issue but with comfortable padding and arms and watched as he took the time to arrange his coat on a wooden hanger on an old-fashioned coat rack. He unwound the plaid scarf from his neck and placed it on a separate hook. His dark hair was still ruffled from the December wind, and its disorder was not improved by his attempt to run his fingers through it.

A quick glance around the plain office showed few personal items. No family photos, no plants, only two framed degrees. She couldn't make out where they were from.

Carmel waited as Darrow took his own chair behind the desk, removed papers from his briefcase and shuffled through them. His fingers were long and squared at the top. Like almost everything else about him, attention had been paid to the manicure but not in a fussy manner, the nails trimmed and smooth with the line of his fingers. They were strongly built hands, sensitive perhaps but not pretty, like the hands of a pianist. The knuckles bore old scars, yet they were competent. These might be the most attractive hands she'd ever seen.

She forced her eyes away, not wanting to be seen fixating on his hands because that would be too weird. Her gaze travelled up the sleeve of his black suit. Why didn't more men wear suits? His was elegant and well-fitting, if a trifle worn around the cuffs. It fit so well it might have been bespoke, specially made for him by a London tailor and, on closer inspection, the fabric looked to be of fine quality.

Darrow was also one of the few men she knew who regularly wore a tie. In fact, she didn't think she'd ever seen him without one. Even that time she'd met him at the art gallery and he was off duty, he'd been done up "like a stick of gum," as Bridget would say, all ironed creases and just perfectly turned out. Today's tie was black with gold stripes running up diagonally, setting off the grey shirt against the dark suit jacket. It was silk, she could tell. No polyester for this man. Was she fixating on his dress sense now? She was feeling lightheaded either from the flu or the pill samples Rhonda had given her. Get with it, she told herself firmly, and raised her head to look into his eyes.

"Glasgow University." A lopsided grin accompanied the words.

"Huh?"

"You were examining my tie. It's from Glasgow University. A graduation present from my mother's cousin Beatrice."

"Ah," she said. The heat of belated embarrassment was beginning to rise underneath her turtleneck, and she needed to deflect the conversation. "What did you take there?"

He looked up at the framed degrees on the wall. She couldn't know that there was one missing. His first love, the degree in Fine Art. That had been put aside with Fiona's pregnancy and their subsequent marriage; he'd had to go on to find something more befitting his wife's expectations. "The usual," he replied. "Psychology, law, whatever took my fancy."

She nodded, relaxing a little. "Me too. I took the same route here at Memorial University. Though I ended up with a degree in Medieval History, not the most practical piece of paper."

A deep chuckle accompanied his answer. He understood about practicality. "No knowledge is wasted," he said. Then he sat up straighter. "Now, you came to see me," he reminded her. "Have you remembered something?"

"Did anyone else come forward yet?" she asked, stalling for time. "Anyone who was at the scene?"

He shook his head. "We're doing a door-to-door inquiry, but not many are owning up to taking part in it."

"Probably too embarrassed to admit it," she remarked. "I would be."

He smiled and waited while she reluctantly told him the ideas she'd had that morning after seeing Vivienne Wilson driving away. The ideas sounded even lamer when spoken out loud, but he remained silent in thought for a few moments as if he was taking them seriously.

"Did they return to the scene after Vivienne left the shelter? It's unlikely, but we have to keep an open mind about that. We couldn't pinpoint the time of his death," he admitted. "Couldn't narrow it down enough for my liking. The temperature dipped below freezing last night, and Wilson's robe was made of wool. It covered just about his full length. We'll be able to have a more accurate reading after the autopsy."

A thought occurred to her, flashing through her mind like a bolt. Her mind was suddenly feeling much clearer now, as if the contents of Rhonda's tablet had rebounded through her brain with added strength. Wow, whatever this stuff was, it was good. She bounced to the edge of her chair in her excitement. "Do you think he could have been killed elsewhere and moved to the field? That the murderer found out about the Affray and thought it could be the perfect cover-up?"

Darrow looked at her, indulgence in his smile. "I think you're suited for this investigation business. Unfortunately, we do know Wilson wasn't moved after death, the blood pooling patterns are consistent with the position of the body."

"Blood? There was no blood," she said. "He was garroted, wasn't he?"

'Yes," he said. "You're correct, there was no blood spilled. But you see, after the body dies and the heart is no longer pumping the blood through the vessels, the blood will act as any liquid does––it will find its own level. In other words, gravity will help it settle in the body." Darrow leant closer as he became involved in the explanation, a natural teacher. "For instance, Reverend Wilson was strangled and left on his back. We know this because the blood has pooled to his back and the undersides of his limbs and head. It's called livor mortis, or hypostasis."

"But if he had been moved, say, if he'd fallen onto his front and was later moved onto his back, wouldn't the blood follow?"

Darrow shook his head. "No, the blood starts to congeal within twenty minutes after the heart ceases to pump. It will fully congeal within, say, five hours of death, so that's why it won't move around even if the body's position is changed."

She was silent. It was sounding more and more like she had witnessed his actual murder. She pictured again the flash of blond curls seen so briefly in the reflected lights of the pitch pine torches. "I'm still certain it was his wife I saw," she said slowly. "The height, the hair, the ... the way she held herself. It had to be a woman."

"Interesting. Do you think men hold themselves different- ly?" he asked as he rested one elbow on the desk, cupping his chin in hand. His attention was entirely on their conversation.

"Yes," she replied. "It's hard to describe. But men, well, it's like they take up more space in their movements, even smaller men do. They use more of the air around them, I don't know. I'm not explaining it well."

Darrow considered her words. "I think you've nailed it, actually. The human male tends to claim more personal space than the female: it's a way of asserting dominance and power."

"And women are socialized into using less space?"

He nodded, then looked at her thoughtfully, in the manner of one seriously considering his next words and their possible consequences. "You know, Vivienne Wilson phoned us early in the morning of the 18th," he said slowly. "Yesterday morning. To report that her husband hadn't come home the night before."

"She could have done that to make herself look innocent," Carmel was quick to point out. She had no reason for liking the woman who had never been friendly toward her. In fact, the woman's doll-like blonde curls, blue eyes, and heavy makeup automatically set Carmel against her. Vivienne reminded her too much of a girl she'd known in school who had used her seeming fragility to manipulate teachers and other children to get her own way. Spoiled rotten, some would call it.

"She seemed quite overcome with grief at the news of his death," he said, slowly shaking his head. "Hysterical, almost. I get the feeling she's led a very sheltered life."

"But I saw her," Carmel said simply. "Sorry. I saw someone like her, saw her with her hands up to his neck." She saw the memory in her mind's eye yet again. In the flickering light of the pitch torches, the second figure had been reaching her gloved hands toward the monk's neck, almost as if she had been going to jump up on his back to get a piggyback ride, except he was leaning back toward her with his own hands clutching at the cowl of his robe.

"I know I asked you before, but do you recall seeing any weapon?"

"Just a flash of white," she confessed. "It could have been very pale skin."

He rummaged around in the bottom drawer of his desk and withdrew an extension cord, a length of white electrical cord.

"That's the murder weapon?"

Darrow smiled and shook his head. "Not this piece of cord, but one very similar to it."

"That can kill someone?" she asked looking up at Darrow.

"Innocuous looking, isn't it?" he said. "And clever. So easy to wipe, not a fingerprint to be had off it, and it's something to be found in every home around the cove. Even the city."

"Could ..." she hesitated to ask. "You said that this was deliberate, in that the murderer had it on them for this purpose. Well, could someone have been carrying it on them, and used it because they saw they had the chance?"

He shook his head decisively. "Who carries around a length of electrical cord? Unless our murderer is an electrician."

"Oh," she said. What he said was true. She had lots of things in her purse at any given time, things that just collected over the months in between purse cleanouts. There was something to meet almost any emergency, even a Phillips screwdriver and a roll of duct tape (the reason for which she couldn't quite recall), but no one carried an electrical cord. She tried to picture a scenario which would lead to that item being casually shoved into the pocket of a monk's robe but nothing came to mind. Did monk's robes even have pockets?

"To get back to the identity of Wilson's murderer," Darrow said. "You didn't actually see the attacker's face?"

"No," Carmel replied. "When the hood slipped back, the person had their back to me. I still swear it was a woman, though."

She next asked the question that had been on her mind since she'd seen Reverend Wilson's wife that morning. "I was wondering. Could she, Vivienne, have carried this out?" she asked him. "I mean, she seems so small."

He stopped to think about the physics of the questions. "Yes," he decided. "She could have reached her arms up, wrapped the cord around his neck, and pulled hard enough. I have a feeling she's not as delicate as she makes herself out to be. And he wasn't a tall man, remember. He had bulk, but not height."

Darrow played with the mouse of his computer for a moment, picking up the black plastic wireless equipment and rolling it back and forth on his hand, as if weighing it. He looked up at her and continued. "But did she do it? That's another matter," he said, shaking his head. "She claims she was at the shelter all evening. Her witnesses aren't saying much, but about that fact they concur."

They continued in this vein for a few minutes, bouncing ideas around between them until a sharp rap on the door frame interrupted them and the half-closed door opened fully. Constable Wright stopped short as she entered the room, her eyes on Carmel. A frown crossed her face momentarily but was quickly smoothed back to a neutral expression. Carmel sat up from her relaxed position in the visitor's chair with a vague feeling of guilt at having been caught at something she shouldn't have been doing.

"Excuse me, I didn't know you had company," Wright said, looking at Darrow. "Just wanted to pass on these briefing notes to you."

"Ah, thank you, Evelyn," he said taking the files from the constable.

She glanced back down at Carmel before shifting her eyes forward again. "The chief wants to see you," she said, holding her ground.

"Better get it over with," he replied, stretching his arms over his head and appearing oblivious to the quiet drama playing out between the two women. "Are we finished?" This last was addressed to Carmel. She nodded.

"Alright," he said as he stood. "Carmel, thanks for dropping in. I'd best be on my way. Constable Wright, can you show her the way out?"

"Gladly," Evelyn said in a low voice as he passed out of the room, then curtly turned on her heel, expecting Carmel to follow.

Chapter 11

S he left the police station with a cold shoulder from Constable Wright, but that was the least of her worries. Putting the rest of her errands on hold, Carmel drove to the lake, for she was feeling the need to think, and the 40-minute walk around the lake was an easy one which wouldn't require too much attention except for dodging the odd puddle or dog poo. A circuit round the lake was perfect for a thinking session.

So the Mississippi Preacher Man was a wife beater. She tried to picture him as she'd known him—not well, certainly, but enough to recognize him. She had always thought of him––when she thought of him at all––as being rather weird but harmless. He had affected the long brown robe of the humble monk. So much for that image, she thought, him with the butler and the SUV, and being a wife beater.

Looking back in her mind, surely she could see the signs of potential abuse, if only she'd thought to look. Or at least a power imbalance between the husband and wife. Vivienne was always done up perfectly, never a hair out of place—one would think she was full of confidence. But she always walked a few steps behind her husband, as if deferring to him. She must have been scared to death of the brute.

Surely the jury would let her off easy, if she could some-how prove the years of abuse. Except that—Carmel stopped, gazing at the ducks on the ground before her as something

Darrow had said sank in. This murder was premeditated. He was right. No one carried around a length of electrical cord hastily shoved in their pocket "just in case" it was needed, like you would a tissue or a credit card.

As she looked for a way around that fact, she could feel the fuzziness descending over her mind again like a wet blanket coating her brain. Maybe Vivienne had seen Wilson striding off in the direction of Snellen's Field, perhaps intent on stopping the pagan mayhem as Christian leaders had tried to do for the past 2,000 years or so. Perhaps Vivienne——finally reaching the end of her rope after years of abuse——had snapped and, grabbing the electrical cord, had run after to him to finally put a stop to her misery. A spur of the moment kind of thing.

But no, that didn't wash either. What reason would Vivienne have had for having electrical cord around, let alone thinking to use it as a garrote? Her thoughts were going round in circles, and they kept coming back to the indisputable fact that this murder was premeditated. And why did she keep forgetting—Vivienne had been with Bridget at the shelter during the time Carmel had possibly witnessed his death. There was no way around that fact.

To think that Vivienne's abuse had been taking place so close to her own home, and no one had realized it. How many more cases were happening around her, the women afraid to speak out or take action because their husbands had beaten them into submission? You never knew what went on behind closed doors. That made up her mind. She was going to help Sharran and the shelter; yes, she was actually going to volunteer her time. Perhaps she could help other women from reaching that boiling point when they could see no other way out of their troubles. Hmmm. Perhaps she could also do a little surreptitious sleuthing while she was at it. The volunteers at the shelter might speak more freely when the police weren't around.

Carmel felt good about this decision. And despite the cotton wool which had descended on her head again, she hadn't sneezed for the past hour. Whatever the miracle drug Rhonda had given her, it was working.

As she walked briskly through the cold mist and drizzle, her thoughts wandered. Today's date was the 19th of December—less than a week from Christmas, and none of her shopping was done. Her suitcase still hadn't appeared at the airport, which also meant she didn't have a single present bought for Christmas. Not that her list was long, but there was Sister Constantine of the convent, the nun who'd played a large part in her upbringing, and Bridget, maybe. Inspector Darrow, perhaps, or would he think that strange? She wished she could read his mind. And now there was Rhonda, her old friend from university days, to think of too—since she was splashing out on a lavish dinner, it would only be right to get her a little something. But what could you get a woman who has everything?

It wasn't until she was driving home and her car had reached the last bend in the road leading to her cove that she realized her problems of Christmas presents could be solved. There was Bridget walking home, the answer to her prayers. Her friend was a potter, and potters made things. Carmel's presents this year would be locally made items——one of a kind useful and practical gifts. Hallelujah!

Stopping to pick her friend up, Carmel immediately broached the subject.

"So do you have any stock left over from the craft fairs?" she asked, steeling herself for a negative answer. The Christmas season was when most crafters made their money to live on for the next year, and if Bridget had had a particularly good season, she might have nothing left by this date. "I need mugs. Or something. Anything, really."

"I've sold out of almost everything," Bridget said. "But if you don't mind a change from my usual work, I actually have a few things of a new design," she continued. "I didn't bring them out to the fairs because I'm still developing the line and didn't want to start selling them before I had the plates and bowls to go with them. You can come down and have a look."

"Is right now good?" Carmel asked.

"As good a time as any," her friend replied.

So Carmel parked in her own driveway and the two walked across the road to Bridget's tiny bungalow. Going down the ancient steep staircase to the basement studio, she grinned as she saw that some additional artwork now adorned the walls. Bridget, an artist as well as a potter, used her wall space as a canvas to test out ideas when she didn't have any wood or paper handy to work on. Carmel could see that she was working out new images involving cats, and had drawn comical stylized felines peering out behind the previous works, the boats and painted crazy quilts and abstract drawings.

"Here they are," Bridget said, rummaging in the back wall storage shelves. Carmel could only smile. How perfect.

Each mug an almost uniform shape, they had been glazed in indigo blue. On some of them, cat shapes had been scraped off to leave them outlined in white. Others had a red glaze over the white parts of the pottery.

"How did you do this?" she asked in wonderment.

"It's called negative glazing," Bridget replied. "Before they go in the kiln, I glaze the whole mug; then I use different tools to draw the image, removing the glaze. Then put on another glaze, if I feel like it. It's a really cool technique," she continued, reaching for another mug. "See—I can get lots of texture, too, depending on the tool I use. This was done with a wire brush." The mug in her hand was without any images etched on, but entirely covered with brush strokes in the indigo glaze.

"How many can I have?" Carmel asked.

"I've got about ten here," the potter said.

"I'll take them all," Carmel replied with a sigh of relief. Christmas shopping had never been this easy. Any mugs that didn't find a home with her various friends and acquaintances she would keep for her own use.

She almost gagged when Bridget told her the price of her combined purchase even after the "friend" discount, but paid up with forced good cheer. After all, each was unique and handmade and she was supporting a local artist. And it was Christmas––goddammit––the season for selflessness.

Her arms full, she left Bridget's to cross the road to her own home when she spied Melba making brisk strides up the hill from the bridge down by her cottage hidden in the woods. The woman, who was all of 75, had a face full of wrinkles but the physique of a woman half her age. Tall and muscular, she also had the most beautiful and melodic voice that Carmel had ever heard. Hence the nickname Melba, after the Australian opera singer of late 19th-century fame.

Melba, who had been christened Assumpta Mary all those years ago in what was now Sid's bar, had the reputation of being a witch. She knew the medicinal properties of every plant growing in her large garden, the surrounding woods, and beyond, and in the bogs nestled in the hollows of the mountains high above the community. The people of the cove didn't bother much with doctors, for Melba had a cure for everything, and had managed all the birthing, sickness, and dying in years gone by. Melba was the keeper of local lore and history. But she also believed there were fairies inhabiting the graveyard between their houses.

You never knew which side of Melba would present herself on any given day.

"Best of the season to you, Melba," Carmel called out, feeling all Christmassy now that she had her gifts bought.

A dark look was thrown her way. "The season of misrule, it is," the old woman muttered.

"No snow yet, though," Carmel replied with a smile, determined to keep the spirit alive.

Melba looked as though she was going to pass right by, but stopped suddenly as she drew near and fixed Carmel with a cold gaze. "Once invited in, the Abbot of Unreason cannot be turned out, and he'll wreak his havoc till he's done," she continued sternly as if Carmel had argued the point. It looked like Melba was having one of her off days.

She nodded to the old woman, started across the road again and was halfway up the steps when Melba spoke again, her low clear voice carrying though the cool air.

"And murder comes in threes."

Chapter 12

T he airline had promised to send her an email when her luggage showed up, to save her constant trips up to the airport, but she didn't have much faith in that. The suitcase could be anywhere between St. Kitts and here—she had taken three different flights that day and could only pray it was at least in Canada. But she would check her email anyway.

There was only one new message in the box. It had the look of spam, for she didn't recognize the sender—strange, for her gmail account was usually good at filtering those out. Even stranger, the sender was identified only as a string of nonsensical letters. Normally she would have sent it to the spam box without opening it, but her eye was caught by the single word in the subject line.

Raven.

Ruscan had been her raven. For reasons still unknown to her, he'd had a raven in midflight tattooed on his left hip. "Voro," he'd called it when she'd asked. "It means 'raven'." But that's all that he would say. His Ukranian friends might, after a night of heavy drinking, let slip the word when they addressed him, but he would never let her call him that.

"Not that word," he would say, his finger on her lips. "Never that, my luba."

Raven.

She focused on the single word in the title until it became all she saw. Raven, in English, not the Cyrillic alphabet. But still. Raven. Ruscan.

If she opened the message, she might be inviting a nasty virus onto her computer. At best, it would be trying to sell her penis enlargements. But if she didn't open it, she'd never know what it signified. If it was a message from her raven, her Ruscan.

She had no choice.

The message inside was a quote, she recognized that much as she quickly scanned down through it. Edgar Allan Poe, if she wasn't mistaken.

"Ghastly, grim, and ancient Raven, wandering from the Nightly shore—Tell me what thy lordly name is on the Night's Plutonian shore! Quoth the Raven 'Nevermore!'"

But what did it mean? She didn't like the tone of it. Ghastly. Grim. Nevermore. This felt surreal, like a bad dream. Perhaps she'd overdosed on Rhonda's pharmaceutical samples and was hallucinating. She shook her head and looked again, but the words were still there.

The mouse hovered over the reply button, then hesitated. If it was Ruscan himself sending this email, then he was hiding. A year and a half after the fact, she had mostly given up all hope of him. Perhaps it was a message from him, to let her know he was out there still, and using the word raven was a code, to let her know he was alive but also to warn her against contacting him. Never that word, he'd said.

If it wasn't Ruscan, if it was the person or people responsible for his disappearance, then she didn't want to be in contact with them.

She had no one to ask about this, nobody who could explain the arrival of this strange quote in her in-box. But she knew one thing. If this wasn't a message from Ruscan himself, then someone, somewhere, thought Ruscan was alive. And if it

wasn't her lover sending the email, then it might be an enemy
of his.

She cancelled the reply, then noticed a link at the bottom
of the message. Praying that her Norton Anti-virus was up to
date and doing its job, she opened it up.

It connected her to the BBC World News site, to a photograph of a scene that looked vaguely familiar. A group of men
standing in front of a columned building, an official building
of some sort, it could be anywhere in the world. Some of
the figures were dressed in fatigues, some in the ubiquitous
dark suits of businessmen everywhere on the planet. It looked
familiar.

Her eyes widened as the memory came back like a dream.
Carmel had been recovering in bed from the attempt on her
life, and Bridget had thoughtfully moved the TV up to her
room for company, leaving it on CNN to cheer her up. In
between dozings, she'd woken up to see this very same shot
on the screen and had thought she'd recognized the turn of
Ruscan's head, but it had been gone in a second. Now she had
time to study the shot.

It was in the Ukraine his homeland and, yes, that figure to
the left could be her lover. Could be. What did this mean?

Chapter 13

C armel had to put it all aside. She put an extra special effort into getting ready for the evening, for it was a rare occasion to be dining out in such a posh place as Oceanica. She dug out a skirt from the back of her closet and looked at it critically. A plain black, figure-hugging cut ending just above the knee: it would work if she could find a pair of unladdered tights.

Why do I never think of tights till I need them? she asked herself in frustration. It was something you always assumed were available in your drawer, until the moment you went to look for them. Unfortunately, she had none in any of the drawers—the only close approximation was a pair of black leggings. Those would work, she decided, along with black knee-high boots and a long white silk shirt belted at the waist. Hoop earrings, makeup, and a thick silver cuff—there, the outfit was complete. Even her hair was well-behaved this evening, falling in soft, brown curls around her face with just the smallest help from the curling iron to tidy up ends that were inclined to stick out.

If I had a big feathered hat, I'd make the perfect pirate, she thought, screwing up her face at the mirror.

Perhaps it was this latest thought which put pirates in her brain, but as she was waited for the time to leave and set about tidying her kitchen, she had the uncomfortable sensation of being watched. Carmel paused by the sink, remembering the inexplicable scares of the summer past when she had moved into the house, including the strange lights outside in the graveyard and the eerie flickers out of the corner of her eye sometimes at night, which Melba claimed were fairies. Darrow had been adamant there were no fireflies in the province, but, she told herself, he didn't know everything. She preferred the firefly explanation to the supernatural. Yes, it was that unmistakeable feeling of eyes on the back of her neck. She turned around sharply as if to take the watcher by surprise, but there was nothing there.

"Don't start this again," she told herself aloud nervously. "This house is not haunted." There were no such things as ghosts or supernaturals. A loud guffawing noise answered her, and her heart stopped beating until she realized it was just the hot water radiators kicking in, the air beating in the pipes. It was a 200-year-old house—there were bound to be weird noises coming from the plumbing. Right?

She drove the distance to the restaurant. Located on land reclaimed from the sea in Portugal Cove, the restaurant owners had caused a bit of a stir when they had started building. Having purchased an old fishing shed perched between the side of the main road and the rocky shore, they had begun to infill from the point where the large boulders crept out of the ocean, ending up with a sizable bit of new land on which to build the restaurant. Yes, there had been some concern vocalized by the rubber-boot crowd, those in-comers of 20 years past who had settled in the picturesque cove and commuted to their jobs at the city's university campus, but the real locals, those who could trace their lineage back generations in the cove, didn't mind too much. That is, until they found out the prices being charged in the restaurant, which were far, far out of their reach. Then they started to mutter amongst themselves, but it was too late then, the land was reclaimed and the building built, so everyone just harrumphed and found something else to grumble about.

Walking through the doors of Oceanica was like entering another world. Soft classical music flowed alongside the smell of freshly made bread, immediately enveloping the guest in an easeful embrace. Dark woodwork against the cream walls lent an air of grace and age to the building, a dignity furthered by the large expensive artworks tastefully decorating the walls. Carmel thought this must be how it was like to walk into one of the gracious old homes on Circular Road, into an atmosphere of secure entitlement and belief in the rightness of wealth.

Through an archway, she could see into the dining room with its wall of windows directly over the water. In daylight there would be a wide vista of Bell Island and perhaps whales and dolphins playing in the tickle, but this dark night there was only the soft reflection of the restaurant's interior with subdued lighting and candles on the tables. It was as if each table grouping was in an alcove of darkness, cushioned by shadows to ensure privacy for the diners.

A young, very beautiful hostess in a slim black dress had materialized by her side with an unobtrusive smile of welcome.

"I'm here to meet my friend," Carmel found herself almost whispering, not wanting to break the spell of the scene. "Rhonda Clerkwell."

The smile widened slightly with recognition. "Dr. Taverstock has her usual table," the vision breathed. "Please follow me."

Another host, a very young and beautiful man this time, silently appeared at her side to remove her coat, and only then was she led into the restaurant itself, to a table set for two on exquisite white linen. Water with just the perfect amount of ice was poured into the crystal glass at the side of her setting. Rhonda was not here yet, but she had perfected the art of timing her entrances years ago.

Most of the tables had diners already seated there. Amazing when you thought about it—the restaurant was located 20 minutes' drive out of the city down a narrow and winding highway, and the prices were reputed to be out of this world, yet they could still fill the place with willing customers. The food must be as good as promised.

She was surprised to see a carafe of white wine appear on the table. The young waiter proceeded to pour a glass for Carmel.

"Oh, no," she said to the man. "I didn't order this. Wrong table, I'm afraid."

She felt the first hint of chill since she had stepped through the doors.

"Dr. Taverstock has a standing order for our house Chardonnay," he informed her, an eyebrow raised, raising himself up stiffly. "Would Madam care for something ... different, perhaps?" In those few words, he managed to convey that this would be a faux pas of the worst order, an insult to Rhonda and to the house itself.

She silently shook her head, easily cowed into submission in these foreign surroundings. "That'll be fine," Carmel mumbled. She could feel a tickle at the back of her throat, and coughed into her napkin in an attempt to head it off. Damn. All she needed was to be barking and dripping all over this place. She fumbled in her purse to take another of the sample tablets Rhonda had provided her with.

The physician floated in on a waft of lightly perfumed air and a confection of scarves and twirling skirts and took the seat opposite. "Thank you, James," she nodded to the young man as he poured another glass and warmly presented it to her.

"Isn't it just divine here?" Rhonda said to her by way of greeting. "Couldn't you just live here forever and ever?"

Carmel didn't need to answer that as Rhonda, true to form, directed the conversation. She also took charge of ordering the meal, for which Carmel was quite grateful. Her menu choices were all exquisite and yes, divine. There were no prices listed by the entrees. If you had to ask, you probably couldn't afford them.

Despite their differences in lifestyle and outlook, the two quickly fell into the comfortable friendship of years past.

"I've been having a marvellous time with my latest project," Rhonda said breezily, moving the conversation to herself.

Carmel smiled. No, she hadn't changed an iota over the years. "Which is?" She was happy to go along with the script.

"I've taken on the Sexual Health contract for this region," she told Carmel proudly. "I'm their only physician, I might add, so I'm kept quite busy with it all."

"And what does that entail, exactly?" Carmel almost didn't want to ask.

"I hold a clinic once a week at the shelter," Rhonda told her. "It's all part of the Sexual Crisis Helpline too. They've moved up the road to the old Rabbittown Theatre. Getting the funding to buy the place was quite a coup, and I'm so happy the province is supporting it. The whole building is being used to address all our needs—the Sexual Assault Shelter headquarters are in another part of the building."

"Can I ask what you do at your clinic?"

Rhonda was happy to oblige. "Everything. Women's clinic, counseling, arrange for transgender operations——you know—sex reassignment. The work is terribly interesting, and runs the whole spectrum."

Sex reassignment? Was that like sex change, transgendered and all that? Carmel knew very little on this topic, and what little she knew she found confusing, and stated this. "This is when gay people want to change their gender, like lesbians want to be men, and vice versa," she said, more in the form of a question.

"No, no," Rhonda replied, shaking her head. "Not at all. Gender actually has little to do with sexual orientation. A transgendered person is someone who feels the usual labels don't apply to them."

"Oh," Carmel said, still unenlightened. "So, this is like, what? Transvestites?" The only example she could think of was Frank N. Furter, the character from the Rocky Horror Picture Show, in his ripped fishnet stockings and leathers.

"Yes, that too," Rhonda replied. "Of course, not all transgendered persons want sexual reassignment surgeries. Nor are all who have the surgeries transgendered."

"Oh," Carmel replied, totally at a loss now. Her complete lack of comprehension was obvious even to Rhonda.

"I got involved with this through my work at the Sexual Health Centre," she said, changing tack. Finally, Carmel could contribute halfway intelligently to this conversation.

"I'm going to be volunteering at the shelter," she said rather proudly. "Sharran's talked me into it." Talk of Sharran and Carmel's adopted community soon brought the conversation round to the murder on Snellen's Field.

"Reverend Wilson will be greatly missed," Rhonda mused. "He was a great businessman. He owned Oceanica, as you no doubt know."

No, this was news to Carmel. Big news. She found it hard to reconcile the luxury of this establishment to the plain, unadorned style of Wilson's church and the congregation.

"But how can that be?" she asked. "They're all so old-fashioned and simple. He even went around in a monk's habit, for God's sake. How could they be a part of this ... this palace of entitlement?" Her voice rose with disbelief.

The diners at the next table lifted their heads at this rabblerousing squawk infringing on their happy bubble. Rhonda leaned over her steaming boeuf bourguignon.

"Lower your voice," she whispered with a cheeky grin. "You don't want to rile the natives."

She continued, sotto voce, enjoying the drama she had produced. "You know, Vivienne is really behind all this," she said, waving her hand at the wealth all around them. "She likes her luxuries."

Carmel considered this. "Okay, that would make more sense," she said slowly. "All the other women in their community dress pretty conservatively, cotton skirts, scarves over their hair. But she's always done up with her hair and her clothes and stilettos, not to mention the makeup––almost like Tammy Faye Baker, for heaven's sake."

"She does take pride in her appearance, certainly," Rhonda said, a little put out at the comparison. "But there's nothing wrong in that." She cast a glance at Carmel. "Wouldn't hurt if more people made a regular effort," she continued, raising an eyebrow.

Carmel knew she had asked for that barb. Rhonda was nothing if not loyal to her close friends. She had always been a bit of a snob, too, so Vivienne with her fine restaurant and designer clothes would definitely be considered a comrade. "So, you were saying," she urged.

"I probably shouldn't ... but, oh, it's common knowledge. I'm not breaking confidentiality."

"Is she your patient, too?" Carmel asked.

Rhonda brushed that query aside. "Vivienne comes from a very wealthy background. Texas oil, I should think," she began. "Had a very sheltered life. She fell in love with her pastor, Wilson, with her father's blessing."

That wasn't the story passed around Wilson's congregation via Bridget. "Didn't I hear some mention that she was a lesbo wild child in Switzerland? Doesn't sound very sheltered to me," Carmel asked. "Isn't that why her father sent her to some sort of bible camp? To get 'fixed'?"

"Where did you hear that nonsense?"

"Sorry, just a bit of gossip from someone who was jealous, I'm sure."

Rhonda nodded sympathetically. "People are very jealous of Vivienne," she agreed. "It comes with the territory––being wealthy and beautiful. It's difficult sometimes." A look of self-pity washed over her face momentarily.

"Anyway, you were saying that Vivienne fell in love with Wilson?"

"Yes, and she followed him up here," she continued. "He was determined to civilize the barbarians through the word of God, and she decided she could do her part by raising the standard of living by example. It was a love match: they were so well-suited."

Carmel couldn't let that one go past her. The facts of the matter belied Rhonda's fantasy. "But I heard he abused her! She was preparing to leave him when he was killed."

"Abused her? What nonsense." The physician put her head to one side to consider. "They may not have agreed 100 percent all the time, that's natural. In any marriage there can be difficult times. I mean, my last husband ... But Vivienne is a very emotional woman. Just because she went seeking asylum at the shelter doesn't mean ..."

"So you're saying she lied?"

"No, but perhaps she was overwrought," Rhonda said. "I'm sure they would have made up, except he ..."

Except he got himself murdered. "The way I heard it was they fought a lot, and her father left Wilson all his money, cutting off his daughter completely, and Wilson wouldn't let her leave."

"That's not true," Rhonda said stubbornly. "And we're very close friends. I would have known. That's just horrible vicious gossip."

"But now Wilson's dead ... Where does that leave Vivienne?" Carmel asked.

Rhonda looked up from her wine, aghast. "Oh dear."

She thought for a moment then continued, a barely perceptible furrow appearing on her botoxed brow. "If they'd had a fight bad enough to send her to the shelter, then he might also have changed his will, or signed his wealth over to his church."

Carmel related the scene at the War Memorial, along with Wilson's words as the waiter approached to remove their entrees and replace them with a deceptively simple chocolate bread pudding.

"Oh dear God," said Rhonda. "He may have signed away her money. How very, very tragic."

Or he might have been intending to do so, which was a good reason for Vivienne to murder him. Except the murdering woman could not have been his wife.

Carmel spooned the last of her heavenly bread pudding into her mouth, closing her mouth to savour the exquisite buttery chocolate silk texture.

"Enjoying your meal, Rhonda?" A soft Texan drawl interrupted her amid a cloud of perfume. "Everything to y'all's satisfaction?"

Carmel opened her eyes and almost choked on the extravagant dessert. There was Vivienne standing before them, a free woman in her stilettoes, makeup, and black Gucci evening gown. The blond hair curled immaculately as always, just like the glimpse she'd had of it the other night. A little red around the eyes, perhaps, but in perfect control otherwise.

How could she have been in two places at once?

Rhonda stood and gave Vivienne a gentle hug. "So sorry about your loss," she murmured softly. "Anything I can do, just call me."

Tears spurted to the woman's eyes, and she held tightly onto her friend's hand. "I still can't believe it," she said. "Who could have done such a thing to that fine man?"

"I admire your strength in keeping going," Rhonda said.

"Well, the show must go on," Vivienne said as she gazed toward the diners, the perfect picture of sorrowing widowhood. Something caught her attention and a momentary frown crossed her face. She clicked her fingers and pointed. The young waiter was on it immediately and straightened the silverware of an empty table setting.

"I'll call you," Rhonda promised.

Vivienne nodded, turned back to the room and sashayed forth, stopping by a table of regulars and accepting their condolences.

"Yes, a tragedy," she heard her agreeing sorrowfully, two tables away. "But one must carry on the good work. Wilson would have wanted it that way."

"See?" Rhonda hissed at her. "Does she look like a woman who's happy her husband is dead?"

Only when she herself stood up did Carmel remember they had shared two carafes of the fine house wine. She would not be driving her car back to St. Jude Without that night, she thought, as she wove her way out to the reception desk. She pulled on her coat as Rhonda settled the bill, then the two went out into the cold night.

The fresh breeze cleared her head a little, but she knew she was still too drunk for driving even the short distance back to her home.

"Come on then, I'll give you a lift," Rhonda told her.

"You drank as much as I did," Carmel pointed out.

"What?" Rhonda said. "Oh, no. I didn't drive. Don't be ridiculous. Jack is here to pick me up."

She led the way to a large black sedan waiting quietly by the door. Carmel remembered something she hadn't done. She ran back to her own humble vehicle and fished out the present she had brought for Rhonda.

"Here you go," she said, climbing into the depths of the car's backseat and handing the box with Bridget's mug inside to Rhonda. "Merry Christmas, and thanks for the meal."

During the short drive, they continued the discussion about Vivienne.

"I don't understand," Carmel began. "How they could be so very different, yet be as happy as you say they were."

"How do you mean?" Rhonda asked as she reapplied her lipstick in a conveniently placed small lit mirror.

"He wore a monk's habit, and preached simplicity. She wears designer clothes and runs the most expensive restaurant in the province," she demanded. "Explain that."

"He loved her," the other replied. "It would be inhuman of him to expect her to live the way he wanted."

"But, a butler? Really?"

"Oh, Franzi," Rhonda laughed. "That's Viv's little indulgence. She needed the company. And Franz also doubles as a chauffeur. She couldn't be expected to drive herself, now, could she? She wasn't brought up that way." This was stated sincerely, with the nonchalance of one born to wealth.

The car stopped outside of Carmel's 200-year-old cottage. Rhonda lifted her head and looked all about her at the dark cove.

"Oh dear God in heaven," she said, horror etched in her words. "Where ever are you living?"

Chapter 14

Vivienne didn't do it, and according to Rhonda, Wilson wasn't abusing his wife. And at the time of her husband's garroting, Vivienne was at the shelter seeking counseling for her husband's violent abuse against her. She couldn't have killed him.

Carmel still had a hard time getting her head around that one, for she had witnessed the murder——she knew she had. Sitting at her kitchen table, morning coffee in hand, she closed her eyes and pictured that snapshot of time burned in her memory. Looking down into Snellen's Field from the road, the pair was standing near the edge of the mob. She could see the back of the woman's blonde head, standing behind the man in the brown robe.

Yes, the woman's hands were up near the man's neck—she had thought at the time the woman was going to jump on him, piggyback style. But he had leaned back toward her, throwing them both off balance. Carmel paused, coffee in mid-air as another memory came to her. Just before the woman had disappeared back into the melee, she had pulled the cowl back over her head and glanced all around her. Had the woman seen Carmel that night? Was she herself now in danger too for being a witness? No, impossible. The road above had been pitch black. She hoped.

But if it wasn't Vivienne, who was Wilson's murderer? Carmel tried but couldn't think of any other blond women she knew around the area. Sharran was way too tall. Rhonda—no, that was laughable. No matter how good friends she was with Vivienne, no way the doctor would go out in those mucky fields in her Jimmy Choos. One of his flock, perhaps? Was he abusing other women too? But those blond curls glinting in the faint light of the pitch torch ... The locks were so blond, the colour couldn't be natural. Artifice was surely responsible for the bright gold of Vivienne's hair, without a doubt, but none of Wilson's congregation habituated hair salons—that went against their whole belief system. Besides, the women of his flock wore scarves over their hair.

A wig. Of course. It had to be a wig the woman was wearing. Carmel's heart deflated, because that meant it could be anyone. A wig with a mask made an effective disguise, especially in the dim light of that night. If one of his congregation was set on breaking God's commandment against murder, they probably wouldn't be too bothered about breaking Wilson's rule against wearing fake hair.

But if it hadn't been one of his own flock, then what other woman would have had reason to top him off? The answer had to lie in the shelter—that was the most obvious. The women there would have known about his supposed cruelty toward his wife. If Vivienne was as much a drama queen as Rhonda, then that was probably not the first time she'd gone crying to the shelter when she argued with her spouse. And anyone involved in the social action surrounding the Anti-Violence group had to feel strongly about the issue of wife beating. Perhaps there was a lone vigilante nut in the group? She wondered if there had been other murders of this nature, unexplained deaths of men who'd abused their women. The police wouldn't necessarily be able to tie the two together, as abused women didn't always go to the police. Bridget had pointed out the reasons. And with the cancellation of the Family Violence Court several years back, they would have even less recourse to get help.

She placed her empty coffee cup back on the table, knowing what she'd be doing that day. A visit to the shelter was in order, officially to register as a volunteer, but also to check out the people who ran the place. Women loved to talk, she knew, being a woman herself, and she might be able to pick up some hint about who would be avid enough to think that murder was the way to solve the problems of violence against women.

This was not going to be easy, she knew.

Chapter 15

S he found the shelter at the back of a large building on Freshwater Road, a small door almost hidden under a dark overhang, just as Sharran had described. At the front were the offices that were the public face of the organization and the women's clinic.

Carmel opened the door into a narrow stairwell, lit only by filtered light from the windows above. The sound of voices grew as she ascended, finally reaching a doorless entry into a space that might have been an old classroom. The large room was littered with old sofas and desks, while a meeting appeared to be in progress at a central round table.

A solid woman with a short haircut and a plaid shirt looked up from the group.

"Can I help you?" she called out. At this, the other four--all women of various ages--looked up. Her eyes met Sharran's welcoming smile.

"C'mon in, Carmel," the minister said, giving a welcoming wave. "Didn't expect to see you so soon." She stood up and strode over to her, clasping her hand in a solid shake.

"Coffee's on, and we're just finished up here," she continued, deftly moving Carmel over to the coffee machine. "Help yourself. Pam, Carmel's our newest volunteer. Want to fill her in on what we do here?"

The plaid-shirted Pam proceeded to give Carmel a very thorough versing of the runnings of the shelter, how the phone line worked, and what volunteers could be expected to do during their shifts. Within an hour, she had very efficiently covered legal aspects, who to let in and when to call the police, among many other things. Carmel's mind was swimming just a little as the list of topics covered was meticulously ticked off by the other woman.

"Of course, you need special training to be on the phone lines," Pam informed her. "That includes suicide intervention, violence de-escalation, and listening skills. We'll be holding classes after Christmas, once a week for a month. You need to do all sessions before you can take your turn on the phones."

"So much," Carmel murmured, looking at the various forms and policies spread out on the table before her.

"It is a lot," Pam agreed gruffly, "but it's serious work. And it's important to do it right."

Sharran had overheard this last bit. "If we can prevent one more death," she said sadly. "Contrary to popular opinion, more murders are committed by a spouse than a stranger. The level of violence in a relationship follows a well-known trajectory—it might start out as jealousy and manipulation, escalate to verbal abuse, and then the physical begins ... Well, you know the story. We want to reach out, help people recognize the signs early on, to cut the cycle."

"It's a big job," Carmel said, nodding and taking her coat in hand. She hadn't had much opportunity to pick up gossip or look for potential murders this morning, for the regulars here didn't spend a lot of time just sitting and yakking as she had expected. The shelter was very efficiently run, no doubt Sharran's influence. At least, she had established herself and could drop in again at a time when they weren't so busy, when the staff was more relaxed.

Pam and Sharran also put on their outdoor wear and moved toward the exit.

"We're heading out to the food bank to do up the Christmas baskets," the tall blond minister told her. "Sure is a busy time of year."

Under the shadowed overhang, Carmel paused to put on her gloves. The sky was a clear blue, with a stiff north wind blowing the clouds away. The temperature was dropping fast.

The familiar silver Land Rover pulled neatly into the chain-link fence parking lot and made an abrupt sweep, readying for a quick re-exit, but then stopped beside the women. The passenger door opened and the newly widowed Vivienne climbed out, her eyes on Sharran and emotion running high in her face.

"Vivienne!" Sharran strode toward her. "How are you doing? I'm so sorry for your loss ..."

"Don't come near me!" Vivienne shrieked, her eyes blazing fury. "You killed my husband."

Sharran stopped short, her arms still held out for the expected embrace.

"All of y'all," Vivienne continued in a rising voice, looking at Sharran and Pam. "If you hadn't lured me into your evilness, encouraging me to act against my husband, he'd still be alive. I'm being punished by God! You Satanists and ... and baby-killers! How could I have trusted you?"

Tears of rage ran down her face, carving channels into her pancake makeup and spreading her mascara. The small woman was out of control, finally overtaken by grief and shaking with anger, the rising wind threatening to whip her bright pink scarf away. Carmel couldn't help but notice that Vivienne wore flats today––not her more stylish heels––surely a sign of how upset she was.

The driver of the vehicle appeared by her side and placed a gloved hand on Vivienne's arm. Carmel could hear him murmuring softly.

"I can't bear it!" Vivienne sobbed, as she turned back to the comfort of his arms.

Beneath his peaked chauffeur's hat, Carmel saw a pair of icy blue eyes staring over Vivienne's bent head at Sharran. This must be the butler. It was a strangely attractive face in that it was blessed with perfect symmetry--yet it lacked warmth. The man's blond hair was so short it was almost shaven, accentuating the pale, graceful neck. Carmel was unable to tear her eyes away, fascinated. Yet at the same time, shivers crept up her spine. The man was beautiful, totally asexual and without colour, like a washed-out David Bowie. A creepy David Bowie.

He urged Vivienne back into the vehicle and firmly shut the door behind her. Without another look or word, he too returned to his seat, and the vehicle sped out of the lot.

Chapter 16

D riving home, all Carmel could think was that Vivienne had the same idea as she did––that Wilson's murder was linked to the shelter. One of those supposedly good and dedicated volunteers had taken on the role of vigilante. Was this the beginning of a movement—would the police soon find more bodies of abusers? She couldn't imagine the good-humoured Sharran or the earnest Pam taking justice into their own hands.

Her small car bounced against wind gusts rising from Windsor Lake and she found herself dropping her speed to regain control, sparking the ire of the drivers behind her. So much for the season of goodwill and peace among men, she thought, not daring to take her hand off the wheel to flip a finger at the car who was furiously tailing her. She was relieved to turn onto the quiet roads of Portugal Cove leading to St. Jude Without. Her car moved slowly against the buffeting winds along the road which hugged the mountain, now splattered by cold rain which was almost, but not quite, turning to hail.

An unfamiliar car was parked in her driveway, a small Chevy from the last century whose rust had almost obliterated the original brown paint job. As she pulled up alongside it, a man unfolded himself from it, huddled against the biting winds. Tall and thin and dressed in an inadequately short black pea jacket, his shoulders were hunched against the biting cold while a long striped scarf flapped colourfully against the gusts.

He peered at her through the drops that were quickly collecting on his thick black-rimmed glasses.

"You'll be Carmel, I'm hoping," he said as she got out of the car. He spoke with a thick Irish brogue. "I've come about the room you're renting. The University put me on to you. Sorry about the lack of notice. I know I should have called first, but my phone is out of juice."

At least, that's what she thought she heard him say between the howling wind and the crack of the (almost) hail against the metal of the cars and the rush of his words. Not having heard back from the university about a boarder, she'd put it from her mind and forgotten all about it. That was way back in the fall, before her trip to St. Kitts.

"Hi." She paused in front of him. "Why don't you come in out of the rain and we can talk?" She hurried past him to lead the way up the steps, and could feel them thudding as he took them two at a time with his long legs.

"I do apologize for bursting in on you like this," he continued as she shut the front door firmly against the wind. She flicked the deadbolt to keep the ancient door from blowing open in the wind. "And it's a terrible day for it. I take it the university people didn't contact you yet?"

She took off her jacket and shook the rain off it. "No, not a word. But you know bureaucracy—there's probably a letter in the mail." She stopped and removed her boots, and hauled out two pairs of thick hand-knit socks from the basket in the hall closet, castoffs of the house's previous owner. She could feel a tickling sneeze coming back.

The house was minimally warmer than outside. He unwound the striped scarf from his neck and removed his black pea jacket. It was frayed at the cuffs and ripped at the pockets. It had seen much better days.

"You can put these on," she said handing him the larger pair of socks. "They'll keep your feet warm."

"The name's Ian Mulrennan." He bent to unlace his heavy black boots. "I'm taking the Master's of Police Studies at the university. It's a fine program that they're offering, don't you know."

"Carmel McAlastair." She took this opportunity to slip into the living room to fold up the quilts left scattered on the furniture. The kitchen ... well, he didn't seem the type to mind a few dirty dishes in the sink. "Come on through, I'll put the kettle on."

He stood at the door to the kitchen and gazed around him through his wet glasses. A tall man, as she'd already noted, but thin, too, and his dark hair stuck out in every direction. His green army-issue sweater was in much the same shape as his coat––frayed at the elbows and hem. He looked to be in his mid-30s, or perhaps he was a hard-worn late 20s. She offered him a tissue to wipe his glasses.

"Oh, thanks for that," he said as he removed them from his face. "Much better now. It's a very charming home you have here."

"It's humble," she said, looking around as she filled the electric kettle. The only new items were the stackable washer/dryer duo sitting by the back door. It was a bit of a squeeze getting past it, but the convenience was well worth it. The kitchen decor, like the rest of the house, hadn't been renovated since the mid-1980s. There was no dishwasher or stovetop fan, and one of the wooden cupboard doors was hanging askew. Funny how you didn't notice these things until someone else was there, as if their presence allowed you to look through their eyes. The room could do with a lick of paint and more.

"It'll suit me just fine," he said.

He hadn't seen the upstairs yet. "I wasn't expecting ... I mean to say, the second bedroom isn't quite ready for habitation yet," she said. "But I can work on that over Christmas."

"Oh." He bent his unruly head and with his finger traced the outline of an ancient ink stain on the oak table. "I was hoping, perhaps, a bit sooner than that." He looked up and sighed. "Y'see, I'm in a bit of a bind. My mate——a musician I was camping out with——well, he's gone on an extended tour of Ireland, so I had to clear out of his place, and, well, I've got his car, but it's not the most comfortable to sleep in, and it being Christmas and all ..."

It being Christmas, she couldn't turn him out onto the streets, the message was clear. She shrugged. It was a nuisance, but as long as he was aware of what to expect, it wouldn't hurt for him to move in early. She could move the old boxes and things being stored in the second bedroom down to the cellar. Or even better, get him to do it, so she wouldn't have to go down there. Carmel brightened.

"If you wouldn't mind helping me clear the stuff out of the room ..."

He nodded enthusiastically. "Not a problem. I'd be glad to help in any way. Just tell me what to do, and you can consider it done."

She poured the boiling water into the teapot. "That's okay then." As she sat across from him, she got down to the business of the monthly rent. Again, he was more than agreeable.

"There's just one thing," he said as she poured two cups. "I'm a bit skint right at the moment." He caught her eye and hastened to explain. "My student grant'll be here at the end of December; it just takes a few days to get through the banks, don't you know. And then we'll get all straightened out money-wise. I don't anticipate any problems on that front, not at all." He nodded his head.

He seemed honest enough, just a little down on his luck at this time. It was Christmas, right, the season of giving. Well, she could help him out. She remembered well enough times when she'd been down on her luck in her life, and now she was glad to pass on the favour.

Carmel reached out and took down the cookie tin, full of seasonal shortbread with little red and green cherries on their tops. She offered them to him. A handful of the cookies disappeared into his mouth as if he hadn't eaten in a few days.

"So Police Studies, eh?" she said. "Funny, you don't really look like a cop." Not that she knew many, just Inspector Darrow, who was never without a tie around his neck. Of course, there was Constable Wright too, but her blond hair and its severe bun were a far cry from Ian's unkempt do.

"I'm not in the police, not at all," he agreed. "At least not yet. Y'see, I studied music at Queen's University, and that got me into computers. In a roundabout way, they're closely related with the mathematics of it all, so I stayed on a bit longer." He paused to take a breath. "And I'm a reader. I love the crime novels. So one day I got to thinking about a program I was working on, and how it could be adjusted with just a few tweaks to be used to solve crimes. So I brought it forward to the Guarda, that's the Irish police force, and they sent me here for this Master's, to develop it in conjunction with the Computer Science Department here."

He was a riveting speaker, his voice full of expression and his whole body taken up with his passion. Intelligence gleamed from behind the thick glasses. She nodded slowly. She had met people like him before, creative, charming, and brilliant to boot.

"So you baffled them with your bull in order to extend your student career."

"And to travel, see a bit of the world before I have to settle down and take a real job," he agreed. He leaned back in his chair. "Tell me now, you wouldn't have a bite to eat, would you? Perhaps a bit of toast and jam. It's just that ..."

"I know," she cut in, smiling as she did. "You haven't had a hot meal in a while."

They continued chatting as she got together the makings of a solid mac and cheese, an old recipe of hers loaded with cheese and noodles, perfect for filling up this hungry student.

"Maybe we can put your computer program to the test," she said, considering. This might be the answer. She proceeded to tell him about the murder in the cove three days ago, what she'd witnessed that night, and all that had happened since.

"I had heard about it, but these details are fascinating," he said. His eyes were round behind his black glasses, the kind of frames that had been trendy for a few years now and were available from all the hot designers. Carmel suspected his were the original National Health issue, or its Irish equivalent, the standard frames given out for free to those who were in need. "Let me just get my laptop out of the car; I can start to plug in the data." He rushed out to his car, returning two minutes later with his socks, sweater, and hair soaked. "It's stopped hailing out there, at any rate. Just rain now."

He gave a damp shiver as he fired up the computer. Carmel looked up from the sink where the cooked macaroni was draining. Ian was a dreamer, one who could create brilliant connections between music, computers, and crime, but he didn't seem to have the sense to protect himself from the elements, and didn't even realize it.

"Hmmmm," he said peering at the screen. "The date, December the 17th, was it? What was the murder victim's profession? Oh, and the costumes, don't forget the costumes."

She layered the noodles, cheese, onions, and breadcrumbs into a pan and set it into the hot oven as he worked.

"Interesting," he said, watching the screen intently as the machine whirred and hummed. "Ah, I hadn't thought of that element. Of course."

Carmel sat down opposite him. "Is it telling you already?" she asked, caught up in Ian's excitement. "It's that easy?" This program could be revolutionary, she thought, saving huge amounts of money for police forces everywhere. And it was happening right here in her kitchen. She could bring the results to Inspector Darrow. An excuse to see him again. "How does it work?"

"It's a bit like the weather programs meteorologists use. You use historical examples to predict the future. If you have enough data from past weather patterns, you can plug in the present data and see what the probable course will be," he said. "Of course, with serial killers, you're also working with the human element, which would include the killer's past, and events which might not appear to have much bearing on the present day," he said, peering up at her through his glasses. "That's the magic of the thing. It takes into account the three basic reasons humans kill other humans: pretty universal when you think of it."

"What are those? The reasons," she urged him on.

"Love (or the other side of the coin, hate), sex, and money," he stated. "Fear is usually the uniting factor."

She thought about that for just a moment. "How about religious wars? There's a lot of murder done in the name of God."

"Love of their concept of God, fear that others do not respect their concept of God. Money, too. You'll often find that scratching a little below the surface of a so-called religious war reveals a fear of lack, and they use the excuse of religion to wipe out the other––the different, the one who is not part of the family. Take the Crusades, if you will," he said. "They weren't fighting for the Christian God, not in a million years. The Europeans just had a good few years, plenty to eat, and the wealthy ended up having surplus sons. They couldn't divide all their lands among the sons—that would finish the family fortunes in no time flat—so they invented religious wars and sent them off, far away. The lads would either get killed, settle down elsewhere, or otherwise make their fortunes. The Crusades were really about money."

Carmel scratched her head. This seemed to be rather sketchy logic, but no doubt the man knew what he was talking about.

"There'll be a few bugs to work out with this, of course. It's always the case with computer programs," he said as he looked up. "And, of course, it can't tell me who did the actual murder. We'd have to put in a lot more data for that, more information than you and I have access to."

"But?"

He stared at the screen for a few minutes longer as the laptop started to beep. He nodded.

"Alright," he nodded, and took a breath. "What I can tell you is that this murder was religious in nature." He pressed a few more keys.

"Religious? But he was a wife-beater. Well, he may have been," she said. "He was a minister, yes, but surely to God no one killed him because of that."

He looked up and shrugged. "Sorry. I can easily understand why you might think spousal abuse was the motive behind his death. It's an emotional topic. However, this program is based on pure logic and science. It is what it is, and this is what it's telling me."

"Can you explain the logic behind this deduction?" Carmel asked.

"The timing is part of it. The murder occurred at the beginning of the festival of Saturnalia, the ancient religious festival, also known as Calends, in Turkey. This, by the way, also involves the tradition of wild partying at Christmas time."

"Excessive drinking certainly fits the bill for that night," Carmel said, wryly, "and many other occasions around here. But the Mummer's Affray isn't based on any religious tradition. It's just a bunch of drunks who got dressed up in mummers costumes one year and decided to start walloping each other for fun. They enjoyed it so much they've made it into a tradition."

"That's as it may be," Ian said, thinking aloud as he sat back in his chair. "But perhaps the need for misrule is like a primal urge lurking under the veneer of civilization. It's in the blood, and the animal inside needs to be let out from restrictions every so often."

"So you're saying that Wilson's death fulfilled a genetic need within the community?" Carmel had her doubts about this. It did seem a little farfetched. St. Jude Without and its inhabitants were weird, but surely not Wicker man territory.

"Plus you need to look at his profession." Ian could sense her scepticism. "Not only was he a fundamentalist minister, a leader of a flock—correct me if I'm wrong, for I never knew the man—but didn't he insist on throwing it in people's faces? The holier-than-thou act? By wearing a monk's robe all the time?"

Carmel nodded. "Yes, that's true enough." She thought back to what she remembered of Wilson the Mississippi Preacher Man. He hadn't been sociable in his caring, not like Sharran or Sister Constantine. Not even like the old priest who was in Sid's bar the other night, Father Wish, who was obviously still part of his community. Wilson, although he lived close by, had seemed to put himself above his neighbours. He had abused his wife (maybe), used the money collected by his church to build a big compound, drove a luxury vehicle—the man even had a butler, for God's sake. The signs pointed to his being more concerned with creature comforts, power, and image than performing good acts. She remembered his quality Italian-made shoes beneath the rough-spun robe he'd worn.

"And the worst part is ..." Ian continued, peering at the screen before him. "This program is telling me that Wilson's murder is only the beginning."

"The beginning of what?"

"Maybe we have a serial killer on our hands." He looked up again, fire taking hold of his imagination. "This is not the end of it, by no means."

"When? Who?" This was huge. If the computer program was to be trusted, it was giving bad news indeed. Perhaps Wilson's abuse of Vivienne had just been a red herring that happened to get thrown into the path of the investigators. Anyway, it had already been proven that she had an alibi for the evening of the Affray. The computer was, after all, examining the facts in a logical manner, based on previous cases. "Are you talking about other members of his congregation? Can we expect them to be polished off in the same way?"

"Hard to tell," Ian replied. "It's just a computer, not a Ouija board. It's saying the possibility is strong that this is a trend, giving the data inputted so far. Like I said, if we had access to more information, we could tighten up the response it's giving me."

"We need to pass this information on, let someone know what to expect," Carmel said, standing up and ready for action. "I can introduce you to Inspector Darrow. Perhaps you could work with him to get better data, to pinpoint the next murder before it happens. Maybe if you had access to everything the police already know, you could even find the murderer."

Ian's gaze slid away. "Darrow, now that would be the Scotsman on the Constabulary, eh? There might be a difficulty there. I've already tried to get him interested in the program, to see if they could help me out a little with the financials, don't you know. He's not a believer; he's old-school: his mind isn't open to the possibilities." He thought a moment and his face brightened. "But we can certainly bring it to their attention. I know just the man--met him in a pub a few days ago. He can get the message across for me and be happy to do it."

"What's the plan, then?" Carmel brushed aside the small voice at the back of her mind that doubted Ian's experience of the police inspector, caught up as she was in this new excitement.

"Can't tell you right now, but you'll see," the Irishman said. "Leave it to me." He sniffed the air. "Is that casserole ready now?"

Chapter 17

There was still no word from the airline about her lost luggage, Carmel discovered after waiting an hour on hold. Not that she really needed her light cotton skirts and sandals right now, not in December on the Avalon Peninsula. Warm woollies and a raincoat were called for at this time of year, and she had plenty of them.

Ian had sorted out his room yesterday evening, removing the empty boxes down to the house's dark cellar which she refused to enter. He'd found an old bureau down there and dragged it up. After wiping the accumulation of cobwebs off, they found that three of the four drawers worked fine, and he proclaimed himself ecstatic with the result. His own luggage hadn't consisted of much, just a worn army-issue duffle bag and a battered guitar case.

It was now ten o'clock in the morning. She hesitated about waking him up, not yet familiar with his schedule. As a compromise, she had made a full pot of coffee, so that whatever time he arose he would at least have caffeine to help him start his day.

Drinking her second coffee in the armchair in the living room, she gazed out the window at the point of land leading out to the tickle between St. Jude Without and the end of Bell Island. It was another grey drizzly day, but the wind had blown itself out and hardly anything moved out there save the ferry returning to Portugal Cove.

And Hank, the black and white tuxedo cat who nominally belonged to Melba but who'd adopted the whole community as his extended family of caregivers. The large cat's belly swayed ungracefully as he hopped from step to step, making his way to Carmel's front veranda. He caught her eye and she could hear a faint mewl through the shaky old window frame, a surprisingly small sound from such a large cat.

"I wondered where you'd gotten to," she said to the cat as she let him in. "About time you came to welcome me home."

He ignored her words and went directly to the kitchen where he waited with great patience by the fridge, staring up at the handle. Fine droplets misted the black fur on his back.

"Good to see you, too. Feeling like an egg today, are we?" Carmel gently nudged him out of the way with her foot to open the fridge to see what she could offer him. He was in luck. With the egg cracked and emptied into a bowl, he indicated with a series of chirps that he wished to dine al fresco, out on the back step.

Seeing the cat made her think again of Melba and the old woman's pronouncement of two days ago.

Murder comes in threes.

Settling back into her cozy armchair by the window on this dismal day, Carmel shivered. She'd always thought the old woman was a little loopy; however, it was commonly believed by her other neighbours, if rarely spoken, that Melba was a witch. She made teas and healing ointments from her woodland and garden gatherings, and she communed with the fairies she claimed inhabited the graveyard between her cottage and Carmel's 200-year-old house. Did she also have the gift of prophecy, of seeing into the future? It was almost believable, especially now that Ian's computer program had given the same pronouncement. Science and superstition were both pointing in the same direction.

Could it be true that other religious leaders were in danger?

She really thought that Darrow should know about this; however, she would respect Ian's wishes and not share it with the Inspector, not until Ian was ready. It was his work, after all; his computer program. But she couldn't sit here doing nothing.

Vivienne, she thought. Okay, so maybe Vivienne didn't kill her husband. However, if Ian was right and this was a religiously motivated murder, surely the first place to look would be within his congregation. Perhaps Vivienne, having knowledge of Wilson's church attendees, might be able to shine some light on disgruntled parishioners, someone who'd broken away from the church or who had a grudge against Wilson. Of course, if the computer program was correct and this was a serial killer bent on doing away with religious leaders, then it could be anyone, anyone at all within the greater St. John's area. But she didn't have the resources to look that widely, so she might as well make a start where she could.

She remembered Vivienne's emotional scene the previous day outside the women's shelter. The widow must be tormented out of her mind, believing as she did that her own actions had brought on her husband's death. Personally, Carmel thought that if she'd been in the same position, she would have been perhaps not overjoyed, but at least a little relieved to have the man gone. But not being a religious person nor a particularly traditional kind of woman, she had no way of knowing how Vivienne's mind worked.

But even a heathen like herself could at least offer the woman sympathy. Stuck in that huge house with no company but a redundant butler/chauffeur, Vivienne might be open to good wishes from a near neighbour. Perhaps she could help to rest her mind, too, by steering the widow toward a discussion of who might have wished her husband ill. The woman had every right to know about the results of the computer program. Who knows if she would be the next target? A logical step in thinking, she prided herself, because whoever had issues with Wilson's misuse of church funds might easily transfer that feeling to the man's wife, who was still living in the house built with his ill-gotten gains.

Carmel had no offerings to bring to Vivienne and she thought that it was customary to bring food to console people. It would certainly be a custom in this cove at any rate where people seemed to eat non-stop, and it surely wouldn't hurt to pop into the bakery up the road from the ferry landing, to be on the safe side.

As she made her way back along North Point Road, her car full of warm bakery smells, she reminded herself of how she would handle the conversation with Vivienne. Besides offering her condolences, Carmel needed to find out who among the congregational circle might have a desire to kill Wilson, and if this disquiet might be stretched out to cover other religious figures.

She turned into the driveway of the house set behind the thick row of bushes which blocked the view of the house from the road and got a good look again at the mansion. It looked like it belonged in a movie set, with its imposing pillars lining the steps up to a double front door, more like a grand house from the American South than a home around the bay in Newfoundland. The outside was stuccoed white and all of the many windows had their drapes drawn shut, as if the house could no longer bear to look out onto the cold December of the North Atlantic.

The Land Rover was parked outside the house, which meant Vivienne was home with Franz. No other vehicles were present, so this should be a good time to visit without interruptions. With an armful of Christmas shortbread cookies decorated with red and green maraschino cherries cut to look like holly leaves and berries, she pressed the bell. A subdued, old-fashioned ding-dong chimed within. She didn't hear footsteps or movement, but the door silently swung inwards.

Franz stood in the half-opened doorway, his right arm holding the inside doorknob as if ready to shut it in her face, wearing a neutral expression. He wore a black suit, his tie a subdued blue. The white shirt had a high collar with the points pressed down—it reminded Carmel of the portrait of Dorian Grey from the turn of the century writings of Oscar Wilde. He had the finest features she'd ever seen on a man. His eyes were an icy blue, so light as to be almost silver, and his blond hair was styled short. His was a face which should have been attractive with its absolute bilateral symmetry, but his chin was perhaps too soft and the skin too perfect and the eyes too cold.

"Madam is indisposed," he said in a clipped European accent and lifted his gloved hand to the jamb as if to prevent her entrance.

"Who is it, Franzi?" A soft drawl came from behind him, and he opened the door a fraction wider. Vivienne appeared at his shoulder, a perfect picture of the fashionable grieving widow from her mid-length black dress to her silk stockings and high black heels. Her eyes were reddened still.

"I've seen you before," she said. "But we haven't been introduced."

"I was at Oceanica with Rhonda," Carmel said. "Several nights ago." She introduced herself. "I just wanted to offer you my condolences, as a neighbour. To see if there's anything I can do for you." She hadn't mentioned the scene outside the shelter, for she didn't think Vivienne had seen her there.

"Please, do come in." At this, Franz stiffened and grasped the door again. Vivienne turned to him. "I may be suffering a grievous loss, but I can still be mannerly," she told him. "Why don't you get the coffee service ready for us and bring it into the parlour?"

He held the door tight still and stared at her with no expression on his features. The two were much of the same height with the added inches of her stilettos.

"Franzi," she said, a hint of steel belying the softness of her voice. "Please do as I request." He gave a curt nod and stepped back.

As she entered into the two-story foyer, Carmel held out the bag of cookies wrapped in their festively printed plastic to him. He took it in his gloved hand with an almost audible sniff, turned, and disappeared into the centre of the house.

She looked all around her at the marble floors and then up, up to the source of the brightness, a glistening chandelier which threw prisms of light throughout the large hallway. Through an archway, she could see the gleaming wooden floors of the parlour, a huge room with seating for at least 20 in the plush sofas and chairs scattered tastefully around. No expense had been spared in furnishing this place. She wondered if the bathroom taps were plated with gold.

Vivienne led her into the room and indicated she should sit on the closest sofa. From here, she could see the deep red velvet drapes firmly shut against the weak December light.

"Franz is very protective of me at this time," Vivienne said. "The police haven't left me alone. And the reporters ... I declare, I am tormented by it all."

"I'm sorry for your troubles," Carmel said, using the time-honoured expression of sympathy. "This must be a very hard time for you."

Vivienne shut her eyes and sighed, nodding her head. "I feel like my world has been turned upside down." She bent her head and paused. "Reverend Wilson and I had our ... differences, sometimes, but they were not insurmountable." Vivienne lifted her eyes again and fixed Carmel with a spec-ulative stare. "You live in St. Jude Without, you say. No doubt the local winds of gossip have told you my story."

Caught unexpectedly, Carmel had no chance to arrange her face in a lie. She nodded. "A little."

The other woman thought for a moment, then her shoulders visibly relaxed as if letting go of a burden. "I might as well tell the truth of the matter," Vivienne said. "Wilson and I were not ... a compatible couple." Her voice was slow in its southern drawl. "I committed certain indiscretions in my younger days, over which I sorrowed greatly when I came to see the light. Wilson helped me though this difficult time, and caused me to feel love for him. I believed he was a good man and so I agreed to marry him, to make my Daddy happy. Daddy was not well, and he worried that I would be alone without a man to care for me. After all, scurrilous gossip travels the fastest, no matter where you live or what level of society, and there weren't many men in my circle willing to take me on for my sins."

Carmel wondered if Rhonda had heard this version of events, and wondered also why Vivienne was opening up to such a stranger as herself.

Franz entered the room and laid the silver coffee service down on the cherry wood table. He poured two cups, handed them to the women and exited again, all without making a sound. Carmel could have sworn he had silently clicked his heels together after giving Vivienne her cup.

Vivienne used the silver tongs to drop in a cube of sugar. "I hope you don't mind me telling this story, but I feel the need to talk. For too long I have been silenced," she said as she stirred her coffee thoughtfully. "I truly believed he was a good man. But then—it was discovered he was taking money from his church, from the good people, the poor, who had sent their last dollars to his televangelist ministry." She looked up at Carmel, again fixing her with that steely gaze. Her voice grew passionate. "He was a greedy man, a weak man when it came to material items. He loved Mammon more than God."

She gave a small laugh overlaced with cynicism. "He atoned for his sins––oh yes, very publicly––and to show he meant it, moved us all up here to these northern reaches. Told the world he was exiling himself to the wilderness, to spread God's word among the heathens." Vivienne sat very still and her voice lowered almost to a whisper. "But then my Daddy died. He left all his fortune to Wilson––not me, his only child." She paused, but then continued in a stronger voice. "Well, you know as well as I do what happens when you give an addict his drug. He rejoiced in the cash. Wilson built this lovely home, a fortress, a jail for me."

It was difficult for Carmel to reconcile this version of the Mississippi Preacher Man with the one she had witnessed, the heavy-laden man dressed in his simple brown robe. Her doubts must have shown on her face, and Vivienne was quick to jump on it.

"You were the one who found his body, weren't you?"

Carmel nodded.

"Did you happen to notice the fine Italian shoes he wore beneath his robe?" Vivienne asked. She saw the answer on the other woman's countenance. "Yes, his piety was all on the surface. He loved his creature comforts. And he grew to hate it here, too—the cold, the unceasing damp, the very rocks of this place. And as he grew more frustrated, he took it out on the one person who was closest to him. I suffered at his hands, suffered greatly with the beatings. It's only through my own strength that I have survived this long." She put her hand to her forehead as she leaned back.

"You're probably wondering if he forced me to wear these fine clothes too?" She gave another angry laugh. "I lost my faith a long time ago, long before he was found out and forced to move up north. I played along when I first got here, only for the sake of appearances. But after Daddy's death, what was the point? I chose to dress like this, live like this—just to throw it all in their pious faces. They couldn't see that Wilson was two-faced—but I could, and by living my life like this I was showing them, flaunting it maybe. They still couldn't see. He had everybody fooled, even you, no doubt."

"Did you have no one to help you? To talk with?" Carmel asked, wondering why if she and Rhonda were such good friends, she hadn't shared her story with the physician.

Vivienne sat up abruptly. "Who was there here? I got so sick of those do-gooders he called his congregation. Flock of the Innocents, indeed. Flock of the Deadly Boring, I called them. I had few equals here, no one to talk with, no supporters." She picked up the coffee cup again, her eyes flicking to Carmel as she sipped. "I couldn't even speak with Rhonda. She was also Wilson's physician, and, besides, Rhonda just sees what she wants to see."

Carmel couldn't disagree with that. "Why didn't you just leave?"

"In my world, a woman's place is by her husband," Vivienne told her, as if scandalized that Carmel could even question this. "Besides, where would I go? I had no money to call my own. No power. You do know that Wilson wouldn't even allow me to drive?"

They both watched as Franz entered the room with an almost feline grace. He bent down and clicked on the electric fireplace without a word. The faint glow coming from it didn't help the room to feel cosier, but only served to emphasize the shadows in the far reaches of the parlour.

"Franzi is my only strength," Vivienne said, as if he wasn't even present. "I demanded, yes, I demanded, from Wilson to let me have some help, at least someone to drive me so I could get out of this dreadful place from time to time." She looked fondly at the butler's back.

Carmel waited until he was out of the room. "Can I ask how on earth you found him, here in Newfoundland?" She'd been curious ever since she first heard his European accent.

"Oh, Franz was an old acquaintance," Vivienne replied, brushing aside the query. She caught herself. "What I mean to say is, he worked down home, and was delighted for the opportunity to come here to be with me."

They were both silent for a moment. The scene had the feeling of having been well rehearsed, the words having run through Vivienne's mind endlessly throughout the long lonely years of this exile, only now being able to be expressed with the demise of her husband.

"I hope they find whoever did this," Carmel said, meaning it with all her heart. "It was a horrible thing."

"Did you know that the police found a message on Wilson's phone?" Vivienne's breath caught as she relayed this information. "Someone told him to go to Snellen's Field to find me. They planned to kill him, to ambush my husband."

Carmel stared at her in horror. "Have they traced the sender?"

The other woman shrugged this away and closed her eyes as if she couldn't bear to think of it. "What do you think?" Vivienne leaned in closer, taking a tissue from the satin covered box. "What hurts is that they dressed up as me," she said, eyes large with unshed tears. "Trying to pin this dastardly deed on me—that greatly adds to my distress. Who hates me that much?" She looked away and dabbed her eyes. "It was my fault, I know. I should never have gone to that women's group. Full of man-haters and baby-killers and ... And lesbians!" She kept the tissue in front of her face as if hiding the sight of strong emotion, and her shoulders shook as she sobbed. "I woe the day I listened to that Sharran. She is the worst of them all, that great bumbling Socialist bitch!" Every syllable was spit out with vehemence.

Vivienne was an emotional mess, even Carmel could see, and she knew she didn't have the necessary skills to counsel the woman. Obviously, Sharran could be no help in this situation. Sister Constantine was the only person she could think of turning to. Even if she was Catholic—the nun's calm demeanour had been a solid rock in Carmel's childhood. But she was way on the other side of the city, and it would take too long to ferry her out here. Vivienne needed someone now, someone close.

Of course—Father Aloysius. Although long retired, the priest still lived in the large rectory by the church on the crest of the hill with other retired priests. It would only take a minute to drive over there and fetch him. He was a kind man, and would surely be willing to help out.

She stood up to take her leave.

Vivienne looked up at her. "They say that you helped the police, last fall," she said. "Will you help them find who did this?"

Carmel looked at her, biting her lip. She had imagined herself as a sleuth and had enjoyed the role for a short time, until she'd been attacked, drugged, and shoved into an ancient root cellar to die. Yes, she seemed to have a knack for stumbling on bodies, but you couldn't call that helping. Not really. She shook her head.

"Sorry, I didn't actually help them that much," she replied. Noting the hope on Vivienne's face fade, she hurried to offer something, any hopeful crumb. "But my new tenant is working on his Master's of Police Studies," she told her. "He's developed a computer program which he says can help point the way to the culprit."

The effect on Vivienne was electric. She sprang up from her chair. "Tell me more," she demanded. "How do I meet this young man?"

Carmel thought for a moment. Ian didn't seem to keep regular hours, and she had no idea if he was still occupied at the university this close to Christmas. "I don't know what his schedule is like," Carmel said. "But I'll pass on to him that you're interested and would like to help. You may even be able to offer more information which can help narrow it down."

"I need to speak with him," Vivienne said. She walked quickly over to the fireplace and pulled a long strip of embroidered fabric that Carmel had thought was part of the décor. A bell sounded in a near region of the house. "Franz, please see this lady out." The interview was obviously over. She turned to Carmel. "I thank you for providing me this comfort. I will meet with your tenant. Now, I think I must rest."

Chapter 18

S itting in her car, Carmel wondered at the sudden change in Vivienne at the mention of Ian and his program, how she appeared revitalized. Grief hits each person in different ways. She remembered how, as a child, the news of her own mother's death had hardly affected her at all, or so it seemed to everyone around her. Yet, a month after that terrible news, at the expected death of the convent's oldest cat, a large ginger tom scarred by his outdoor life and who had lived a full fifteen very happy and murderous years—at his passing, Carmel had cried buckets for a whole week.

She had offered new hope to Vivienne, but still the woman must be carrying a great load of grief. Off to Father Wish then, to see if that good man could help her deal with her anger and other overwhelming emotions.

The large wooden structure was plain and built at a time when the church had attracted a large number of young men as a career choice. Nowadays, however, there were fewer who could agree to the demand for lifelong celibacy, and the big white house was used to house the retired priests, those who had served their lives for the church. Many such structures had been built around the island from the same blueprint to house convents and priests, but most had been auctioned off to be turned into B & Bs or office buildings, the upkeep on the big houses too much for the fewer number of priests these days.

There was only one car in the lot—a bright red Kia. Not an expensive make of car, but the colour was an unexpected choice for a priest. She didn't know if it was Father Wish's or not. Wood smoke was rising from one of the tall chimneys on the roof, so someone was home.

She approached the grand porched door, confident in her welcome. The modern buzzer sounded loudly through the house, but there was no answering sound of footsteps. The door stood barely ajar, as if the last person leaving the house hadn't quite bothered to pull it all the way shut.

Careless, she thought, and gave the door a push. It was stuck, the old wooden frame having swollen a little over the years. That was no doubt why it hadn't been properly closed. She gave it a shove with her shoulder and it opened freely.

"Hello?" No one answered. She projected her voice to carry up the sweeping staircase to the floor above. "Father Aloysius, are you home?"

I'll just leave a note then, she thought, and looked around for a notepad. Surely there must be one handy somewhere, a leftover relic from the time before telephones, when the rectory door would never be locked and folks would leave their messages. The hallway was bare, except for two faded prints hanging on the walls. She glanced up at the closest one fondly. The old fisherman in his sou'wester sat facing the artist as he rowed, bringing his two grandchildren across a body of water. She had lost count of the number of times she had seen this same print hanging in halls and living rooms. It had been popular once upon a time.

The first door to the right was open, and she could see the fire crackling within the tiled fireplace. Whoever it is must have just left for a moment, she decided. Maybe gone to the little boy's room.

But on opening the door fully, she saw that the occupant was still present. Sitting in a large comfy chair facing the fire, his head lolled to one side as he gazed unseeingly toward the mantle. This was not a natural death. There was no mistaking the protruding tongue, the dark purple of the face, and the bulging eyes. She'd seen that same look just a few days ago, on the Reverend Wilson, the Mississippi Preacher Man. There was even an end of white electrical cord draped over the chair back.

Her throat closed up, the welling scream escaping only as the smallest sound. She glanced around the room, her eyes moving in darting motions, but there were no other occupants, no one waiting with a length of electric cord ready to pounce.

She did the only thing that made sense, the only possible action, and took off through the hallway and massive front door and down the steps to her car where she locked all the doors.

The open front door gaped at her.

With shaking hands she hauled her cellphone out of her purse and sat blankly, looking at its display. What was she supposed to do with this? All she could think was Darrow. It took only a moment to retrieve him from her contacts and push the right button to dial.

He answered almost immediately.

"Darrow here."

The sound of his voice, that soft comforting Scots accent, relaxed her throat and a sigh escaped. She hadn't even realized she hadn't been breathing.

"Carmel?" he asked, his voice sharp. "What is it?" A small part of her brain, one removed from the present crisis, noted that he must have entered her into his contacts too, for he couldn't have recognized her voice from the sigh.

"Yeah," she said. "It's me. I've found ... Oh God."

Darrow let loose a muttered curse at the other end of the line. "What? Not another ...."

She nodded. "Yeah. I think it's ..." She couldn't say Father Wish's name. That would make it true. Irrevocably and utterly true.

"Where are you?"

"At the rectory in Portugal Cove," she said. "It's the big white house next to the church, the Holy Rosary Church, on the hill up from the ferry. Past the ferry, past the restaurant ..." Now she'd found her voice she couldn't stop babbling.

"Yes, I know it," he said, cutting her off. "Listen, we'll be out there right away. Stay there."

After she ended the call, she remained sitting in her car, looking out the windshield across the tickle to Bell Island. She remembered back to the end of August when she'd first arrived, how the town and surrounding woods had seemed to pulse with life and colour. The bright green of meadows, the deep blue shades of the water and sky, even the rocks glistened white in the late summer sun. But now all was grey. The road below her, the water of the cove farther down from that, as far as she could see––yes, even Bell Island––it was like looking at an old black and white photograph, just varying shades of the same drabness. A heavy mist beaded the glass in front of her until she could no longer make out the outline of the island in the distance. Everything was blurred now.

The blue and red lights cut through her thoughts in an unexpected swath of colour, and the knocking on her window brought her back to the horrible here and now. It was Darrow. She reached over and unlocked the passenger door. The rain was coming down now at a steady pelt.

"Look, lass, you've got to stop doing this," he said after he'd folded himself into her small car. "I'm having a hard time explaining to the station why it's always you that finds the bodies." His eyes creased. His humour was just what she needed to bring her back to normality.

"Believe me, I don't go looking for them," she said.

"Go through it with me," he said, his manner kind. "Tell me what happened, what you saw."

There wasn't much to tell. She didn't go into what had gone on before to lead her to be looking for Father Aloysius, just how she'd found the dead priest sitting ... Oh God, how awful the scene had been, how absolutely bloody awful.

Darrow remained silent for a moment after she'd finished speaking.

"You sure you recognized the priest?" he asked.

His question took her by surprise. Did she actually recognize the dead man? Had she looked at his face in the split second she'd stood there in the open doorway to the parlour? She shook her head. "I was looking for Father Wish, and I expected to see him," she said. "I really don't know who it is, I guess."

He again advised her to stay put in the car while he joined the investigative team at the rectory. She started the car to get some heat going. It wasn't snowing out, not yet, but the wind had plenty of bite to it. She could feel it, even in the car.

Here it was the 21st of December and not even a scattering of the white stuff out around. The Avalon Peninsula didn't always have a white Christmas, not every year, despite the province's reputation for having winters that typically could last four or five months long. Sometimes the snow didn't happen until mid-January, and a mild winter could mean living in a constant state of melt and slush underfoot. Sometimes, though, the snow could start early November and if it was a colder than average year, the snow wouldn't melt but would keep on coming and pile up until the drifts were over your head. It depended on the year, on the weather patterns. But there was usually something falling from the sky regardless, whether in solid or liquid form.

And here was Inspector Darrow again, so soon. She unrolled her window.

"It's not who you thought," he told her. "He's been identified as another priest living here, Father John. Go on home now. We'll call you into the station later for your statement. I don't need to tell you, but please don't discuss this with anyone."

With that, he patted the frame of her car and turned back to his investigation inside the house.

Chapter 19

"**Y**ou were right," she told him as he poured the tea into two mugs. Ian hadn't been long awake by the looks of him––his black hair standing every which way, and the yawns he was giving off despite the fact that it was just past mid-day on the shortest day of the year. The sun was already lowering somewhere south, behind the wet blanket that was smothering the cove.

He listened with an avid ear as she told him the story of finding the dead priest. It helped to be able to talk about it, helped to get the vision and its ghastly details out of her head. It wasn't until she'd finished, that she remembered Darrow's request to keep it quiet.

"But this is confidential, mind," she added, hoping thereby to absolve herself of guilt.

But the cat was out of the bag. The Irishman was overjoyed with the news and took it as proof that his computer program was working, forgetting that they were talking about a real life murder, the victim's cooling body in the old rectory not one mile from where they sat.

"And you were doubting my work. I could see it in your face," he crowed. "But as I've told you, this is a scientific method of deduction. It will change police work, bring it into the 21st century. And about time, right? The bloody dinosaurs will have to listen to me now."

"You should really bring this to the Royal Newfoundland Constabulary now," she said, getting caught up in his excitement, forgetting again so quickly that she wasn't supposed to say a word about the details of the murder. "Inspector Darrow will listen to you this time, I'm sure of it. He's pretty open-minded." She took out her cell, ready to call him.

"Darrow? That bloody Scots haggis-eater? I'll not be giving my work away free to that porridge wog, that kilt-wearing cross-dresser. Not a dime he offered me, not a penny. He's so tight his arse squeaks when he walks! Scots—don't get me started."

Carmel's finger hovered over the call button. This was a side of Darrow which she hadn't yet come across. It didn't sound like the Darrow she knew.

"Right when I first got here. I was looking around for funding, you know, to help pay for the work—it doesn't come cheap, my time and effort. Do you know what he said to me?" Ian was in full outraged spate. "He says to me, he says, 'That's all verra good and weel, but we dinna have the budget fur research. Try hawkin' yer wares doon the road to the RCMP.'" This was possibly the worst Scots imitation Carmel had ever heard, coloured as it was by Ian's strong Irish brogue. "Like I was a bloody salesman, and not the genius that I am. That black Prot bastard! Jaysus, what a Neanderthal! He's living in the Dark Ages; he can't see progress when it's slapping him in the face." Ian shook his head. "No, I know the very man who'll be interested in this gem I've got. Someone who can appreciate the proper value of my work, if you know what I mean." He leaned closer to Carmel, winked and tapped the side of his nose.

She didn't really, but let it go. "Who's that then?" she asked.

"A little man I met in the Georgetown Pub," he said as he rose from the table. "He's got the means to bring this to the attention of the real people in charge. And that's where the money is." He shoved on his shoddy pea coat and grabbed the keys to his old Chevy and the ever-present laptop. "I'll be seeing you later, then."

Chapter 20

The house was very quiet after Ian left. He certainly could fill a space with his talk and his ego. Left on her own, the full horror of what she'd found that afternoon came back to her.

Garroted. Carmel knew from her own wandering studies in ancient and medieval history that the garrote had been used as a form of execution by the Romans before the time of Christ. Darrow had also told her that modern-day specially trained soldiers were taught this skill and how to improvise a garrote as necessary.

Now religious figures in Portugal Cove were being garroted. Ian's program had predicted that Wilson was only the first in a series. This second death changed things—it wasn't co-incidence, it couldn't be. She wished Ian hadn't rushed off so quickly, for if he'd only taken the time to input this new information in his program, they might be able to narrow down a loose description or profile of the murderer.

And there was also Melba's prophecy to keep in mind—that murder comes in threes.

If the computer program was accurate, then these murders were directly linked to the callings of the victims. But there must be something else that linked them—the perpetrator couldn't be just killing off religious leaders willy-nilly. That wouldn't make sense. There would be no point to it surely, and there were a lot of clerics in the world. Why start here, in Portugal Cove?

Hank was scratching at the window, looking for a late afternoon snack. She let him in and searched through the fridge for some leftovers, but it looked like Ian had already scrounged everything she'd put aside for the cat. Hank would have to be satisfied with another egg beaten in a bowl.

"A computer is artificial intelligence," she told the cat. "It emulates the human brain and logic. So it stands to reason that I should be able to reason it out, if I think hard enough. Right?"

To start with, she needed to figure out what the two men––Wilson and Father John––had in common. They were both men, and white. They were both spiritual leaders. She cast her mind about, looking for more similarities. One was active, one retired. Wilson was from Mississippi, Father John––he was Irish, she thought, remembering the only time she'd ever seen him. It was in the local post office, and he'd been yarning with the clerk. She distinctly remembered an Irish accent. Or was he merely from the Southern Shore of the Avalon, where the brogue still ran thick in people's mouths even after centuries of being separated from the motherland. So possibly, both men were not locally bred, although this last was uncertain.

Her mind harkened back to Ian's insult of Darrow as a "kilt-wearing cross-dresser." Ah—they both wore long robes, she added mentally. Although Father John, being retired, probably didn't wear the clerical garb of the Catholic priest except on special occasions. If that was the link between the two, this could be the beginning of a spree against men who wore dresses. A sort of strange sexual hate crime? At least that would rule out anyone from the shelter, for they were very open-minded there about expression of sexuality and gender.

She shook her head. This was stretching it a bit far, really, because the wearing of robes was for religious purposes, rather than denoting sexual tastes or gender biases. Although there had been some mention of Father John having been moved from parish to parish in his earlier years—that usually meant he must have been doing something the church frowned upon, and that was usually sexual in nature. But really, since the whole Mount Cashel scandal, that sort of thing didn't happen anymore, did it? The populace no longer held church leaders in such esteem and the Catholic Church just didn't have the power in the community that it used to have even 30 years ago. Once upon a time in this province, the Church and state were inextricably linked though family ties and education. Newfoundlanders remained colonial in their attitudes long after the rest of the English-speaking world had broken free of the yoke of the Crown. Some philosophers attributed this to the centuries-old hold the fishing merchants had held over fishermen——each year leaving them deeper in debt with never a bit of cash.

But this philosophizing wasn't getting her anywhere. There had to be something else——something she wasn't see-ing——that linked the two men and their deaths.

They were both balding.

That was the best she could come up with. "That's pathetic," she muttered. She hefted Hank up off her lap where he'd settled and carried him back through to the kitchen. It would be a quiche for supper tonight, as there was still only eggs and cheese in the fridge. She turned the TV news on to accompany her preparations. No doubt local reporter Smythe had already caught wind of the latest murder and she wanted to know if he had any more information she could use.

A young female intern was co-hosting the news tonight. Most of the regular news announcers and reporters would have started their Christmas vacations already. This was the intern's chance to shine, and she took the opportunity very seriously.

"We have breaking news. Another cleric has been found murdered in the small town of Portugal Cove. The tragic death of Father John O'Driscoll has rocked the Catholic community there. Father John served many parishes in the province over his career, and was enjoying a well-deserved retirement, living in the Rectory of the Holy Rosary. More on this terrible event and with some new developments, here is Gerald Smythe."

The camera panned to Smythe, who for once was not haunting the site of the murder but was inside the studio itself. He strode onto the set with his hand lifted in greeting. Sitting down, he straightened his trademark bow tie and grinned professionally into the camera.

"Thank you, Kelsey. A couple of days ago, the province was rocked with news of the death of Reverend Wilson, a humble man known to many, and easily recognized by the simple brown robe he wore. He was the leader of a congregation known as the Flock of the Innocents——a small evangelical church located in the town of Portugal Cove. Now we are faced with the equally gruesome murder of Father John, a well-loved retired priest of the Catholic persuasion."

The camera angle changed and Gerald swerved to greet it. "Yes, I said murder——that foulest of deeds. Naturally, the Royal Newfoundland Constabulary is releasing no information at this time, but my source tells me that Father John, like Reverend Wilson before him, was garroted."

Carmel raised her eyes from her cheese grater. Wow, heads were going to roll with this information being leaked. Inspector Darrow hadn't wanted the general public to know that the two deaths were related in any way, or they'd have general panic to deal with on top of solving the murders. She shook her head. In this day and age with the hacking of computers and even cellphones, nothing was sacred or secret anymore. Look at the Royal family and their woes. She didn't envy Darrow his task.

"Yes, my gentle viewers, there is a clerical strangler on the loose. The members of the most respected profession––our clerics––the keepers of our morals, are being slaughtered, one by one. Are we going to stand for this? Of course, the police say they are doing everything in their power to get to the bottom of this. They point out that Christmas leave has been cancelled and all available manpower is on this case."

He gave an almost imperceptible eye roll and continued on his dramatic way. "But I ask you, are they really? No, I tell you, no, they are not. I have proof that they are ignoring the one tool which can help them tie up this case." The camera switched angles again, and Gerald moved swiftly with it. It must have been choreographed ahead of time. "You see, there is a computer program invented by a young genius named Ian Mulrennan from Ireland––now a resident of our province––which actually foretold the next death. Not the details, certainly, it couldn't pinpoint who would be the next cleric murdered, but that there would be one, yes, without a doubt."

Oh dear God. Say it wasn't so. The block of cheese slipped from her hand onto the counter. Suddenly she wasn't hungry anymore.

"And when offered access to this program, were the police interested?" Gerald shook his head. "No, it takes a man of vision to recognize the possibilities. Here is my exclusive interview with the man of the hour––Mulrennan––just moments ago. I apologize for the lack of editing of this interview, but I felt this needed to be shared today."

The screen filled with a darkened room, a pub by the looks of it, showing figures hunched over video games and others lurking in the shadows. She recognized it alright—it was the Georgetown Pub, and it hadn't changed much since she'd lived around the corner on Maxse Street as a student, in a huge unheatable shared apartment, mostly memorable for the Purple Jesus drinks parties held around the none-too-clean bathtub. It had been cheap accommodation at the time, but now all of the Georgetown neighbourhood was gentrified, or on its way to becoming so. Oh yes, the Georgetown Pub, which had reluctantly begun to open its doors to women in the late seventies, but had resisted giving in to the upwardly mobile influences surrounding it—it remained a beacon of homeliness, perhaps in homage to its humble beginnings as the local pub for the city's early trash collectors. It was an unpretentious place and the beer was cheap—trust Ian to have homed in on this spot.

The camera panned and came to rest upon her new tenant, an empty pint glass resting on the table at his elbow. He looked like he'd already emptied it a few times in the short space of time since he'd left her house. Guinness—the breakfast of champions, indeed.

"Ian, I understand you've developed a computer program which is set to change the world, enabling police forces to solve crimes just by inputting data. Tell the viewers about it."

"Well, the genius of the thing is it's really quite simple, and it builds on similar software already being used by police." He was only slurring his words a little as he looked past the camera lens to Smythe. "The probability factor comes directly out of the data cluster, the variance will be correlated to the ..."

"Alright, alright," Smythe said. "Spare us the technicalities. Why not illustrate what the program can do using the latest murders out in Portugal Cove as an example?"

"Well, basically how the program works is, you feed in all the known information about a crime—the victim, the location, the time of day, anything at all really. More information will help narrow down the probabilities exponentially, of course." His eyes must have caught those of Smythe. "Ah, yes. Well, when I heard about the death of Reverend Wilson, I inputted all the data I could find, and as I have a very reliable source close to the murders, this was more than John Q. Public would have access to. To pare this down to the simplest facts, the verdict was that Wilson's death was the start of a series of murders, somehow connected through the man's occupation which was that of a spiritual leader."

Carmel swallowed hard. She was Ian's 'reliable source.' Darrow was going to be very unhappy when he saw this broadcast.

The camera moved to include Smythe in its range. His close-set eyes and small mouth expressed pure glee. "And this was before today's death of Father John, was it not? You predicted a serial killer."

"Oh, yes indeed, it was." Ian leaned back into his chair now, basking in the camera's lights. "Yes, the prediction was made yesterday. Y'see, Wilson was garroted, as you may or may not know. And my source tells me that today's murder, that of Father John, was also garroted with the self-same electrical cord."

"I didn't say that," Carmel said to the TV, swept by a feeling of outraged justification. "You're making that up, Ian Mulrennan. I said no such thing."

Smythe's eyes were as wide open now as they could get. "Really? Keep going," he breathed, nodding.

Ian's eyes slid to the empty glass and he gave a dry pathetic cough. "If I could just whet my whistle a little," he said. "I'm a little skint today, perhaps you could ..." Smythe made an impatient gesture with his left hand. An unseen media flunkey whisked the glass away and almost immediately replaced it with a full one. The cream foam of the Guinness head gleamed in the bright light and Ian warmed his hands around the tankard for a moment. "That's much better," he said after taking a deep swallow and wiping his mouth with the back of his hand. "Now, where was I?"

"The same murder weapon was used on Father John."

"Ah, well now, that might be a debatable point, don't you know," Ian said, looking a little worried but his brow relaxed after he took another sip. "At any rate, my sources tell me he was garroted in exactly the same manner as Wilson. So, this is proof indelible that my program is successful. And I'd like you to let your viewers know that I'm in the process of developing an App, so that anybody can solve crimes using their phones. Now, wouldn't that be a blast? All I need right now is the proper funding, and, Gerry, I was thinking maybe you could organize a bit of crowd funding for me ..."

The screen cut him off in mid-spiel and switched back to Smythe comfortably ensconced in his studio chair. "There you have it, folks," he said, his small mouth pursed in smug satisfaction. "You saw it here first. A software program that actually predicted the murder of Father John, yet this valuable tool has been ignored by the Royal Newfoundland Constabulary, particularly by Inspector Darrow, the one man who could certainly use it." His smile grew spitey as he remembered the bollocking Darrow had given him the previous summer for getting himself strung up in the ravine. "Oh, yes, Darrow could use any help he can get, as we all know."

Now she was in for it. Just when Darrow was warming up to her, she'd betrayed his trust, and in such a public manner. As if she'd deliberately aligned herself with the two idiots in town whose feelings had been hurt by his blunt ways. She really had no one to blame but herself, and that stung most of all. How could she ever rectify this situation?

It was time to talk with Sister Constantine.

Chapter 21

The next morning, she saw that Ian's car had not made it back to the driveway over night, which meant he had found somewhere else to lay his head. Just as well, for she had still not simmered down after yesterday's news fiasco. She was comforted only by the thought that the Irishman hadn't yet coughed up the rent payment, which meant it would be morally okay to toss his mouldy old duffel bag into the fresh snow which had fallen overnight. Carmel gave her car a little more coaxing, and the engine finally caught. She used the wipers to clear the windshield, hoping that the wind would knock the other windows clear as she drove into town. Damn, it was cold outside. Looked like they would have a white Christmas this year after all.

Sister Constantine, now at an age some would call elderly (although the term could never be applied to this active healthy woman) had moved out of the stone convent by the river with the other few remaining nuns when the building had been bought up by the government to use as a convention centre. Carmel smiled at the irony of the words every time she thought of it, from convent to convention hall. All the retired nuns had moved into Presentation Convent up by the Basilica. With two stories and a span of seven windows, it was another large stone building, such a rarity in this city famous for wooden houses, yet its grand size was reduced in scale by the towering Basilica next to it. To celebrate the season, there was a simple wreath placed on the front entrance doorway.

The convent was located just a few streets over from the Georgetown Pub, and she was sorely tempted to drive around looking for Ian's car, and perhaps find him inside, frozen after an enforced camp out in the winter night. Serve the bugger right.

But this was no way to be thinking when she was on her way to visit Sister Constantine. Carmel sighed and parked her car at the bottom of the sloping parking lot, squeezing in before yet another funeral goer could take the spot before her. Attendance at regular services might be dropping over the years, but the Basilica was still the most popular spot to host a funeral. You couldn't beat it for atmosphere.

The convent door opened just as she rang the old-fashioned bell set into the stonework, and a kindly woman dressed in scrubs let her in. A nurse, perhaps, or one of the cleaning staff––hard to tell as they all dressed the same these days.

"She's expecting you," the staff member said, ushering her into a small parlour down the hall where a fire burned in the marble-tiled grate.

Carmel stopped on the threshold as the sole occupant of the room rose to greet her, at the sight of the smiling, unlined face, her eyes wise with years of experience in human affairs. Still the same face after all this time, her hair a burnished white glow like a halo in the soft December daylight. That hair was once upon a time a subdued brown, rarely seen beneath the harsh wimple, only at night when the world was locked away and Sister Constantine and the other nuns turned into real people, real women. They had become Carmel's family, with their mugs of hot chocolate and plates of heavily buttered toast, dressed in housecoats and shawls, they and all the community gathered to watch the latest American shows on the black and white TV. Sister Constantine had been delighted when the order at long last decided to catch up with modern times and drop the starched headdress in public, although she had continued in her simple dress.

She fell into Sister Constantine's arms, not even bothering to remove her coat as she hugged the nun tight.

"There, there," the nun murmured, while at the same time pushing her away to inspect her fully. A quizzical look appeared in her eyes. "Why don't you sit down and tell me all about it?"

With those kind words, the waterworks started. Carmel hadn't even realized she wanted to cry, but cry she did as she sobbed out the story of the past five days, and it took a good fifteen minutes. Meanwhile, a tray of tea and fresh-baked scones had silently appeared on the low table in front of the sofa where the two women sat.

"So," Carmel finally sniffed, wiping her nose one final time. "That's what's been happening with me." She looked up with a watery smile. "How are things with you?"

Sister Constantine laughed. "Not nearly as exciting, tucked away here in the convent," she said. "Just the usual parish intrigues." She started to pour two cups of tea from the silver service. "Now, why don't you take off your coat and stay awhile?"

They drank the first cup sitting silently in contemplation, as was the nun's wont. She had always insisted that tea's excellent healing benefits must be allowed to settle the mind and calm the nerves, preparing for the real conversation which would follow. And it was a fine cup of tea which deserved to be savoured, the good sister's personal blend from the tea shop downtown.

"I did watch the news last night," Sister Constantine admitted. "Poor Father John, God rest his soul. He had his trials in this life." She then looked over her glasses at Carmel rather sternly. "What I want to know first is, what is your relationship with that young Irishman?"

"He showed up on my doorstep, looking for a room to rent," she answered. "He was nice and funny, and I agreed because he seemed like he'd be good company. But now ... I'd just like to shoot him, quite frankly."

The older woman seemed satisfied with that answer. "Good, so you're not going to get mixed up with him any further, in an intimate manner," she said, pointedly.

"Oh, Sister, no, not like that," Carmel said, although she did find herself blushing a little. There had been a time when a man of Ian's looks and charm would have drawn her like a magnet, and she resented the nun for reminding her. "Besides, he's way too young for me."

"So now let's talk about this policeman," the other continued relentlessly. "What is your relationship to him?"

Carmel shook her head. "No, no," she said. "Nothing there. I mean, we get along really well, but I think I've scuppered that friendship now. He's probably royally pissed at me."

"Pity," Constantine said. "I think he might be a good one for you. It's high time you settled down. It may not be too late to have children."

"Sister," Carmel said, becoming exasperated, yet at the same time realizing this is what it must be like to have a mother. She was 43 years old, and had no intention of starting a family. "I'm really not interested in Inspector Darrow. Stop trying to get me married off."

"I just want you to be happy," the other said, a pious note momentarily entering her voice. "You lost the last one, too, although he sounded like he might be from the Russian mafia, so just as well. He wouldn't have been Catholic, I don't suppose."

"Ruscan was––is Ukranian. He hated the Russians," Carmel said, trying not to grit her teeth. "He was agnostic, if anything. And I didn't lose him, he ... he disappeared."

"In midflight, yes. Strange thing for a man to do."

She had no rebuttal for that, for if Ruscan, her lover, had not disappeared because he'd been murdered by his supposed enemies, then that meant he was still alive and had left her alone and without explanation, on purpose.

"So, Inspector Darrow," the other continued. "Tell me—he did ask you not to spread the word about how Father John was murdered?"

Carmel stared at the faded Aubusson carpet underfoot, and nodded.

"Hmm," the other said. They both knew she had made her point, so she relented. "Now, these two murders. Interesting, don't you think?"

"It's awful," Carmel said, glad to have the conversation move away from herself and her failings. "Someone is going around killing clerics. We have an anti-religious serial killer in Portugal Cove."

Sister Constantine pursed her lips in disagreement. "You really think so?"

"It does look like that, Sister. I mean, surely you're not saying that two murders, so close in time and location and method, are coincidental, are you? The only thing linking the two are that the men were both religious figures. Believe me, I've been searching in my mind for something else that links them, but there's nothing, except they both wore long dresses and were balding. And white, but most people in the cove are white, so I don't think their race counts."

"It's called a cassock, not a dress, dear," the other said, an automatic response but her mind was on something else. She paused a moment before continuing. "Yet the two men were so fundamentally different as people, there's no way I can believe their murders could be linked."

"What do you mean? I've heard nasty things about both," Carmel replied. A thought struck her and she continued slowly as she gave form to this new idea. "Perhaps our serial killer is only going after bad clerics, people who have done harm, abused their position of power. Now, that's what is linking them."

Sister Constantine shook her head. "Oh, no, you're wrong there. I knew Reverend Wilson. We've worked on many social initiatives together." She spoke very decisively.

"That doesn't mean he didn't abuse his wife in private."

The other glared over her spectacles, in full nun mode now as if in front of a class of fourth-graders. "I've personally known more abusers in my lifetime than you ever will, Carmel McAlistair, and I'll thank you to remember that. If I say he wasn't an abusive man, then he wasn't."

"I heard it from the horse's mouth. His wife Vivienne herself told me," Carmel insisted truculently, too stubborn to let it go. "And yes, he did do bad things, at least to her. He put on a good show in public, but he was really horrible. Did you know that at the time of his murder in Snellen's Field, she was actually at the women's shelter, seeking counselling and planning to finally leave him?"

The nun sniffed. "Vivienne. There's a name for women like her, and it's not one we use in this house."

"Oh, come on, give her a break," Carmel replied. "So she wears pancake makeup and high heels and is dolled up like Tammy Faye, but look at it from her point of view. She really tried to make it work with him, followed her husband out here to the cold and relative wilderness. She's a broken woman, Sister, my heart goes out to her."

"She's a spoiled princess, that one," Sister Constantine said, effectively ending that line of conversation. "Now, dear, you haven't tried Sister Amelie's scones. She made them especially for you when she heard you were coming. You really must stop by the kitchen to say thank you before you go."

Carmel knew from long experience when the other would not be swayed, so gave up her argument and ate the scones. And they were very good, a taste reminiscent of her childhood.

"I almost forgot," she said. "A present for you." She handed the wrapped package to the nun.

"How many times do I need to tell you that we do not celebrate our Lord's birth in the commercial manner?" Sister Constantine asked her in a mock-scolding tone even as her hands were carefully undoing the wrapping paper before folding it to put away for later re-use. "Oh, how lovely," she said, examining the present. "I think," she added with a trace of doubt in her voice as she held up the brightly coloured mug. This was one Carmel had chosen just for her, with red poppies shining amongst the cobalt blue glaze, her favourite of the ten she'd purchased.

In return, Sister Constantine had given her much to think about. This icon from her childhood was rarely wrong, but how could the murders not be related?

Chapter 22

T he snow was lightly falling as she followed the graveled road back to St. Jude Without, ready for lunch. The little cove was peaceful today—no bikers and their loud machines ripping through the silence, no teenage girls hanging out by the boulders, even Clyde Farrell's farm dog was not patrolling the lanes. Given the snow, Vee Ryan must not be doing any laundry, or perhaps she had a clothes dryer to handle her son's constant stream of discarded T-shirts and jeans which she seemed to spend her waking hours attending to.

Ian's rusted Chevy was back in her driveway, developing a pristine coat of white the longer it sat there. Just the sight of it made her clench her fists around the steering wheel. She would see to it that he moved out that very day. He could sleep in his car, for all she cared because he'd had no business spreading that bit about how Father John had died to the press. To anyone.

She flung open the front door, ready to face him as he stretched out on the sofa, resting his filthy socks on the fabric as he did so. She was fully prepared to lay down the law, her law and give him the boot. But he wasn't where she expected him to be.

Carmel followed the smell of bacon frying into the kitchen where Ian was beavering away at the stove. The toaster popped, adding a warm note of bread to the olfactory over-load. Sausages, eggs, bacon, tomatoes, mushrooms, onions, and fries sizzled away on the stovetop, cooking within three different fry-pans. She hadn't known she owned so many. Hank was keeping him company and closely overseeing the operations from his perch on the counter, his lip hooked up in his fang to give his trademark grin.

"What are you doing?" In the few days he'd been here, she'd never seen him attempt to make anything more than a cup of tea. Using her teabags, milk, and sugar. But the ingredients for this meal hadn't been supplied by her. No way. She hadn't bought a tomato since last summer, and she knew she didn't have bacon and sausages in the freezer. Where had this largesse arrived from?

He turned with a welcoming smile, not looking in the least bit hung over. "Ah good, you're home then. Me and the cat thought we'd like to surprise you with a hearty full British. Minus the beans, now, for you don't seem a beans-for-brunch kind of person, if you don't mind my saying," he said. "I made a trip to the grocery store. And I've got your rent cheque finally. You're a saint, you really are, letting me stay here without giving you a penny surety. There's not many who'll do that for a soul down on his luck these days."

Hank turned to her also, looking pleased as punch at discovering that this new friend could cook decent food. He'd had enough of raw eggs and she could see the bacon-lust in his eyes. "Shoo!" she scolded him to cover her confusion, sweeping him off. "Get down off the counter. Ian, how can you let him up there? That's disgusting, I prepare food there."

"Ah, he's just trying to help, y'know. Besides, he cleaned his paws before he jumped up. I made sure of that."

She could feel her resolve weakening by the smell of the cooking food. Better get it over with, so she took a deep breath. This wasn't going to be easy.

"Hold on to your cheque, Ian," she said, standing by the table. "This isn't going to work out. I think you'd better move out."

His shoulders sagged and the light died from his eyes in an instant. "Oh," he said in a very small voice. He turned back to the stove and began to transfer the food onto three plates. "I've done it again, haven't I?"

Carmel kept her jaw firm and said nothing.

"Here, eat this up. It'd be a shame to waste good food. We can maybe talk it over when we're finished," he said sadly. He left Hank's plate on the counter where the cat had reappeared and set to chowing down on the meat. Carmel glared, but both cat and man refused to meet her eye. Ian sat before his plate. Carmel had no choice but to follow suit. He had gone to the effort, after all. The first bite of home fries had almost reached her mouth when Ian spoke again.

"So close to Christmas, an' all."

She bit down on the hot, crunchy potato, but guilt sucked the pleasure and the spicy taste right out of it. Looking across the table at him, she decided that he was pathetic, like a puppy waiting to be kicked. The food sat in front of him, untouched.

It was snowing and cold out there. His first Christmas in a strange land. He was young, or youngish, and his only sin had been to believe passionately in his creation, and try to make money to pay his bills. The worst of it was, she couldn't even tell him why she was so pissed at him, for she'd had no business passing on Darrow's confidences in the first place.

What would Sister Constantine do right now? She pictured the nun sitting across from her, glaring over her half-glasses.

Sighing, she put down her fork. "Oh, forget it," she said. "Stay for the season. Just give me the cheque. We'll see how it goes."

Like the star on Cabot Tower on a black night, his face lit up again and his eyes twinkled as he tucked into the meal. Back to his old self in a flash, he chattered throughout the meal.

"But I've been thinking, where is the famous Christmas tree?" he asked. "I thought all Americans had a tree and stockings in front of the fireplace, but you haven't got a single decoration up. Sure, we do more back in County Kerry than I've seen here."

This was Canada, not America, but it was true what he said. Back in the city, and in neighbouring Portugal Cove, people decorated the outsides of their houses too, sometimes in competition to have the brightest and most colourful display, setting up the Holy Family and their menagerie alongside Santa and his reindeers. Even during the rolling electrical blackouts which could happen during winter storms, folks would fire up their generators and insist on having their Christmas spirit shine through the night.

Here in St. Jude Without, not so much. She herself hadn't bothered with Christmas, just having gotten back from her trip, and with only herself it had seemed silly to go to the effort of getting a tree. But elsewhere in the community, there was not much evidence of the season. She would have expected Vee at least to have a crass and tasteless display with which to offend the eyes. But no, as in so many other ways, it was as if the 21st century was passing the small cove by. The darkness of the cove was creepy, when you thought about it.

And Ian was hoping for a full Christmas experience. Did this mean she, as a landlord, was expected to provide Christmas dinner to this waif from another country? She'd never cooked a turkey before, let alone made gravy. This could be tense. She busied herself with wolfing down the excellent brunch provided with the money he had squeezed out of Smythe's TV station in exchange for Darrow's confidential information. It was the best breakfast/brunch she'd had in a long while, if she could overlook the slightly sour taste of guilt.

"Christmas decorations," she said aloud after she'd finished. "I may have had some, years ago, but honestly, I've been on the move so much over the past years that I just don't bother with it all. It's just more junk to carry around." And Ruscan certainly hadn't pushed for the North American-style celebration, being content for them to share the traditional

Ukrainian Christmas Eve meal with the small community of his compatriots in Taiwan, the lavishly embroidered table-cloth laden with the twelve dishes cooked by others. Their Saint Nicholas had remained a religious figure––no jolly fat man for them.

"No matter," Ian said, brushing it aside after she confessed she'd never cooked a turkey in her life. "I can pop in on my friend Gerry. I'm sure he'll be having the whole Christmas Day hoo-ha. He's a very generous lad, is Gerry."

Carmel tried to imagine Smythe's reaction to the shortened form of his name, and smiled. There were rumours he'd been born "Smith" and his name had somehow morphed on his journey up the journalistic ladder. 'Gerry' just seemed too undignified for the image the reporter held of himself.

Which made her think. Did she really want Ian to remain under the influence of Smythe? It seemed somehow in her best interests to keep the two men away from each other, to prevent––if she could––the two of them making trouble for Darrow.

Of course—the church was the answer. She would intro-duce the Irishman to the pub next door—a drinking estab-lishment so close by that it would keep him out of Darrow's hair, and maybe he'd be able to wrangle an invite to Christmas dinner from one of the regulars, thereby getting her off the hook. Life was suddenly looking much brighter.

Chapter 23

I an stood outside the church, entranced by the rosette window which glowed in the night, the only sign that Sid was open for business.

"It's absolutely bloody brilliant," he said. "The holiest of communions, taken among the fellowship of man. And right next door. What a prime location it is." The Irishman was turning out to be a bit of a poet, waxing eloquently, especially after he'd uncorked a bottle of rum he'd picked up on his grocery run.

She opened the door to the bell tower leading into the church body. "Coming in?"

"Lay on, MacDuff, and damned be him who first cries, 'Hold! Enough!'" Ian bellowed as he charged his way into the pub. And she'd thought he was just a computer nerd, not realizing the hidden Shakespeare nut inside the man. Well, the crowd inside would either lynch him or love him; there were no back doors on them.

He paused at the threshold, looking around the bar with delight. All the regulars were already inside, each in their allotted place. The bikers to the left up by the altar, the pool players to the right under the lights, Clyde the farmer in his corner pew. All eyes turned on Ian, faces stony at this loud interruption. Okay, it might be a lynching, Carmel thought as she swallowed nervously. She wondered how she was going to smooth this over with them all. Ian wasn't so worried.

"Hell is empty and all the devils are here!" Ian roared, his arms flung wide as he embraced the room.

Silence greeted him, until a voice by the bar called out.

"Midsummer Night's Dream?" It was Sharran, leaning against the bar.

"No, it's not," the head biker spoke out, looking over at her with incredulity. "It's The Tempest, you fool. Didn't they teach you anything in the Protestant schools?" He rolled his eyes and tch'ed at her ignorance.

"The large hairy one in leather wins the prize," Ian called as he strolled down the aisle. "Barkeep, give the man an ale for his knowledge." He had already hauled out his wallet and the biker's face broke into a toothy smile. Smythe's payoff wasn't going to last long, Carmel thought. She must remember to get that cheque off him before it turned to rubber.

Well, there would be no lynching there tonight—that was a relief. Almost everyone in the room was looking on the Irishman with smiling faces, and there was an animation in the buzz of conversation she'd never seen before. When they realized they'd seen his face on the news the previous night, their delight rose to even greater heights, for it wasn't every night there was a real live TV star in their midst.

Almost everyone, yes, but not Phonse. He sidled over to her by the bar, keeping his eyes on Ian with a frown on his face.

"Who's your friend?" The Christmas lights by the bar which were up all year round glowed green on his blonde curls, masking the grey of time. His black eye stood out even darker in this light.

"My tenant," Carmel replied. They both watched as Ian and Bridget made a brief moment of eye contact across the room, then their glances dropped away simultaneously. The two younger members deliberately did not look again in each other's direction, yet they drifted toward each other as if in a much rehearsed dance, each knowing the other's moves by heart. When they casually bumped into each other at the bar, they began a light flirtation, then just as casually danced off to opposite ends of the room, her to her biker friends, he to the pool table. Carmel had a feeling they'd both already made plans for the other.

"I don't like him," Phonse said, his frown deepening.

Carmel turned to look at him. "You haven't even met him," she said.

"He's awfully loud." The scowl on his face was just plain unattractive, and she had a hard time seeing the gorgeousness that she had crushed on last summer. Maybe it had faded with his tan. "What's he doing here?" he asked.

"You're a fine one to ask that question," she said. "Why are any of us here in the pub? A little drink, a little company, that's why pubs exist."

His scowl deepened. "No, I mean why is he here, in the cove? Why did he choose your house to rent from? You can't tell me there aren't better places, more convenient places in the city." His eyes hadn't left the Irishman since they'd entered the building.

Carmel had no answer to that. Ian had gotten her name from the university, hadn't he said something about that? Strange, though, that no one from the housing office had phoned to let her know, but perhaps it had gotten overlooked in the Christmas rush to get out of their offices. She'd make a point of asking him, later on.

"I don't have a good feeling about him," Phonse stated.

She turned again, to look at him fully this time. This was not the Phonse she knew and loved/hated. For one thing, he seemed pretty sober. For another, he looked truly troubled, and the Phonse she knew was rarely bothered by anything which didn't touch him directly. "Is it Bridget?" she asked. "Are you worried about your cousin?"

It was his turn to look at her. "What's she got to do with this?" he asked, his face as blank as if he hadn't witnessed the courting ritual which had just taken place.

"Nothing, I guess," she replied with a mental shrug. So it didn't bother him that Bridget and Ian had made a beeline for each other like two magnets unable to change direction, so powerful was the inevitability of their coming together. It bothered her, if only for her friend's sake, but Bridget surely wouldn't want any interference from her. She'd seen the look in her redheaded friend's eye when she'd first laid her eyes on the Irishman.

Carmel and Phonse watched as Ian picked up an odd pool cue, a mismatched one that unofficially belonged to Phonse. Without a break in his patter, Ian was obvious challenging the other pool players to a friendly bet, mesmerizing them to agree to his terms and then astounding them by bouncing the ball off four walls of the table and sinking it into the hole closest to him. Another round of beer was bought, and not paid for by Ian. It was almost like watching a magic show, seeing the man in action, she realized. He was a master pool player, while he gave a top-notch and entertaining performance.

"I've had enough of this," Phonse muttered. He grabbed his coat hanging by the pool table, glaring at Ian as he did so, and left by the side door, the smoker's entrance.

After a time, Ian drifted back to his landlady's side, where she was chatting with Sharran.

"So what are your plans for Christmas Day, you two?" the blond woman asked them.

Ian watched Carmel expectantly as she struggled for an answer. "Mmm, maybe go watch a movie?" she offered.

"No way!" Sharran looked shocked. "What about Christmas dinner? It's his first Christmas here, and you're not going to feed him a proper dinner?"

"She's never cooked a turkey before, y'know," Ian confided to Sharran. "And she doesn't even have a tree up in the house."

He wasn't standing close enough for Carmel to dig an elbow in his ribs. She hoped he could feel the glare she was sending his way.

"Well, I'll be cooking a turkey," Sharran answered. "Why don't you two come over to my house? I'll have enough there to feed an army." She was a loud and exuberant personality, and her voice naturally carried through the hall. A few wistful heads turned toward the bar where they sat. The four bikers (plus their hanger-on), both Clyde and his dog, and some strays along the wall were staring now. Sharran was a generous person, and being a freelance United Church minister, she was trained to be sensitive to the needs of others. "Hell," she said, looking around and putting her hands on her hips. "Why don't we just hold Christmas dinner right here in the church?"

This announcement received a warm reception, and a thrill of good feeling raced through the bar with smiles all round. Who knew there were so many lost souls in the cove?

"Sid," she called out to the dark, dour bartender who stood behind the altar, one hand absently smoothing his long moustaches. "Guess what, Sid? You've just been nominated to play Father Christmas!"

And so it was decreed. A communal Christmas dinner would be held in Sid's pub for all the loners, transients, and strays of the cove, and even for those who just didn't like their families and preferred to spend their holiday time with friends. Sharran quickly dispatched the organization of the large event by assigning everyone to a task which would bring the whole thing together.

The bikers and their young hanger-on would scour the Salvation Army and the Dollar stores for decorations to give the hall a festive air. Others would clean and scrub to make sure the place came up to Sharran's standards. Clyde said he knew the perfect tree to cut. Ian was very anxious to be a part of this, the most sacred of traditions. It was an unlikely pairing, but even Clyde, who Carmel knew for a fact was the crabbiest person in the whole of St. Jude Without—even Clyde Farrell and his dog––had both fallen under the spell of Ian's Irish charm.

Chapter 22

For the first time in what felt ages, but had only been five days or so, Carmel woke up full of energy with no sniffles, sneezes, or cough. She'd finally shaken off her cold, just in time for Christmas. Perhaps having a Christmas to look forward to helped, for she hadn't truly celebrated the season for years and the light dusting of snow which had fallen overnight brought back memories of youthful Christmases in the convent when she was a young girl. The sisters had never been into the material aspect, but a tree had always magically appeared in the nuns' private parlour on Christmas morning, decorated with pre-war glass decorations saved so carefully through the years. Birds with long glittery tails peeked out from the innermost branches, along with brightly painted Belgian baubles. The collection had grown over the years as nuns came and went on their international journeys. And there had always been a stocking under the tree for Carmel, a mandarin orange stuck in the toe, with some chocolate coins and a candy cane, and small presents designed to intrigue a little girl.

That there had been two murders close to St. Jude Without quite fell from her mind in the brewing excitement. Her mind was instead on other things, for she was in charge of making desserts for the celebration. Sharran had given permission for her to buy a fruitcake instead of making her own, for no one wanted to take chances with that honoured tradition. Besides, by all rights, the cake should have been made months ago and left to mature in a wash of rum. But a chocolate cake, of course, that would be popular and easy enough to create. Even Carmel could be relied upon to do that, and perhaps a fruit flan with custard and glazed fruit on the top. She found herself humming as the coffee brewed.

The day was warming up outside. After making a grocery list for everything she could possibly need (extra potatoes—you could never have enough roast potatoes for a mid-winter feast), she set off to town. Being in the Christmas spirit now, she decided to give herself a present and stopped into the used skate store. Yeah, it had been 25 years since she'd been on a pair of ice skates but she was feeling invincible, bold, and in love with life. She remembered the thrill of fresh air rushing through her hair as her teenage self glided free and weightless on the ice, the air cold on her face but her body perfectly warmed by the workout. She was feeling young again.

She parked her car in the small lot behind the Colonial Building, and walked the short way to the Loop, a marvellous creation of outdoor ice in the center of Bannerman Park. There were few skaters there so early in the day, and the fresh ice shone, a smooth ribbon looping around the old bandstand, beckoning her on. Christmas music filled the air.

Skates laced up tightly, she continued to sit on the bench, the smile now plastered on her face like a grimace. Now it was time to launch. What had she been thinking? That she could just hop on skates after a quarter-century and fly like her young self used to? Yes, that's exactly what she'd thought. She tested the ice beneath her skates while she sat, moving her feet back and forth. It was really slippery, like ice was supposed to be. And now she was going to stand up and set off. By herself. There were no side rails to hold on to at the Loop, nothing within grasping height, she saw, as she looked ahead down the track.

Hmmm. Maybe she should wait until she'd worked up the confidence. Perhaps this was sort of like waxing your own legs, you knew if you waited long enough, eventually you'd find the courage to make the rip.

Or perhaps she could pretend that she'd already done it, already skated proficiently around the ribbon a few times, oh, say ten times at least, and now had to get a move on, busy day ahead. Great day for it, she would call to the skaters who were just arriving. The ice is perfect today! She must have been sitting there for at least twenty minutes now—that was long enough. She bent to begin the unlacing process, all the time berating herself for being such a chicken.

A pair of men's skates slashed to a stop too close to her feet, the slurry spraying over her legs. Show-off, she thought.

"Carmel?"

Oh no, someone she knew. She was caught. She wondered if she could pretend to have finished her skate, and peered up to judge the situation.

Phonse stood there, unwavering on his ice skates, the morning chill flushing his cheeks and his eyes matching the bright blue of his toque. "You've been sitting here awhile. Gonna get up for a skate?"

"Erm..." she replied. Oh, just her luck. He would have the biggest kind of laugh when he saw her going arse-over-teakettle on the ice.

"Come on, skate with me," he urged, holding out an unmittened hand.

"Oh God," she said at last. "I'm sorry, Phonse. I thought it would be a good idea. I went out and bought skates this morning, but I can't do this. It's been 25 years. There's no way I can start again."

He squatted down on his skates to bring his face to her level. How did he do that without falling flat on his face? "Good for you," he said, taking both her hands in his. "You're very brave. Hey, you've come this far. It's a shame to waste the morning, right? Now, keep hold to my hands—I won't let you fall."

His bruise from last week was hardly noticeable in the winter sunlight. His eyes held hers, steady and trustworthy, and he seemed to understand her fear and hesitation. This was a side of Phonse she never knew existed, a gentler one. A Phonse who saw beyond his own little world, one who could see the distress of another and not make a mockery of it, but could work to help her overcome her fears. This was... rather sexy.

His arm encircled her as he helped her upright. She stood stiff, petrified, unable to move her legs for fear of falling.

"One foot at a time," he said. "You can do it."

So she did, and almost glided. She just had to remember to push off with the other foot. And it was working: the world was sliding past her.

"That's right, slowly does it." His hand was firmly grasping hers, engulfing her felted mitten. She felt safe. He kept his pace exactly matched to hers as they negotiated the first bend.

She was relaxing now, too busy concentrating on moving her feet to hold onto her fear. And then suddenly she was sailing on her own, and laughing aloud.

"You're doing it!" She looked over at him and turning, wobbled a little, but he was there again at her side, offering a steadying hand. He took her arm as the second bend approached. Then suddenly they were back at the starting point. She'd done a full circuit.

Her confidence was growing exponentially, and she moved away from him, pushing up the speed. Phonse laughed and overtook her, flying free himself and gliding ahead, far ahead. He skated like a boy, the side-to-side swish-swish learned in hockey to get the skater to the opposite end of the ice in the fastest time. She, on the other hand, had been a figure skater, and the graceful moves came back to her as naturally as... as riding a bike.

They did a few more turns of the Loop, he more than her, sometimes grabbing her hand from behind and forcing her to move faster until he let her go again, laughing as he sped away. She found herself skating in time to the music, almost dancing on the ice (but no daring moves) and during a waltz he put his arm around her waist and they skated in time, swaying to the beat, and she found she could nestle right into his shoulder.

No wonder she'd had such a crush on the man when they'd first met last summer.

But her ankles were aching, the hitherto unused muscles burning, and she had to sit down for a spell. He joined her not long after.

"Had enough for the day?" he asked.

She nodded. "I'm going to have to work up to this," she said. "But you don't seem to be having any problems with it."

"We play hockey every week," he said. "All of us from the pub formed a team. It's just for fun, not a serious league, but it keeps us up to speed."

"What, even the bikers?" she asked. "And Sid?" She couldn't picture it.

"Oh, yeah," he replied. "Usually have a few brews afterwards."

The 'few brews' were probably the whole raison d'être for their games, but she declined to comment. He'd been so nice.

"Want to go for a coffee?" he asked her.

She found that she did, yes. So they got in his truck and he stopped by the Jumping Bean on Duckworth.

"It's almost too nice of a day to sit inside," he observed as they waited for their coffees.

"Too cold to sit out," she pointed out to him. "And they don't have their tables set up out there."

"No, but ..." He turned to the young woman pouring the drinks. "Can we have those to go?"

·····•·•····

He drove them to the top of Signal Hill and parked overlooking the ocean's wide expanse. Even in late December, there were blue notes among the grey on the water, with the white rime lining the shore. A supply vessel chugged its way south-east, off to the oilfields impossibly far away over the horizon of water.

"That guy ..." Phonse began.

"You mean Ian," Carmel replied. "My tenant. Who you don't seem to like."

"It's not that I don't like him," Phonse protested. "He seems likable enough." He paused. "Too young for you though."

"What?" She turned to him in outrage, only to see a small teasing smile on his face. "Not planning on sleeping with him," she said. "I don't even know if I'll let him stay past Christmas."

"Yeah?"

"He's nice and all, but I don't know. He's not too reliable. He hasn't given me the rent cheque yet," she said.

Phonse sat in thought awhile before he spoke. "Don't you find it weird that he showed up right after Wilson's murder? Him and his computer program which can predict a serial murder."

"And?"

"Well, he predicts another murder, and, bingo, one happens."

"You're not saying ..."

"Look, I saw him on TV with Smythe. The man's out for a buck. He wants to sell this computer program of his, and he's not getting any bites from the police or he would have sold it to them already. Correct?"

She nodded slowly. "Yeah."

"Okay. Is it past the realm of possibility that he did the second murder, just to fit into the known facts of the first? That would make his program a viable asset."

"No," she said. "No, Phonse, no one's that devious. This is murder you're talking about. I can't believe... No. Absolutely not." She was still shaking her head.

"What do you know of this guy? I mean, really, besides what he's told you himself?"

She opened her mouth to reply, but had to catch herself. She'd accepted Ian's word that he was a grad student, and that the University had given him her name. He carried a guitar case, so she'd assumed he played the guitar—but none of this meant anything, for it wasn't corroborated by outside sources. She'd watched him input data the other night into his program, supposedly, but did she even know that the program existed? Perhaps he had even killed Wilson, just to start the ball rolling.

What had she gotten herself into now?

Chapter 23

"**I** didn't mean to upset you," the new and gentler Phonse said to her, giving her a worried look. "I just want to make sure you're okay."

They sat in silence for a while. Carmel was wondering at the change in Phonse over the past few days. He'd been acting so out of character. She decided to approach the subject by easing her way in.

"Surprised you guys don't have any Christmas decorations up," she began. This was a legitimate opening, for she'd seen the inside of his mother's house last summer during an interview Smythe had held with her on-camera. Their house was a tribute to kitsch, with its china kittens and wood-burned plaques and hand-carved gingerbread around the windows. She expected at least strings of coloured blinking lights around the eaves of their house.

His face crumpled. "Carmel, Mom's gone," Phonse blurted out as if unable to hold it in any longer. He sat looking straight ahead at the ocean depths, his eyes awash with tears.

She turned to him in horror. "What? No one told me," she said. "How did it happen? I'm so sorry, Phonse." In a small place like St. Jude Without, any news tended to spread quickly.

"She took a flight, of course," he said, looking at her strangely, any hint of sorrow gone from his face. "She's not going to drive all the way to the mainland this time of year, now, is she?"

"Oh, gone that way," she said. "I thought you meant gone—dead." Wouldn't be such a loss to the world, really. Vee was possibly the nastiest person she'd ever met, and their relationship hadn't been helped by the fact that the woman thought Carmel had designs on her son. It had only been a crush, really.

"Her? Ha! She'll be round for years. She's tough as old boots."

"So..."

He sighed. "That's why I didn't put up any decorations," he said. "I didn't have the heart. It's my first Christmas without her. Ever."

"Oh." Forty-five years was a long time never to have spent Christmas on his own.

"She went to Florida, to visit Uncle Frank." Frank was the previous owner of Carmel's house, the one who'd left behind the pirate books and other odds and sods she hadn't yet bothered to turf out. "She said she couldn't face another year of snow. She'd finally had it."

"And the cove let her go?" Carmel asked, remembering back to the first conversation she'd ever had with Bridget. *'If this place was in your blood,'* the redhead had told her when they'd met, *'you would never leave, for St. Jude Without held on to its own.'* But then again, Bridget also believed in a weird mishmash of fairies and ghosts, so you had to take anything she said with a grain of salt.

"Well, she's not gone forever, now, is she? Mom'll come back in the spring."

Too bad.

"But what are you doing for Christmas dinner, then?"

The dark look settled back on his face, and he shrugged.

"Well, you have to spend it with us," she said. "One more is no problem."

His eyes darted hopefully over to her.

"Sharran's organizing a big dinner at the church," she explained.

"Oh," he said, in a disappointed tone. He thought about it some more. "Oh." This time it was more positive. "Cool."

"Everyone's coming," she said. "Got anything to bring?"

"I got the makings for a boiled dinner," he replied. "Salt beef, turnip, and cabbage—I'll do up a pot and bring it along."

"There you go," she said in an encouraging tone, although hoping he wouldn't expect her to eat it herself. She'd never acquired a taste for that popular dish. "And while you're at it, why don't you put up those Christmas decorations outside your house? The cove is as dark as a tomb. We'll want to be able to look out the windows of the church and see something cheerful."

"Damn it all, I will," he said, slapping the steering wheel with his hands. "Carmel McAlistair, you just made Christmas for me!" He leaned over and taking her face between his hands, gave her a long and searing kiss, the kind she'd been dreaming of last summer which he had never delivered. Thank God I'm over that crush, she thought to herself as she unwound the truck window—the heat was blasting in the cab.

"Damn," he said. "Now I feel Christmassy."

Chapter 24

I t took three trips up the steep steps to unload the bags of groceries and wine she'd picked up. Just after she'd struggled to the top with the last load, Bridget's door opened across the road. Carmel paused to watch her new tenant stroll out of Bridget's bungalow, the door left gaping wide behind him. He took a deep breath of the fresh air and let it out in a loud sigh, a dreamy smile on his face all the while.

"Let me help you with those bags," he said when he spied her, running across the road and jumping up the stairs two at a time. Ian grabbed the bags closest to him and while she was unlocking the door, turned to face the cove. He began belting out a Christmas carol——or was it a love song——in his best Irish tenor. He lifted his arms to embrace the morning as the song rang out. "It was Christmas Eve, babe, in the drunk tank..."

The sound of Bridget's door slamming stopped his music, and he gazed down at it in a fond manner. "Now, that's a woman," he said. "Nothing like a redhead."

Oh God, Carmel thought. Now she had a lovesick Ian on her hands. With any luck she could pawn him off on Bridget for good, get him to move in with her. Although the door slamming didn't look like an auspicious sign.

"Bring these into the kitchen," she called after him, making her way down the hall, "and shut the door behind you."

He hummed the rest of the Pogues' song as he followed her.

"What do you say to a nice bit of brunch?" he asked.

"Again?" Carmel asked. "Didn't you do that yesterday? The dishes are still in the sink."

"Not to worry, I'll take care of them lickety-split," he replied, already rooting through the fridge. He resumed his humming, dancing to his own music as he made his preparations. A whole hearty British meal again, she saw. Lord, how could anyone eat all that food two days in a row? She'd have to take up running again, not an easy thing to do in the Newfoundland winter, but the calories had to be burned off somehow.

"Would you mind putting on a pot of coffee?" he called over to her. The combined odours were again rising, and they awakened hunger inside her. His efforts must even have woken the cat up from wherever he'd been sleeping for Hank appeared outside the window and began picking at the screen with his claws. Ian let him in, while he set the table for three, still dancing and humming.

"He is not sitting at the table with us," she said, thinking it was time she put her foot down again.

"A cat at the table? Now what a fanciful idea," he replied. "That place's for my darling Bridget; she'll be along any minute." Indeed, the artist appeared not a moment later, unbrushed hair caught loosely back in a ponytail.

Lovestruck Ian might appear to be, but the same could surely not be said about Bridget. She largely ignored the Irishman and his nonstop chatter, allowing him to serve her as she set to eating in her purposeful way. The woman had an amazing appetite, Carmel knew. She always seemed to have something in her mouth but never put on any weight. Carmel found that she herself couldn't manage to eat very much today, despite the delicious aromas, as memories of yesterday's brunch were still clinging to her hips. And she really needed to remind Ian about the rent payment.

"The cheque!" he said, patting down his pockets but coming up blank. "It must be in the car. I'll run out and get that now."

"No, finish your meal first," she said, a little abashed. "It can wait."

"Don't forget about tomorrow night, Carmel," Bridget spoke up for the first time. "You're coming with me. I have to work on the help lines."

She'd forgotten all about her promise to Bridget made before the Christmas dinner plans, before the second murder, when it didn't seem she would have much to occupy her over Christmas. Darrow wouldn't want her help now, she had no doubt, not after what she'd done. He would know she couldn't be trusted. "But don't I need training?"

"S'alright," Bridget said around a mouth full of fries. "Just come and watch. And keep me company."

"But tomorrow's Christmas Eve," Carmel continued weakly, a thin whine entering her voice as she thought of all the preparations she had promised Sharran.

Bridget lay down her fork. "Domestic violence doesn't take a holiday," she said with not a trace of humour in her voice. "In fact, it tends to increase around this time of year because emotions run high."

At that moment, Carmel would have given anything to have the old Bridget back——the pre-militant one, the woman who was only concerned for her own cove and family and didn't give a rat about the problems other people created for themselves. Sharran was a force for the good, yes, but she had a lot to answer for.

"Speaking of which," Bridget continued. "I'll also be manning the Mental Health line while I'm at it. The regular volunteer for that shift has gone on vacation."

Carmel's cell rang and she grabbed it. "What?" she said into it.

"Yeah, would you come down and give me a hand putting up the decorations?" It was Phonse. "I need someone to pass stuff up to me when I'm on the roof."

Carmel looked at her half-eaten meal, then at Bridget who was ignoring Ian, and Ian who had resumed his chatter, ignoring the fact he was being ignored. Phonse's worries of the morning came back to her. What was Ian doing here in the cove? He was charming everyone, that was sure. The man might have an ulterior motive for everything he did. Even this play with Bridget. He might just be worming his way in, for the sole purpose of selling his program. Even murdering.

"Be down there right away," she said. The house and its occupants were pressing in on her—she needed to escape.

....

Phonse was already up on the roof, hammering at something unseen.

"I'm here," she called up, her hands in her pockets. It was growing chillier as the sun passed its zenith.

"Hand me up that box there, would ya?"

She struggled to carry the large carton up the ladder. It was heavy and full of little bits of wood and strings of outdoor lights. He took it from her as she approached the top of the ladder.

"There," he said. "Stick around. I'll just be a moment longer. I can do this with my eyes closed now."

She considered staying at the top to watch, but the wind was getting up and his work didn't seem exciting enough to brave the cold. From below, she listened to the hammering and thumps, and the grating of wood being moved with accompanying grunts. Finally, Phonse's head appeared over the roof edge as he hooked the strings of coloured lights around the perimeter of the eaves.

He grinned over at her as he finished up. "I'm doing Mom proud this year," he said.

And I hope she appreciates it, Carmel thought.

He put the ladder carefully away in the crawlspace beneath the small house, and then stood up. "Listen, I asked you down here, cause I want to talk something over with you," he said, not quite meeting her eyes.

What now? she wondered, but couldn't think of anything. She followed him as he walked down to the empty wharf. The boat was not in dock, having been put away somewhere safe for the winter. He paused, looking over the tickle to Bell Island, then took her hand and helped her jump down onto the rocks which passed for a beach in these parts. No sand, just large boulders surrounded by their rocky offspring. The pebbles crunched underfoot as they walked along.

"I've been thinking a lot since Mom left," he began. "She's not going to be around forever. I know it kills her not to be here with me this Christmas, but she's got a right to live her own life."

Carmel suppressed a shudder as she remembered the accusations flung at her by Vee Ryan last summer. That woman didn't live life so much as screech her way through it like the Wicked Witch of the West, spreading malice everywhere she passed.

"I know she wants to move down south at least part of the year. The winters here are getting to her," he continued. "She'll only go if she knows I'll be alright. So that's why ..." He turned to her and without warning grabbed her by the waist and hefted her up on top of the nearest boulder so that they were at eye level. He smiled into her eyes. "Let's get hitched."

Both his actions and his words took her by such surprise that she didn't get a chance to regain her balance on the precarious perch. He let go of her in order to half-kneel at her feet in a dramatic pose, but as her mind was reeling, her foot attempted to gain footing on the ice-covered rock yet failed to get a purchase. And down she went, landing like a cat on all fours. Unfortunately, humans aren't built the same way as those of the feline persuasion, not having the unattached clavicles which allow for grace on landing, and she could have sworn she heard a crack as her weight fell heavily onto her left wrist before it slipped into a wedge of stones.

"Ow!" She yelped more in surprise than pain at this point. "What are you doing to me?"

He pulled her left hand out of the small rock cleft, leaving the mitten behind, and she couldn't help the scream. This was real pain.

"Don't blame me if you can't stand on a rock without falling over," he said defensively as he helped her upright.

She glared at him, leaving him in no doubt what her answer was to his question.

"How come I'm always the one who has to go to the hospital with you?" he complained as he climbed into his truck. "Two days before Christmas. You know how much stuff I have left to do?"

"Just shut up and drive," she said. "And we're not going to the General, we're just going to the clinic up on Portugal Cove Road." She winced as her wrist kept up its deep throbbing. The emergency room might be the best place for her, but it was a much shorter drive to Rhonda's clinic. And she couldn't wait to get rid of Phonse.

Chapter 25

"Ouch! She couldn't help squealing as Rhonda prodded her wrist, flapping it back and forth.

"Wiggle your fingers," the doctor commanded and watched as she did so. "Okay then; it's not broken."

"I heard it crack as I fell."

"Then go to the hospital." Rhonda turned to look at her, and seeing that Carmel was near tears, relented and smiled at her. "You might have a hairline fracture. We'll keep it bandaged up and make sure you don't move it. Here, I'll show you how it's done." She firmly and deftly wrapped the wrist in an elastic bandage.

"I won't be able to do anything with my arm like this," Carmel said. "And it's Christmas."

"Oh, you'll be fine," the doctor said, brushing away her concerns as she affixed the limb to a sling. "Get someone else to peel the vegetables." She went silent for a moment. "I don't suppose ..."

"What?"

"Well, I suppose you already have plans for Christmas dinner, don't you?" she asked. Her tone had changed from brisk to wistful.

This sounded almost like a plea, and she wondered if she'd read it correctly. The doctor had a large family and circle of friends, all centred around Circular Road, the street of old money in the city, and she would most certainly have a full social calendar for the whole season as the group danced from mansion to mansion. "What are your plans?" she asked her back. "I guess your parents are doing the whole seasonal round as they usually do."

Rhonda let out a sigh. "Not this year. Mummy and Daddy have split up again. Unfortunately, they can't agree as to who should get Landmark House, so neither has moved out. It's ... it's too long of a story to get into, but there won't be any festivities this year. I can't bear to be around them when they're like that."

"Ah," Carmel said. The domestic affairs of Rhonda's parents were not something that reached the gossip columns, but she knew that behind the facade it was not a happy home. Every few years, one or the other would feel a need for a bit of drama, as if their wealth wasn't enough to keep them occupied, and it was never a pretty sight. "A bunch of us are getting together next door for Christmas dinner," she told her. "It's not anything fancy. It's in St. Jude Without ..." Rhonda hadn't been impressed by the small community the only time she'd seen it. "But you're welcome to join us."

"Really?" Rhonda looked up at her. "How absolutely cozy it sounds. How lovely! I'll meet all your friends and see this famous pub." She turned to wash her hands. "What can I bring? What time should I show up?"

"Well," Carmel paused to think. "Everything is taken care of for the main meal and food. Why don't you surprise us?"

"That's a delightful idea," the other said, her shiny hair bouncing as she dried her hands. "I know just the thing. How many people?"

"Maybe 20?" Carmel replied, not quite sure of the total number of people expected for the feast. "Possibly more. Sorry I can't be more exact." Oh boy. This was going to be an interesting mix indeed. The hairy tattooed bikers and Rhonda in her designer dress all sitting at the same table. Whatever would they find to talk about?

·········

The next day was a two-coffee morning. For one, she thought it might help dull the pain of her wrist. Rhonda had warned she might have discomfort, but this was a constant ache and the acetaminophen wasn't touching it. Two, she had to make a list and plan her day very carefully, for it was going to take twice as long to do her chores singlehandedly—literally.

Rewrapping the bandage hadn't been too hard. She held on to one end with her left as her right did the business as tightly as she could get it. The sling, however, caused much grief as she stuck herself with the safety pin in her shoulder three times before she gave up. The other arm would be useful anyway, even if she couldn't use her hand, for things like steadying the bowl and removing the cake from the oven.

"All these preparations—how do you make a cake with just one hand, let alone ice it?" she asked Hank, her only audience. It was cold again outside, below zero Celsius and the wind was whistling through the old wooden window frames. Hank was spending a lot of time at her place although he was Melba's cat. No doubt, he was hoping for another baconfest from Ian, his new best friend.

The cake wasn't going exactly to recipe: it was impossible to separate eggs using only one hand. At least the cat was making himself useful cleaning up the messes. She recalled seeing an egg separator advertised on TV once and thinking at the time what a ridiculous kitchen implement it was, just another consumer product with which to clutter up the kitchen drawer and to waste money on. If only she had her time back, she would also have stocked up on cake mixes, too. But no use crying over spilled eggs.

And truth be told, her mind wasn't really on the cake preparation anyway.

The second murder had changed things. A lot. Vivienne had been at the shelter when her husband was killed, and had been with Carmel herself during the murder of Father John, so that ruled her out. Franz too.

Who had been at the Affray on that fateful night? Phonse, yes. However, he might be a lot of things, but just not a murderer. She remembered back to last summer when he had been a suspect in the investigation.

The bikers had also been present on the night of the 17th. Well, she'd seen one there, but where one was, they all usually would be. But the bikers and Sid—they tended to mind their own business. Hairy, tattooed, and rough-looking, yes, but surely their style would be more a one-on-one, face-to-face knifing. If they had a murdering style, that is, which really, she was coming to doubt. One of them could recognize a Shakespeare quote, for God's sake, although that fact alone didn't make him less of a murder suspect. Shakespeare had dealt in a lot of bloody gory deaths.

Phonse's words about Ian kept coming back to haunt her, no matter how hard she tried to push them aside. The seed of suspicion was sprouting by the minute. Ian, and the possibility that he had committed the second murder just to prove his program right, in a crazed effort to sell it.

But the Irishman had just awoken when she had returned to the house with the news of Father John. Or so he had made it appear. Vivienne's drapes had been drawn in mourning while she'd been in the woman's house, and Ian could have easily slipped over to Portugal Cove and done the deed without her noticing his car passing by. If that was the case though, he must have done his homework ahead of time, finding out who to target next and where to find the priest.

Which still left the original murder to be solved. And from that point, her mind made the next obvious, horrible leap, thanks to Phonse's suspicions. The whole thing could have been set up by Ian from the start. He had been in the city since the fall when he began his Master's, or so he claimed. He would have just gotten here at the beginning of September when the newspapers were so full of the happenings in St. Jude Without. The whole series of incidents might have sparked the idea in his mind when he realized that Darrow was not receptive to funding research into his work. Perhaps the idea grew to set up a series of murders which his program would predict and 'solve,' making him a hero and allowing him to sell his work to the highest bidder, anywhere in the world.

He's just out to make a buck, Phonse had said. And this could make him a lot of bucks.

She could have opened her door to a murderer, a man worse than a serial killer because he was driven by pure greed. Where was Darrow when she needed him? She hadn't heard from the police officer for four days, not since they'd talked in the parking lot near the rectory. The day she'd passed on information she had no right to talk about, passed it on to Ian of all people. Though, of course, he may have already known the details of Father John's murder.

Carmel took a deep breath and steeled herself as she picked up her cellphone and tried to bring up the Inspector's number with one hand while holding the phone down with her injured arm. She had to tell Darrow her suspicions, and confess, all while she was at it. This would not be easy.

But there was no answer. A creak overhead signalled Ian's presence so she hung up without leaving a message, for she didn't want to alert the Irishman to her suspicions. In fact, she didn't want to see him or have anything to do with him and it would be no good to confront him directly, not when she was here by herself. The timer on the oven went off. She lifted the cake pans from the oven, then fled over to Bridget's house. She had to warn her, too.

It was already glooming over when they made their way into St. John's and the shelter for their shift on the phones. Bridget drove her car, as there was no way Carmel could manage the stick shift and the wheel at the same time. As the car entered Portugal Cove, Carmel attempted to explain her theory to Bridget, who was having none of it.

"That's the stupidest thing I ever heard," the redhead said. "Ian? He's a twit. He's charming, but a twit nevertheless. He wouldn't have the ability to plan that far ahead."

It didn't sound as if Bridget was blinded with love for the man; still, he'd spent the night with her, so she must have some feelings for him. Carmel told her as much.

"Oh please," Bridget replied. "That's just sex. And he's fun to be around. Do you think I can't see his faults?" She looked over to Carmel as she paused at the ferry entrance on the main road. "Being a murderer is not one of them. Yes," she continued, holding up her hand to stem Carmel's objections. "He's a bit over the top, has no ability to manage money, and can't understand why he pisses people off. But no, he is not that devious and well-organized. End of subject."

Bridget refused to be drawn into the topic again. Carmel sat back in the passenger seat in frustration. She would like nothing more than to turn around and go back home to nurse her aching wrist, but there was a murderer in her house, so this was the better option.

"Isn't there a way to reroute the shelter calls to one of our houses?" Carmel asked. Really, with modern technology it should be easy enough. "Then we could, like, do things in between calls." Like, get ready for Christmas dinner, for which she had optimistically promised to do too much.

Bridget appeared shocked by the suggestion. "No," she said. "For one thing, there's the call logs—we have to log in every call. How could we pass that on to the next shift if we did it from home?"

"Of course, the all-important call logs," Carmel said, under her breath. She tuned out Bridget's long list of reasons why they had to be at the shelter, which lasted right to the moment they pulled into the parking lot behind the brick building. Bridget was taking this whole thing too seriously.

Pam looked up from her phone as they entered the room. She gave them a curt nod as she finished the call, then stretched. "At last," she said. "I'm off then."

"Anything we need to know?" Bridget asked.

"Yeah, the cops said there's a report of a domestic over on Hamilton Avenue," Pam said, consulting her notes. "But no charges are being laid this time. Might want to pass it on so that whoever's on the lines tomorrow can expect to deal with it when they've all sobered up." She left shortly after that, eager to start her own celebrations.

In between the infrequent calls, Bridget ran through the procedures for each type of call. "They say you need to have the whole training course before we put you on the phones, but personally I think on the job training is the best way to go. Besides, there's no real counselling done by us," she said. "The only thing we can do is listen and provide contact phone numbers. All that is listed right here, anything you could possibly need."

"In case of suicide threats," Carmel read aloud. "Oh God, are we really expected to deal with that?" She suddenly felt very inadequate. "How about if I say the wrong thing and cause someone to jump off a bridge? I'm not sure I'm ready for this responsibility." In truth, there was something behind this worry. Carmel was conscious of having a history of saying exactly the wrong thing at exactly the worst time. Ruscan's disappearance could be taken as proof of that. She didn't want to be the one to push someone over the edge.

"Then don't say anything," Bridget said. "Your instructions are written right there. Ask if they have a plan, and get as much information as possible as to the location if they sound really serious." She poured water into the coffee machine to make a fresh pot. "The thing is, if someone calls the help line because they're suicidal, they're really looking for help, for someone to talk them out of it."

There wasn't much to do, even with Bridget looking after both phone lines. As it was her first night, and she really hadn't had the proper training yet, Bridget took the calls on speakerphone, showing Carmel by example how to handle each call. The few calls ranged from inquiries as to where one could find free condoms on George Street to a mother worried that her son was on drugs. Nothing really exciting, so Bridget occupied herself with tidying up some filing leftover from the week. Carmel attempted to wash the stained coffee mugs and other dishes—with only one working hand, it was a slow job.

The minute hand on the clock had been dragging for the past hour and their shift was drawing to a close, just 30 minutes left before their relief came on, when another call came through.

"Get that, would you?" Bridget called from the depths of the stationery supplies closet. "Put it on speakerphone for me."

Carmel's heart started to race as her adrenaline pumped into action. Okay, okay, which button turned on the speakerphone? She didn't want to hang up on her first call. She punched a button and success! She could hear breathing at the other end, against a faint background of music.

"You've reached the crisis line," she told the caller, reading from the script. "How can I help you?"

The caller continued to breathe noisily, and then she heard what sounded like a gurgle and a swallow.

"I did it," the voice said finally, slurry with booze. She tried to identify if it was a male or female speaking. Oh God, what had they done? Taken an overdose? Carmel looked for Bridget to save her, but she was still tucked away organizing tape dispensers and counting pens.

Just go with the script, she told herself. Keep whoever it was talking. "What did you do?" she asked, forcing herself to sound relaxed.

"I killed the bastard!" The voice rose to a squeak on the verb. "Both of them," he or she added.

"Do you want to talk about it?" she stammered, unwilling to deviate from the written form she'd been given. "I'm here to listen."

"I took the electrical cord and I strangled him," the other said. "He was sitting there all smug and comfortable, like he never done nothing to hurt no one in his life. But he ruined mine!"

Oh sweet Jesus. This was the murderer from Portugal Cove. It had to be. The Clerical Strangler. Carmel knew, because she'd discovered Father John's body, but the police hadn't released the information that the priest had been sitting in his parlor when he died. She hadn't even told Ian about that.

Bridget came rushing through the room and hit the 'record' button on the specially equipped telephone. "Keep them talking," she mouthed.

"Okay," Carmel said.

"I'm listening," Bridget mouthed again, pointing to the script.

Carmel cleared her throat. "I'm listening."

"Thought he was going to get his treat," the voice slurred. It was a young person, or youngish at any rate. "He sure did get a surprise!" The person on the end of the line began to laugh hysterically, an almost braying sound, as if the caller didn't know whether to laugh or cry.

"Where are you calling from?" Bridget jumped in.

The only answer was a click and the dial tone as the phone was disconnected. The two women were left looking at each other.

"What do we do now?" Carmel asked. "Is there a script for this?"

"We call the police," Bridget said. "That's standard procedure when we believe someone has been or is going to be harmed." She looked up before she started dialling. "You think this one is for real? That whoever it is really did the murders?"

Carmel nodded. "Yeah," she said. "That bit about Father John being found in his parlor ... No one would know that but the police. And the murderer."

There'd been no trace of an Irish accent in that voice on the phone. It wasn't her new tenant.

Chapter 26

C onstable Wright was on duty that night. Of course, this police officer was not aware that Carmel was the one responsible for leaking the information about the manner of Father John's demise to the press, but she still found it difficult to make eye contact with the constable. And there was no way she could ask about Darrow.

Evelyn Wright deftly removed the tape from the machine after listening a few times to the short recording and placed it into a plastic zip-lock bag. She was questioning Carmel closely about the exact wording of the conversation she'd had with the caller before the record button was started when Darrow himself walked into the room. The temperature in the room dropped several degrees, and it wasn't just from the rush of freezing air that accompanied him.

He listened without comment to what both Bridget and Carmel had to say, and only after they finished, did he speak. "Did either of you recognize the voice?" The question was addressed to them both, but he was looking only at Bridget, who shook her head.

"I ..." Carmel started to answer, but caught herself. The voice had seemed familiar—but where she'd heard it before she couldn't say. She didn't even know if it was male or female. She only knew that it wasn't Ian.

He was finally looking her way, his eyes hard and questioning as if he didn't really believe anything that was going to come out of her mouth. He waited.

"I think I've heard the voice before," she said. "I just need a few minutes. I'm sure it will come to me."

"Ms. McAlistair, might I remind you this is a murder investigation. We are under strict time constraints."

Like he needed to remind her.

"And I don't need to add that nothing of this is to be repeated outside this room," he said. "Do I."

That wasn't a question. No, he was right, he didn't need to add that. She had learned her lesson.

"And no details are to be discussed with the media."

"I didn't..." She shut her mouth. It was no use protesting. She had told Ian, and Darrow was quite aware of that. Ian had gone to the media, not her, but it was still her fault.

"If on further reflection anything comes to you, please contact Constable Wright," he said before leaving. In other words, he wanted nothing to do with her, and she was not invited to call him directly. She should take him off her speed dial.

Chapter 27

Christmas Day, and her tenant wasn't a serial killer. She had that much to be thankful for, anyway.

Yes, it was a white Christmas. A fresh fall of snow blanketed all the surfaces of the cove and the sea was steely grey. Smoke from the woodstoves trailed out of the chimneys to hang in the air. There was Phonse's rooftop Christmas display, the paint from the wooden figures fading after years of exposure to the winter salt winds. The only other colours visible were the few houses and cars in the cove, a deep red here, a bright blue there, as if the scene was a black and white photo colourized by an unseen hand.

The only sign of life out there was Clyde's black dog. He must have gotten loose again, and was snuffling and rummaging through the snow like a 100-pound puppy, littering the sides of the lane with doggy snow angels. There was probably pony poo under the snow. Yep, the dog had found a trophy and was headed back triumphantly home to the farm with a frozen puck held high in his mouth.

Carmel hummed carols to herself as she attempted to peel a whole bag of carrots singlehandedly. It was doable, after a fashion, for she could use her fingers to hold the carrot still as the other hand wielded the scraper. It was just a very slow process. The potatoes—well, the peel was where all the vitamins were, so she could get away with just washing them.

"You can't be at that now, not with your wrist out of action," Ian said behind her. She hadn't heard him get up. He gave a yawn. "Leave it, now, and I'll do that when I've had a coffee."

Carmel was happy enough to quit the job and join him at the table. She wasn't at all uncomfortable with him now that he was no longer a suspect.

"Merry Christmas," she said to him.

"And a very merry one to you," he replied.

"I got you a present," she said. She handed him the mug loosely wrapped in tissue paper with a sticky-back bow holding it all together. That had been all the wrapping she could manage that morning.

He held out the mug with a white and blue cat on the side. "Why, it looks like wee Hank! Thank you, I'll hold this dear forever."

"Bridget made it," she said.

"And that makes it doubly special to me," he said with a smile. "And now, here's a little something for you."

She took his offering in her hand. It was a CD jewel case with a black and white photocopied image of an alley downtown, the one that used to be known as Birdshit Alley before they cut down all the trees where the starlings gathered. The picture angled down the steep concrete winding steps. A backdrop of cartoonish graffiti framed four figures, one of which was Ian, dressed in his shabby pea coat and a silk top hat.

"You're in a band?" Carmel asked, looking back up at him. "What kind of music do you play?"

Ian inclined his head modestly. "It's been described as garage-punk traditional," he said. "With a smattering of Euro techno-pop. But we just call ourselves the Back Alley B'ys." He pronounced the last word as a Newfoundlander might, with a long i sound instead of the oy. "It's just a bunch of the lads getting together for the beer, don't you know."

She could believe that, knowing Ian. "I'll have to give it a listen. Any Christmas songs on it?"

He laughed in reply.

"Oh well, we won't play it tonight at the dinner," she said, also grinning.

"Might not be Sharran's cup of tea," he said, nodding.

"Speaking of which, did you go with Clyde to get the tree yesterday?"

"We did indeed and what a fine tree we found," he said. He leaned in closer. "Have you ever done this thing? I mean, go out into the wilderness to get the perfect tree for the perfect celebration? For I believe——and correct me if I'm wrong——but it's the tree which makes the Christmas."

Carmel didn't necessarily agree with this sentiment, but he was on a roll, so she simply nodded. She had, in the past, had occasion to go tramping through the snowy woods to find the perfect tree, and hadn't enjoyed the experience at all. First of all, there was the tramping through deep snow, off the beaten track, and the snow getting inside your boots and melting but then freezing again. When your poor feet were good and cold from doing that, then there was the standing around while some anal person insisted on looking at each tree in the woods from every single angle to determine the most suitable one. By this time, you were ready to go to Canadian Tire to purchase a good old plastic tree, but then the real work began, the sawing down (which took forever when no one owned a power saw). Now your feet were blocks of ice but your entire upper body was sweating and you were feeling slightly feverish, and only then were you allowed to turn back toward home, but this time you were slugging back through the woods and snow lugging a most uncooperative tree behind you through the bushes and over the rocks.

However, she appreciated that he had enjoyed the excursion, and didn't try to dampen his enthusiasm.

"And there it was before us," he had continued, not realizing she'd been lost in thought. "The most marvellous, the most stupendous tree of all, standing on its own in the field. With two quick cuts of Clyde's saw, it was down and in the back of his truck, and off we went to Sid's."

"That doesn't sound much like wilderness," she said. "And, uh, whose field was it?"

"I don't know, it was over near St. Phillip's way, one of those big estates overlooking the ocean. They had lots of trees there, they won't miss one. But they weren't home. Clyde made sure of that," he assured her. "By the way, how did your volunteering go last night?"

She let him change the subject for she didn't want to think on the possible repercussions of the tree theft. But she also couldn't tell him any details about the last phone call of their shift. Look what had happened the last time she'd spoken out of turn.

"Alright, you know, nothing too exciting," she said. No, she was not going to mention a word of it.

"Nothing exciting?" he asked. "Well, that's a shame. Or maybe it's not, come to think of it. But the tree—you'll love it; it's a fine specimen."

At least, Carmel thought, at least the tree was now safely tucked away inside the church. There was little likelihood that it would be seen by anyone other than the folks of the cove, and they were very good at keeping secrets. There was that to be thankful for.

After the vegetables were made ready and popped in the oven to roast, the two worked companionably on icing the cake. Carmel read out the ingredients while Ian carefully measured and mixed.

"I don't think the butter's soft enough," he said, raising his voice over the motor of the small hand mixer. "It's still all lumpy. You can't have lumpy icing, now; folks won't like that."

She frowned at the bowl and motioned him to turn the beaters off. "Try mashing the lumps with a fork," she said. "You're right, I should have taken the butter out last night to warm up. It's too cold."

By the time the bigger pieces of butter had been smushed down, the icing was growing stiff from overbeating. They managed to get it all on the double layered cake anyway, by Ian holding and turning and Carmel slathering the sides and top.

"It doesn't exactly look like a Martha Stewart production," she said, eying the cake critically. It was lacking the soft waves of the recipe's picture—the icing was almost the texture of fudge by this time. "Still, we'll put a few of those red and green cherries on, and it'll look Christmassy, anyway."

Chapter 28

T he church was done up splendidly in true old-fashioned Christmas glory. Foil accordion streamers hung from the corner to corner, the type that hadn't been sold since the late 1970s that Carmel remembered as a mainstay of the convent holidays. A plastic sheet printed with a merry Santa Claus covered the smoker's door, while fake snow covered all the windows in decorative drifts. Tinsel hung from the tiny lights outlining the bar until Sid looked like he was peering out from beneath a glittering silver fringe. The bikers had truly gotten to work and shown their Christmas spirit, having scoured the Salvation Army Thrift Store for anything seasonal and cheap.

The tree, of course, was the attention-getter in the room. Placed to the right of the front door, the darkest corner of the room, it glowed with perhaps a thousand white and coloured lights, each set twinkling at a different beat. You would almost think it was a living creature, with the illusion of movement caused by those lights, that is, until you looked at it straight on. Then the mad twinklings might set off an epileptic fit if you watched them too long and tried to discern a pattern. Instead of an angel or a star, it was crowned by a large fibre-optic creation which sprouted even more pulsing colours for the eye. Every tiny branchling was hung with a bauble––so many that the tree itself, pride of Ian's first North American Christmas, was hardly visible.

A nod was given to the Holy Family, too, this being an old church and all. Almost-complete nativity scenes decorated some of the window ledges, and three-foot high wooden cut-outs were spaced out along the north wall. Even the natural world was represented in a plastic sort of way, with fake garlands hung along the bar and bottoms of the windowsills. Last but not least, a large star of Bethlehem glowed yellow above the bar, as tall as a man, complete with a streaming comet's tail. Carmel couldn't hazard a guess where that had come from.

All the tables had been placed in the centre of the hall to create one large, long place for the community to gather and eat. Large pieces of plywood had been cut up and placed over the tabletops in order to give a standard shape surface—no doubt this bit had also been organized by Sharran. White tablecloths, or perhaps they were old sheets, were being placed over it as Carmel approached the bar, her chocolate cake wedged between arm and good hand. The pool table had also gotten the same treatment.

Almost everybody from St. Jude Without, or connected with the cove, was present. Many of them milled around looking aimless in the now-unfamiliar surroundings as their usual spots were otherwise commandeered for the celebration. The pool players hovered near the buffet table out of habit, not quite knowing what to do with their cue-less hands or with their spouses, and the bikers grouped near the smoking entrance where their table usually sat. Clyde's dog and the young biker wanna-be were the only ones not at a loss. The large black beast was extremely well-behaved, heeling at the farmer's side but never taking his eyes off the food safely high on the bar. The young man was not so well-behaved, having imbibed more of his share of booze or some other drug already earlier in the evening. He staggered around, greeting all like old friends and making inappropriate remarks which were largely ignored.

"I'm surprised young Daniel made it this evening," Ian remarked to Carmel as he placed the large bowl of carrots next to the potatoes. "He was in no fit state last night, I can tell you."

"What's his story, anyway?" Carmel asked, watching the young man. "He's a new addition since I came back."

Ian had, in the very short time he'd lived there, ensconced himself within the life of the cove, and knew as much gossip as Vee. He also was on a first-name basis with almost everyone in the bar. "He's the nephew by marriage of Billy." He indicated the man Carmel thought of as the head biker, the tallest one who seemed to take the lead in everything the group did.

"Father Wish said he had a hard time of it growing up," Carmel said.

"And that he did," Ian agreed. "Bounced from a broken home to foster homes all over the city. Heavily into drugs. Billy's trying to help him straighten out his life but it's an uphill battle, I can tell you. And I call him young, but he's not really. He's in his mid-20s. You'd never say it to look at him."

Carmel watched Daniel a moment longer. He had a scrawny build, a painful thinness in the way you don't see so often these days, as if he'd not had the proper nourishment he'd needed growing up.

"We're going to do this buffet style," Sharran called out to the growing crowd, interrupting their conversation. "Sid is carving the turkeys, and I want all the dishes for the main meal set up there." She turned to Carmel. "Leave the cakes on the bar for now. We'll get to them later."

Modern Christmas carols rang out through the speakers, keeping the mood lively and upbeat. Sharran instructed everyone to line up in an orderly fashion, giving out paper plates and napkin wrapped utensils as she did so.

At the last moment, the front door was flung open and Rhonda floated into the space, followed by a man in a black suit. She shrugged off a tiny mink cape which the man hung up on the coat hook for her. Next to the Christmas tree, she

was the second most dazzling thing in the room. She wore a
mid-length gown of silver lame and beads which clung to her
every curve. As she paused by the entrance, next to the tree,
she reflected the twinkling lights back into the room.

"Not too late, am I?" she called out when she spotted
Carmel. Her blonde locks were sprayed into an elaborate
arrangement held up by diamond clips.

"Come on in," Carmel said, moving forward to greet her.
"You too, Jack. Plenty of room and food." She recognized
Rhonda's driver from the other night, then took her friend
aside. "Don't you ever drive?"

Rhonda looked at her with surprise. "Drive? I can, of
course," she said. "Can't everyone? But why should I, when I
have Jack?"

Carmel laughed. Typical Rhonda—why do something
when there was someone else hired to do it? "Grab a plate
from Sharran, there, you guys."

It turned out that introductions didn't have to be made,
for Jack already knew the bikers and indeed many of the
men in the room, as he'd grown up in St. Phillip's, the next
community south of Portugal Cove. As for Rhonda, she floated
everywhere, not needing to know people before she spoke
with them.

And there was room around the table, despite the large
crowd. Carmel found herself at the end with Bridget and Ian
to one side, Sharran at the head of the table on her other.
She looked around for Rhonda, and gave her a wave when she
spotted her friend down at the other end seated by the bikers
and Father Wish. Phonse was nearer, seated beside Clyde and
the pool players, while Sid sat across from him. There were
faces she didn't know, especially the women who must be
attached to Sid's habitués, but all were friendly.

"Before we begin to eat," Sharran said as she stood up.
"I'll say a short grace." There was much clinking as forks and
knives were hastily set back on the plates, and guilty glances

darted around as mouthfuls were quickly swallowed. Everyone stood up with her and bowed their heads in time-honoured tradition. "We give thanks for this day, this meal to be shared in the company of our community, friends, and family. Yet we remember also those who are not with us, and we pray for their souls, and also for forgiveness to those responsible for these crimes." You could have heard a pin drop in the hall. In the silence which followed, Carmel shivered, and wondered if the murderer was in the hall that evening and heard Sharran's generous request for them to be forgiven.

"Amen." All at the table mumbled an answering "Amen."

"Now let's chow down," Sharran said, grinning around the gathering and breaking the sombre mood she had created. And so the community resumed their meal.

"Oh," Rhonda cried out at the end of the long table. "The Christmas crackers! Jack, give out the crackers. We can't have dinner without them." The silver crackers (which happened to match Rhonda's dress) were speedily dispatched and, amid much merriment, the crackers were pulled, toys examined, and paper crowns placed on everyone's head.

There was plenty to eat, and loads left over even after all second and third helpings were taken. An enormous plum pudding appeared, appropriately ablaze, and the obligatory spoonful given to all. Finally, the various cakes and sweets were dug into and enjoyed, then the company sat back and groaned with relief that the feast was over.

But they weren't allowed to wallow for long.

"Let's get the place cleaned up and sorted," Sharran called out. "Then we can start the dancing!" Dancing in the bar, that was a first. Sid's church and this congregation had never seen the like of this woman, but everyone went along with her ideas because, well, because she was so much fun to be around. Where she came from, and how she happened to be hanging out here in St. Jude Without, Carmel didn't as yet understand, but Sharran's presence had certainly been accepted by the cove. Even though she was a United Church minister.

Of course, it didn't take long to toss out the paper plates, throw the silverware into a large container to be sent to someone's dishwasher, gather up the leftovers, and disassemble the table. Some folk drifted up to the bar to renew their refreshments, others meandered their way outside for cigarettes.

Dropping the last handful of the paper napkins and plates into the industrial-size garbage bag, Carmel's eyes and ears were caught by a ripple spreading through the crowd. She looked up, and there was Vivienne, pausing at the front entrance as if deciding whether or not to come in.

Everyone in the place recognized Wilson's wife, of course, although few from St. Jude Without had ever had occasion to make her acquaintance. They just didn't move in the same circles, and they weren't the church-going types except when roused by Father Wish for the holy days.

Within moments, Rhonda materialized at Vivienne's side and the two embraced. The southern belle then made her way on to Carmel's group next with Franz the butler-cum-chauffeur trailing behind her. She had deftly avoided Sharran and Bridget, not that the artist noticed for she was too busy ignoring Ian. "I thought I might drop in and find you here," Vivienne said. "I didn't realize I'd be crashing a party."

"It's okay," Carmel said. "The more the merrier, I'm sure."

"I heard the news," the other said in a low voice. "About Father John." She glanced about her. "What do you know about that?"

Carmel shrugged, feeling a little guilty. "Nothing more than what's on the news," she extemporized, not wanting to confess that she was the one responsible for the media knowing.

"But I heard you found his body too." This was almost an accusation. "And he was killed in the same manner," Vivienne pressed on, her eyes like steel. "I just don't understand what's going on here."

"Yes," Carmel replied. "I found him. Right after I left your house that day."

Vivienne's shoulders relaxed a little. "He was murdered while you were visiting me?" she said. "So now the police can stop hounding me. There's no way I can be accused of this."

The other nodded. "The media are saying it's a serial killer," Carmel said, "one who is targeting clerics."

"Which reminds me," Vivienne said, "where is that new tenant of yours? The one with this computer program everyone's talking about?"

Carmel was happy to call out to Ian. He left Bridget reluctantly, watching over his shoulder as the redhead wafted over to Billy. "Ian, this is Vivienne Wilson."

His eyes came alive as he focused on the blonde. Carmel had told him of Vivienne's possible interest in funding his project. Another of his many talents appeared to be the ability to smell money.

"The computer programmer," Vivienne said, holding out her gloved hand palm downwards. "How delightful to finally meet you."

Ian took the proffered hand in the spirit intended, grasping it lightly and executing a small bow. "And I you, Mrs. Wilson."

"Oh please, call me Vivienne," she said, glancing coyly up at him. "I have a feeling we're going to be good friends, very good friends indeed. And I want you to tell me all about this wonderful program you've been developing."

The Irishman started on his spiel. Vivienne waved him down when he began on the endlessly fascinating (to him) technical details.

"Oh, yes, yes," she said. "But what have you produced? I mean to say, what is the program telling you about my husband's murderer?"

"Both murders," Ian nodded knowingly. "As predicted, we're dealing with a serial killer. If only I had the means to develop it further, the money to really sit at it and devote all my time, I could really ..."

He was cut short by Vivienne. "But is it pointing to the murderer? Now, with Father John's death, what is it telling you? How has that changed things?"

"Well, it needs a few tweaks, of course," Ian said. "And that doesn't come cheaply. Now Carmel was telling me you might have an interest in funding this research ..." He put his arm around her and led her to a private corner. Carmel watched them with a smile. She had no doubt that Vivienne would be able to take care of herself and not be steamrollered into anything she had no intention of doing. She might look and act like a delicate flower, but there was steel beneath the southern belle facade.

By now the tables were cleared, the leftovers packed away, and a small space cleared for dancing in front of the bar. Jingle Bell Rock blared out of the speakers. It was one of Carmel's least favourite Christmas songs, but it was lively and Sharran started off the dancing.

"Come on, everybody!" she called over the music, dancing by herself. Some of the women pulled their men up onto the floor and the old floor was soon pulsing to the rhythm.

Phonse had materialized by her side, nursing his beer as he watched the dancers. "Saw your friend Darrow in town," he said, glancing over at her.

"Not my friend," she said. She turned to Sid behind the bar and asked for a top-up.

"You guys seemed pretty cozy," he continued as he also turned toward the bar, his arm now touching hers. "But haven't seen him here lately."

"No," she said. "Why would he be?" Phonse's body was warm through her thin sweater. He smelled clean tonight for a change.

"He didn't appear too happy when I banged into him in town," Phonse said. "He didn't seem to think you guys were friends either."

"What are you getting at, Phonse?" she asked, moving slightly down the bar to get away from his touch.

He slid down the bar after her. "I ran into him at the Duke," he said. "Him and that missus, the blond police girl."

"Constable Wright," Carmel informed him, turning back to face the dance floor. "And I don't think they call themselves 'police girls.' The term is 'police officer.' They're partners; they work together as a team."

"I think they've got something going," he said. "You know. Partners not just at work, if you know what I mean. Wink wink, nudge nudge." He elbowed her to bring home his point.

What? Darrow and the uptight Evelyn, who never had a hair out of place? She couldn't see it.

"Nice girl, that," he said.

Carmel disagreed, but declined to say so. Evelyn had never been friendly to her—but why should she be? The only time she'd seen the constable was when she was stumbling upon dead bodies, making more work for the police.

But Darrow and Evelyn. They worked closely together, no doubt there was a bond between them. Had she imagined anything between herself and the Inspector? She remembered the two hours they had inadvertently spent together before she left for St. Kitts last fall––the art gallery and the shared pizza. She had enjoyed his company. They'd found a lot of common ground.

She was beginning to feel a little glum.

The music changed to a slow song, The St. John's Waltz. One of the most romantic songs ever, in her book. Sharran stood on the dance floor, her hand held out toward the bar and an expectant look on her face. Sid removed his apron and joined her on the floor. They make a good-looking couple,

Carmel noted, as the realization clicked in her mind. The two were in love.

Ian was dragging Bridget up to the floor, too, his eyes gazing at her in adoration as the redhead looked away, a small smile on her face. Was everyone in the place partnered up? Everyone but her.

"Want to dance?" Phonse murmured in her ear as he placed his arm around her. He took her good hand and her bandaged left arm rested on his waist. He was a surprisingly good dancer, leading her at just the right pace.

"My offer still stands, you know." She could feel his voice rumble through her chest as he softly spoke the words, his breath soft on her neck. He still had that magnetism she'd fallen for last summer, that inexplicable physicality that melted her, even now when she knew him better. Knew what a scoundrel he could be. The wine and beer had relaxed her body and she leaned her head against his chest. "You and me—it could be good."

He started singing the words to the song softly in her ear as they danced to the end of the music.

A loud shrill of laughter burst over the last notes of the song, a hysterical cry which shook her out of the reverie Phonse and the alcohol had induced. She'd heard that voice before. Carmel looked up with a start, her eyes meeting Bridget's. "That's ..."

Bridget nodded. "It is."

The murderer who had phoned the help line last night. They both looked over to the source of the strange laughter, and saw Daniel, the young biker wannabe, stumbling from the toilet, his nose smeared with white. He was chortling to himself as he made his way to Billy, who was watching the young man with a look of consternation on his face. As Daniel passed Clyde's dog, he made a face and swerved to kick the creature in the ribs, but wasn't coordinated enough to inflict any damage. The large black dog rose from the floor and gave a warning growl.

"Phone Darrow," Bridget hissed to her in the space between songs. Carmel stood still on the dance floor, all thoughts of loneliness gone as she stared at the two men in leather jackets. Billy was shaking his head and looking like he was about to give up on his nephew by marriage. "Quick before Bill throws him out into the snow!"

Carmel ran back to the bar where she'd laid her purse and took out her cell. She fumbled at the buttons and it seemed to take an age before she could hear the ringing.

"Please answer," she whispered. "Don't ignore this call." At the very last moment, it seemed, she heard a click and his voice.

"Darrow," he said, managing to convey a lot of displeasure into that one word.

"He's here," she said into the phone. "I'm so sorry for phoning you, but I don't have Evelyn's number and I still had you on speed dial. Please come, the m ... murderer ..." But it was Daniel, that mixed-up foolish young man. Yes, he was the murderer, or claimed to be. "That voice, we just recognized him."

"Where are you?" Darrow asked, his voice sharp.

"At the bar," she said. "At Sid's. We're having a Christmas dinner for the cove ..."

"We're on our way," he said. "Don't let him leave."

She clicked off the phone and looked over to where the bikers were standing. Billy had by now lifted the younger man up bodily by the arms and was shaking him.

"Clean up your goddamn act!" Billy was furious. The other three bikers just looked on and shook their heads. "Can't take you nowhere, can I? We're all having a nice time here, a civilized time, and you got to be getting into your drugs and acting like a jerk!"

He set the younger man on his feet with a thud. Daniel wobbled and caught himself, wavering between bravado and a real desire to get back into Billy's good graces. Good sense seemed to win out, for he sat in the nearest chair and slumped. Tears started running down his face.

None of the other celebrants had paid much attention. The music had started up again by this time, another waltz she vaguely knew, and the floor was filling up again, as if the scene had never happened. Even Vivienne was up there, Carmel noted, dancing with her chauffeur Franz. They were an odd couple, her so soft and feminine, he so straight and stiff, wearing his white gloves even now in the relaxed holiday atmosphere. They were sharing a secret smile as they looked into each other's eyes so closely, so intimately. Carmel hadn't realized the two were the same height—Franz being so narrow had appeared to be so much taller. The strange thing was, Vivienne appeared to be leading in the dance.

She didn't have time to wonder on this, for Darrow was soon at the door with Evelyn right behind him. Darrow for once looked as though he might have been relaxing, his tie was still loosened under his coat. Evelyn was not in uniform, but a soft velvet black dress with a parka thrown over it and winter boots on her feet. They must have been dragged out of their own Christmas celebration, Carmel realized, and wondered fleetingly if they had been dining together.

Evelyn was examining the tree with a suspicious scowl on her face. Carmel hurried over to meet them.

"It's the young guy, over in the corner with the leather jacket," she said in a low voice. "I knew I had heard the voice before. It's him."

"Daniel Connolly," Evelyn said in disgust as she turned to look. "Might have known." She took a pair of handcuffs out of her beaded evening bag.

Darrow didn't seem so ready to judge. "Are you sure?" he asked. Carmel couldn't tell if he was just ascertaining or if he didn't believe her.

"That laugh was hard to mistake," she said.

He shook his head. "It doesn't fit," he said. "It just doesn't fit."

"It's him," she said again, insisting. "The killer."

He nodded to the constable. "We'll take him in." The two walked over to where the bikers sat.

Carmel watched in trepidation as they approached the table of bikers. There were four against two. Four burly men, for she wasn't counting Daniel, who was now a sobbing mess, set against Darrow and the petite Evelyn. Billy stood up and crossed his arms and watched the two police officers as they made their way across the room. He looked pretty pissed off.

Darrow nodded to him and took him aside as if in consultation. The two men spoke, and nodded, and spoke some more until Billy shook his head in despair. He watched in silence as Evelyn placed the cuffs on Daniel with no resistance and began to lead him away. When the two had left the building, he could no longer be quiet.

"That little asshole! After all I've done for him, he pulls this kind of crap." Billy turned to the bar and ordered a large one.

Most parties and celebrations in the cove broke up with a fight, but a police arrest was just as effective. Now the serious drinking could begin.

Chapter 29

Carmekll accompanied Darrow to the door, but the man seemed to be lost in thought.

"You don't think he did it?" she asked, searching his face for an answer.

"I have no doubt he's guilty," replied Darrow after a pause. "What he's guilty of, we have yet to ascertain." He looked up to see Phonse hovering behind Carmel. "Just a couple of things," he said, drawing her closer and lowering his voice. He looked up at the fine tree in all its gaudiness and fingered the nearest branch. "This tree," he said. "It's a white pine."

She followed his gaze and swallowed. "Erm," she managed to say. Of course, the tree.

"We had a report of a tree theft yesterday, out in St. Phillip's," he said. "A white pine, much like this. We'll be checking into that complaint." He looked at her meaningfully. "Tomorrow, when there's time."

"A tree theft," Carmel said, shaking her head. "The lowest of the low. I hope you find the scoundrels who would do such a thing." Damn Ian and Clyde and their lazy thieving ways. "You said there were a couple of things?"

Darrow looked down at his feet, shuffled then up at her again, meeting her gaze. His dark eyes reflected the rainbow colours from the tree lights. He cleared his throat. "You said you have me on speed dial?"

·····•··•····

Boxing Day. The day after Christmas, when all the excitement was over for another year. Some stalwarts clung to the tradition of the season lasting until January 6, the twelve days of Christmas, and could not bear to take down the decorations until Old Christmas Day had arrived, but for Carmel who was never much of a fan of the season, the celebration was now over, and good riddance.

Over and done with, like the snow which had graced the cove yesterday. A fall of ice and rain last night and a temperature hovering at 0 degrees Celsius meant that there was a coating of ice over everything. Ice on the cars, ice on the roads, ice on her veranda, with a coat of cold water to polish it off. She would need the steel grips on her boots today, those brilliant creations of rubber and metal which turned her winter boots into studded tires.

Unable to bear the greyness at the window any longer, she turned to her computer and idly checked her email. The airline had promised to send her a message when and if her luggage ever turned up. She didn't have much hope for it today, it being a statutory holiday.

Again, there was only one new message, this time from a different sender. Her eye was caught by the single word in the subject line.

Raven.

Like before, she had to open it, but again, the message made no sense.

Come, the croaking raven doth bellow for revenge.

"What!" What the hell was that all about? She sat and read the words again. Croaking raven. Was it hurt? Bellow for revenge—did that mean he was angry? But at whom? The only clue she could find was the ancient verb doth, which meant "does," loosely speaking.

She quickly opened Google and typed the words in, to see what that great source could make of the message.

So, a quote from Shakespeare, from Hamlet. But what was it saying? Ian knew Shakespeare, perhaps he would understand the reference. She hauled him out of bed and sat him in front of the computer while she fetched him a coffee.

"Explain it; what does this mean?"

"Come, the croaking raven ..." he repeated as he rubbed his eyes. He shivered a little, sitting on the leather seat in just his underwear. "Christ, Carmel, I don't know. Hamlet, yes, from the play scene. It's, let's see ..." He sat back and sipped from the warm cup. "Hamlet is impatient, telling the lead actor to get on with his business. Y'see, he's having a play enacted in which a wife murders her husband, in order to trap his new father-in-law, to see by his reaction if he murdered Hamlet's father." He looked over at her. "That help?"

She shook her head. "Not really. Who's the raven in the play?"

He considered this for a moment. "Hamlet, himself, I think. Or, if you want to get really specific, it's another of Shake-speare's jests, a play on words, harking back to the original story, sometimes called 'Ur-Hamlet', in which ..."

He got no further, for she had stood up. "No, no. I don't think we need to delve that deeply into it." She paused for a moment in thought. "Revenge. Croaking. Those are the words that are important. But who is this message from?" She paused, sidetracked for a moment. "How do you know all that stuff anyway?"

Ian shrugged. "The life of a terminal student. You come across a lot of bits of knowledge when you refuse to leave university." He removed himself and his coffee and crawled back upstairs to bed.

She curled up in the chair he had vacated and studied the message again, but could get no further ahead with it, no matter how much she puzzled. There was no other link included this time, nothing to give her any clues. Was it from Ruscan? Was it about Ruscan? Perhaps she should reply to it. Or perhaps not. She remembered how he had disappeared so totally and so simply, on the overnight flight to Hong Kong. Maybe someone was looking for him for revenge of some sort, had tracked her email down, thought she knew where he was. What would she be inviting into her life if she replied? She hated the uncertainty.

Again, she was unable to stop herself from hitting the reply button. But what to reply?

Who are you?

Like that would help. The person at the other end could say they were anyone and she wouldn't be able to tell the difference. She erased the words.

Is this Ruscan? She hadn't changed her email address in years. It could be anyone at the other end. Maybe she should just give her phone number, encourage the person to call her, and then she would be one step closer.

But then the person would know where she was by the area code. If it wasn't Ruscan, then who knew what she would be inviting into her life?

Of course, if she answered the email at all, a person with a bit of sophisticated equipment could narrow down her location. She erased the words again in an unexpected wave of anger. What right did this person have to be playing games with her? She was sick enough of secrets. It either was Ruscan or it wasn't. She'd done nothing wrong, had no knowledge of his whereabouts and had no interest in getting mixed up in international intrigue.

Is this some kind of a joke? And she hit send before she could change her mind and turned away from the screen.

Chapter 30

C armel had passed on the message about the tree last night to Sharran, the only half sober one of the lot remaining in the bar, and could only hope that action had been taken. Speaking of whom, she'd totally forgotten to give the woman minister a present last night, even just a token to acknowledge her gratitude in the organizing (and cooking) of the turkey feast for the cove. As there were still a number of Bridget's mugs left, this was easily taken care of.

She left the car where it was and decided to walk. Setting off on her walk with the YakTraks firmly over her boots, Carmel noted that the pine needles strewn around the ice on the church's parking lot. At least that had been taken care of, although she wouldn't put it past Constable Wright to bag up the fallen needles as incriminating evidence to be used against the cove. Now that the murders had been solved, the police would have time on their hands to chase after other, less pressing crimes.

A fine mist was drizzling again by the time she reached Portugal Cove. There was no action that she could see up the driveway to Vivienne's house. The silver Land Rover had a fine sheen of ice over it that showed it hadn't been moved since the previous night, and the curtains were still drawn.

Strange, Vivienne dancing last night so soon after her husband's death. And dancing in public too, with her butler. Something about that whole scenario was bothering her, something she couldn't quite put her finger on. That smile on the woman's face as she looked into Franz's eyes, almost triumphant. That same smile on her face as she had watched Daniel led out by the constable. Well, grief hit people in strange ways.

Just passing Oceanica, she changed her mind about walking. The car would have been much warmer and drier, even with the layer of ice all over it, but she was almost to Sharran's house now so there was no sense turning back. She glanced up at the rectory next to Holy Rosary and saw a forlorn figure standing in the rain, one she recognized. It was the young reporter from the news station. They'd met last fall standing over the ravine where Smythe, his boss, had been strung up and left to die. She veered up the long driveway.

"Josh, is that you?" she asked.

The young reporter turned with a doleful face.

"What are you doing here, standing out in the rain?"

He shrugged wetly. "I didn't have anything else to do, so when I saw the cops back here, thought I'd see if I could get anything else from them."

She looked up past him. There was a police car parked by the steps, right next to Darrow's own sedan and she wondered if the news of Daniel's arrest for the two murders was public knowledge yet. If it wasn't, well, she didn't want to be the one accused of leaking it with the media. Not this time. "Any new developments?"

"Not that they're sharing."

Hmmm. Best not to say a word. "Did you have a good Christmas?"

He sighed. "If you call a turkey sandwich from Breen's and NetFlix a good time, then yeah, I guess I did."

"Oh, Josh," she said, feeling sorry for the lad despite her distaste for him. It wasn't his fault. He was the protégé of Gerald Smythe, who was teaching the young man everything he knew about tabloid reporting. Shallow and sensational, that's how

Smythe liked to deliver the news. "Were you working over Christmas?"

He brought himself up proudly. "Yep, someone has to be responsible for any breaking stories. News doesn't sleep you know, and it doesn't take holidays."

As she had feared, his words were straight from the mouth of Smythe. "Any family in town?"

"No," he said, his face dropping as he remembered once again his sad situation. "They all live on the west coast. It's my first time away from home for Christmas."

His first time away from family, and no traditional dinner. But Sharran had had lots of leftovers, she knew, and had packed them all up to be redistributed to the shelter. That kind-hearted woman would never say no to a sad story like Josh's.

"Here's a present for you," she said, delving into her bag. The second mug had been meant for Sid, if he was around, but Carmel didn't think he would care.

The eyes of the young man brightened. "You got me a present?" From the glow now on his face, she knew that it didn't matter that the present was just a mug. Just the fact that someone cared was present enough for him.

"Here," she said, handing it to him. "And there's a Christmas dinner waiting for you over at Sharran's, too, if you don't mind it being leftovers."

A field separated Sharran's residence from the parking lot, but they followed the road to Sharran's two-story house on Beachy Cove Road. It was a longer route but easier walking at this time of year. He was actually a likeable enough young man, she found as he chattered on the short distance to Sharran's. Self-absorbed perhaps, but then again, who wasn't? He was even making jokes about his own dolour.

They walked up the steps to the old clapboard saltbox house. The wooden storm door was open and folded in on itself, as if the last person to enter had not been too mindful of what they were doing. At least the main door was shut properly. If it too had been ajar, Carmel would have run a mile after her last experience with open doors.

Just as she reached her hand to knock, the two heard a loud scream come from within. It was almost simultaneously accompanied by a terrible thumping noise which seemed to go on and on and on. Carmel and Josh looked at each other in horror before he acted. Thrusting his present at her, he opened the door with one hand while reaching inside his jacket pocket with the other.

There was the United Church minister, lying in an unmoving heap at the bottom of the stairs just inside the house. For long seconds, Carmel could only stare at Sharran before she looked up, up the stairs, where Sid stood with his arms outreached and mouth open as he stared back at her.

"Holy shit, it's the Clerical Killer!" cried the reporter.

She turned to look at Josh but was blinded by the flashing of his camera lights in the darkened narrow stairwell.

"I caught him in action!" he cried. "Yes! This is my day to shine!" Josh turned to leave, but remembered his present and grabbed it from her arms. "Run!" he yelled over his shoulder as he did just that, slipping and sliding over the icy field to his car in the church parking lot, not minding the rain and ice one bit.

Carmel turned back to the stairs. "Sid?" she asked in a small voice. "What happened?"

He didn't have a chance to answer before the blond woman at the bottom of the stairs stirred and looked up.

"Oops," Sharran said, holding her arm. "That was a tumble." She began to laugh, a chuckle which quickly grew into a deep belly laugh. Sid made his way down the stairs, shaking his head. "Good thing I have lots of padding," she laughed again as she looked up at him. "Nothing broken."

Sid shook his head. "God looks after fools and drunks," he said, which made her laugh even harder.

"Are you okay?" Carmel asked the woman, pretty sure she was.

"Too much mulled wine," the woman confessed. "I held back last night, being in a semi-professional capacity and all. Thought I'd make up for it today." She started laughing again. "What was all that flashing light? I didn't hit my head, did I?"

"No," Carmel replied. "That was Josh, ace reporter. I think you're going to be famous tonight." She held out the plastic bag holding the boxed mug. "Merry Christmas."

Chapter 31

S he could see Darrow watching her from the Holy Rosary parking lot, his arms crossed and looking over toward her. He didn't have a welcoming smile on his face, but she trudged through the field toward him regardless.

"What?" he asked when she reached him. "What's up with that reporter?"

"Sharran took a fall down the stairs," she said. "He thinks Sid killed her. He thinks Sid is the Clerical Killer."

"You didn't tell him about Daniel?"

"No, I didn't." It wasn't her business. "Didn't you send out a press release?"

"Not on Christmas Day," he said. "Besides, there's been a bit of a twist."

She waited. He didn't have to tell her anything about the police investigation, but she could always hope. Carmel clutched the collar of her jacket and held her hood with the other to stop the horizontal rain from burrowing inside her clothing. He looked at her hands as she did so.

Darrow shoved his own hands into the pockets of his dark trench coat as the rain and wind picked up.

"Got time for a coffee?" He flicked his head in the direction of the cluster of businesses which had grown up by the lineup for the ferry. What had started out as a bar once upon a time had over the years morphed into a cafe, grocery store, bakery, pizzeria, and general old-fashioned hardware store.

Bell Island had become popular as a residence for commuters, but the government ferry services had not increased to handle the load, so there were always long line-ups for the ferry. The business opportunity on this corner of land had boomed exponentially with a captive audience waiting to cross the tickle. The only day they ever closed was the 25th of December, and even that was flexible depending on the needs of their customers.

She nodded. The rain was starting in earnest now and beginning to drip down her face and neck. "I walked over, so let's take your car."

On the short drive from church to cafe, she felt she had to clear the air between them for it had been weighing heavily on her mind. Carmel took a deep breath. "I'm sorry, okay? I'm so sorry I passed on the details of Father John's death to Ian. I just got excited about the computer program he's developing, and I didn't stop to think he would bring that news to Smythe, of all people." The results of her action, the betrayal of his trust, could have had serious implications for him professionally, she knew.

He pulled into the parking area lining the front of the cafe. "Smythe, of all people," he agreed as he switched off the engine then turned to her. His eyes were softened by the hint of a smile on his face. "What's done is done," he said. "It helps that I'm getting a small revenge tonight."

The wind was chilly despite the rain outside, and the cafe was warm, causing evaporation to blanket the windows and bar the grey view of the ferry and the water. There were few customers, but the coffee was fresh and hot.

"You might want to let Josh know that he didn't discover the Clerical Killer," she said as they brought their drinks to a booth by the window. They hung their damp coats on the hooks placed on the booth ends. "You know he's just dying to have a big splash-up story for the news tonight."

Darrow considered this while a small smile crossed his face. "I'll arrange for a press release," he said. "I think about 6 p.m. would be good timing, don't you?"

The evening news started at six on the weekends and holidays. By the time the release hit the media, Josh would already be on-air.

"That's really mean," she said, matching his smile as she remembered how the young man had rushed to take pictures without stopping to see if he could help Sharran, his story more important to him than common human decency. Yet he'd had the presence of mind to grab his present back before dashing off, too. "I like it."

The waitress brought over two scones for Darrow. Being a holiday, the kitchen was closed and no hot food available. Carmel watched as he scarfed them down as if it was the first thing he'd eaten that day.

He gave a low chuckle as he wiped the crumbs from his mouth. "Might teach him to get his facts straight before he airs a story, no matter how sensational it is. No doubt Smythe has steered him wrong in that regard." Darrow was wearing a sweater over his shirt and tie instead of his usual suit jacket. The light over the table cast a yellow glow, softening the lines of his face and creating an intimate space.

"So, Daniel was the one," Carmel said. "I must say, I'm sort of surprised at that. He doesn't strike me as having the wherewithal to be——I don't know——planning ahead like that, somehow."

"You don't think he's a killer?"

"Yes and no," she said slowly. She remembered how the young man had kicked out at Clyde's dog. "He's not right in the head. Maybe it's the drugs, or whatever. It just seems that it would take a lot of planning and imagination to kill like that, and I don't think he would be capable. Do you know what I mean?"

"He doesn't have the executive thinking capacity?"

She nodded.

"You're right there," he said. "Tell me again, what were his words when he phoned the help line two nights ago?"

"He said, 'I killed him,'" she said, laying the emphasis on killed just as the voice on the phone had. "Then he said, 'I killed them both'—almost as if he was correcting himself." She looked up at Darrow.

"Daniel recanted his confession, once he sobered up from the drink and drugs," Darrow said. "Of course, he'd left prints all over Father John's study, especially on the back of the leather armchair, even on the electrical cord. He couldn't explain those away."

"So he did it," she said.

"The second one, yes," Darrow said. "And there's a history between the two. Father John's last parish was in a small town in central Newfoundland. Daniel had been shipped out there as part of the foster system, as no homes in the city would take him. He'd run the gamut, and his behaviour was just too wild."

"You mean, they sent him away from his family and friends?"

"Completely isolated from what supports he had, yes," Darrow agreed. "It must have made him so much more vulnerable to the priest's approaches. In exchange for booze and cigarettes, Father John––well––you know the old story, I don't need to go into the details."

Carmel sat back, appalled. She had known young teenage boys like Daniel when she was growing up, and had heard their boasts of the free alcohol given to them by a certain member of the clergy and the weekend camping trips. The lads didn't go into any other details, but there had been whispers among her group of the price they paid for these pleasures. "In this day and age?" She was incredulous. "Didn't this province already go through all this? I thought ..."

"Unfortunately, yes, it appears to have been going on," he said. "Human nature being what it is, I say the abuse of power will continue to go on, just in different forms. This corrupted form of sexuality is usually a learned behaviour. If we can stop it at its source, then we might have success eventually, over the years." He stopped to consider. "But I may be wrong."

"So his murder of Father John was, well, revenge."

"It was a copycat murder," Darrow continued. "He heard the details of Wilson's murder, listened to Smythe's interview, and decided he could get away with it."

"So Daniel knew where Father John was living and must have known his habits," she said. "He would have known the priest would be home alone at that time."

Darrow paused and looked out the window. The fog on the glass was dissipating now, and the afternoon sun starting to peek out from amongst the clouds, cold and clear. He could tell by the flag on the ferry that the wind had also dropped. The calming weather meant they were probably in for a storm, a nasty one, before the night was out.

"The priest played a large part in Daniel's life at a very vulnerable time," he said. "He offered him acceptance, and love, in a fashion. I would say they kept in contact through the years."

"What? After the man abused him and messed up his mind?"

There was a sad smile on Darrow's face. "Daniel was largely on the way to being messed up before he met Father John," he said. "Unfortunately, he became more messed up as a result, yes."

"How can you be so sure Daniel didn't also kill Reverend Wilson?" She played with the dregs of coffee in her mug, watching it swirl around in a circular pattern as she searched her mind for a reason, any reason, the young man could have had to do away with the Mississippi Preacher Man. She was looking for a link between the two, something perhaps that the police had missed.

"For one thing, he had no reason to," he replied. "None that I can see. And for another, he had an alibi for the time of

Wilson's death. In fact, the best of alibis. He was in our lock-up downtown after trying to hold up the gas bar on Pennywell Road." He smiled. "The young lad is not the brightest in the bunch," he continued. "He didn't cover his face, and since he lives around the corner, the staff knows him well. After they chased him off, the owner called us and told the officer where they could pick Daniel up, at his own apartment. So, yes, he could not have murdered Wilson that night."

They both sat in thought for a moment, then Carmel stated what was on both their minds. "That leaves a murderer on the loose," she said.

"It's been a week now," he said. "And we don't feel any closer to catching him or her. It's safe to tell you this, is it?"

"Yes," she said, knowing she fully deserved this. "Yes, it is." She gave him a small smile, which he returned. A beam of afternoon sun was full on them through the glass.

"It's a puzzle," he admitted. "So many people were at the Affray, yet so few are coming forward. And those who would have been mixed up with that––well––they had little to no dealings with Reverend Wilson. There is only that text sent to Wilson, telling him to go to Snellen's Field that night."

"That's untraceable, isn't it?" She remembered Vivienne telling her.

"From a throwaway phone," he said. "And I have no doubt that phone is now in the Robin Hood Bay dump, buried deep. Even if we had the resources to look for it, I have no doubt it would be difficult to trace. Our murderer planned this carefully and wouldn't have left fingerprints or any other telling signs."

"Vivienne and her driver were at the shelter," she said, thinking of the blond woman. "And someone dressed up as her. That makes it particularly horrible." The image of the person in a wig with their arms grasping Wilson's neck would take a long time to leave her mind. If only she'd known at the time what was happening, in the midst of the Affray, she could have stopped it and gotten help for the man.

"Yes, dressed up as a woman, thus concealing their identity in a crowd of others who had also concealed their identity for fun," he said. "Quite a brilliant move, really, when you think of it."

He yawned suddenly. Carmel remembered how quickly his scones had disappeared, and wondered how well he was taking care of himself. His Christmas dinner must have been disrupted last night by her phone call.

"Ian's making moose stew tonight," she said on impulse. "Why don't you drop by? You look like you could use a hot meal."

"That's tempting," he said. "But I don't think your tenant would be too happy to see me again."

She brushed that aside. "Think of it as payback for his telling Smythe," she said. "Besides, he's a really good cook when he puts his mind to it." She thought for a moment. "And he's in love now. He probably won't notice you're even there if Bridget's around."

"This moose," he said. "It's a legal moose then, is it?" He was no doubt referring to the questionable origins of the pine tree decorating the church last night. "Shot by someone with a license to hunt?"

"He had nothing to do with the moose," Carmel was quick to respond. "Phonse gave him the meat from his mother's freezer." No sooner were the words out of her mouth than she realized this might not be the best assurance that the meat was legally obtained in the right season with the proper license. Phonse had no problem with smuggling illegal beer, and might have a similar loose view of poaching moose. At least, the police might think so.

Darrow looked sceptical. "Perhaps the less I know, the better," he said. "But I would appreciate a good feed of stew. I don't often get a chance to eat moose."

The sun was shining when they left the cafe and the wind was down so it almost felt warm outside, although there was still plenty of water and slush on the road. Carmel opted to walk back to St. Jude Without and they agreed he would drop by for supper.

"Just one thing," Darrow said before she turned away. His Scottish accent strong was suddenly very noticeable, even on those few words. He cleared his throat. "I believe congratulations are in order?"

Congratulations for what, she was about to ask. However, she was slowly learning to put a filter on her words, and so she quickly and silently examined everything in her life that was congrats worthy. Nothing showed up.

"For what?"

"Oh, dear," he said. "I hope I haven't put my great foot in it."

"What are you talking about? Am I supposed to have done something?"

"You and Phonse...?" he asked. "Hmm, I've made a mistake. The music at the Duke was loud that night; I must have misheard his words."

Phonse, that jerk. Had he told everyone they were getting married before he even asked her? Had he assumed she would jump at the chance of being the next Mrs. Ryan? She gritted her teeth when she remembered his cavalier treatment of her after she'd fallen from the rock and sprained her wrist.

And Constable Wright? She wanted to ask. Was there anything between the two of them, or was this just Phonse's overactive imagination at work again?

A smile lit Darrow's face as the sun finally struggled out from behind the cloud bank. "Or perhaps it was a misrepresentation of facts," he said softly. "Cheerio, then."

Chapter 32

A misrepresentation of facts, indeed, she fumed as she strode along the gravelled road. As the sun broke out and the cloud cover disappeared, the temperature dropped suddenly just like tearing the blankets off the bed on a frosty morning. She walked quickly, both to work off the temper Phonse had caused yet again, and to keep her body warm.

The whole case was full of misrepresentation of facts. It had all started with the ridiculous Mummers Affray at Snellen's Field, when grown men had donned costumes in order to hide their identities as they took revenge on the neighbours and families for imagined slights and to generally be in the midst of havoc.

And concealed identities. Ruscan must have concealed his identity in order to disappear from her life. There had been no body found on that airplane, and it couldn't have been thrown off mid-flight, that just wasn't possible. He must have had another passport on him, in preparation for this switch. He had meant to do what he did, but who did he become, and why couldn't he tell her of it? She wondered if she had indeed meant anything at all to him, or if she herself had been part of a previous disguise. Perhaps his name wasn't even Ruscan Milanovic.

Father John, now that was an old story of a pretense, and of abuse too. Acting as a holy man yet warping the very souls he was meant to save. For a long time, the Catholic Church had been the only power in people's lives. It was an old story of trust betrayed.

The Mississippi Preacher Man had not been what he seemed, either. He had abused his position of televangelist before, and had been abusing his position since, too. Pretending to be a man of God, yet abusing his wife, her money, and the trust of his community of simple souls.

And yet... Sister Constantine had firmly come down on his side, and stated he was a true man of God. She was not usually wrong.

Nothing was as it seemed. Even Rhonda was part of it, with her newfound work with transgender issues.

Vivienne seemed to be the only link, but she was possibly the only person in the whole lot who was unabashedly, unashamedly, herself. This southern belle was painfully truthful: she had bared her soul to Carmel when admitting she did not have a good relationship with her husband.

And what was going on with Ruscan?

She reached her home without reaching any conclusions about anything at all, and her brain was tired from the fruitless effort. Carmel was starting not to care about any of it, even Ruscan. She really wanted to have a nap.

But it was not to be. Ian had commandeered the kitchen for the creation of his moose stew, and both he and Bridget were playing the radio loud on a heavy metal station. The sound would echo throughout the whole house. He called to her before she made it up the stairs.

"The airport called for you," he said as he appeared in the kitchen doorway. "A reminder about your luggage. They'd like you to pick it up as soon as you can. They seemed a little annoyed at you."

"Like I've been purposefully losing my luggage and leaving it in airports all over the globe?" Right. She'd go pick it up before they sent it off to Outer Mongolia. Even if it was Boxing Day and technically a statutory holiday. So she grabbed her coat again and turned back out the door to her car.

The coughing noises her car had been making hadn't cleared up yet. She wondered briefly if she should ask to borrow Ian's car, but quite frankly, his sounded much worse than her own.

But perhaps she should have, for as the car struggled and wheezed its way up the steep hill out of town, it gave a final cough and shuddered just by Murray's Pond. Of course, the nearby greenhouse and country club were closed, likewise the gas station she'd just passed. The day was gathering in and the cold wind had not stopped. Carmel pulled her coat tighter around her and kicked the closest tire then got back into the car while she examined her options.

It would have to be Ian to the rescue after all. But he wasn't answering his phone, and neither was Bridget. Their phones were no doubt in their coat pockets hung in the hall closet while they danced to the ear-splitting bass of AC/DC.

"Crap!" She yelled out into the wind and the fields, but there was not a soul to hear her, not even a crow. Now chilled to the bone, she knew her only option was to head back down the steep hill to home. She wouldn't be able to get a taxi to come in from town to bring her home, not without being charged triple the fare.

She was so sunk in despair she hardly registered the quiet buzzing of her phone, feeling only a mere vibration in her pocket.

"Carmel? Just wanted to phone and thank you for inviting me to that delightful dinner last night," Rhonda's smooth voice came over the phone. "You've no idea what a lifesaver it was for me to get away from the family. I don't think I can stand these dramas anymore. Next, year it's Bermuda for me, I don't care what ..."

"Rhonda," Carmel said, breaking into the flow. "I need you. Come pick me up. My car broke down just by Murray's. Please."

"Oh," the other replied, after a pause. "I'm not sure about that ..."

"Please," she insisted again. "I'll invite you for dinner again. Ian's making a stew. He's Irish, so it's sure to be good." Perhaps she was grasping at straws, but weren't the Irish famous for their stews? As long as she didn't have to walk all the way home, she didn't care who she misled. A loud smattering on the windshield told her that the skies were now hurling ice pellets at her.

"Okay," Rhonda's voice picked up enthusiasm. She, like Bridget, loved to eat, and never seemed to gain an ounce. "I'll leave right now. It'll take me awhile to drive in from town."

"Thank you," Carmel whispered before closing off the phone.

Chapter 33

S he didn't really have that long to wait. Rhonda pulled up with a jerk and a protest of brakes across the road, one tire on the shoulder as a nod to an attempt to pull off the road.

"Jack's off today," the doctor called as Carmel slid her window smoothly down. "Wouldn't leave his television, not even for you."

"You do have a license to drive, right?" Carmel asked as she climbed into the passenger seat.

Rhonda paused for a moment as she cast her mind back. "I'm sure it was renewed," she said. "My secretary is quite good about looking after those things. Anyway, hop in. It'll be fine. I've been driving since I was twelve, you know."

Yes, on the old woods roads and beaches surrounding her family's summer estate out around the bay, where there were no living obstacles in her path and no icy slopes to negotiate. Carmel secured the seatbelt and prepared to hang on.

It was the shortest time she'd ever driven down that winding road into Portugal Cove, yet every second was etched on her mind in slow motion. Rhonda kept up a constant stream of chatter and she was one of those people who like to look at the person they're chatting with, perhaps to constantly gauge their reaction to the words. Carmel had never understood that need, especially when the person was driving a vehicle.

"The road!" she finally exclaimed, exaggeratedly pointing out the windshield as the road veered off sharply to the left by Indian Meal Line. "Look at the road, not at me."

Her friend, miffed at this inattention to her words, grasped the wheel and swung it hard, the vehicle sliding on the icy road until it was going down the hill sideways. "Look what you did," she scolded after she righted the car again. "Were you even listening to me?" Rhonda continued her chatter and passenger-watching, while Carmel watched the road for her and clung to the overhead strap. Her foot was automatically pressing on the brake pedal, as if that would help with Rhonda's driving.

They sailed through the ferry lineup, Rhonda blowing her horn at those in her way, then she gave an extra push of the gas to manoeuvre up the short but steep link to North Point Road. On this relatively flat road, Carmel could almost now relax except they were entering into the twisty mountain road leading to St. Jude Without. Thank God she was on the mountain side and wasn't forced to look over the cliff as Rhonda negotiated the bends.

"Vivienne is leaving tonight," Rhonda informed her as the Mercedes jerked its way past the woman's driveway. "I can't say I blame her. She's had nothing but grief since she moved up here. She's got the restaurant for sale, and she'll be putting the house up too. No need for her to stick around to look after that."

"Road, please," Carmel said as a reminder, then resumed the conversation. "Guess she's all right financially now she's got her father's money again."

"There might be some tie-up with that, apparently." Rhonda looked over at her as she imparted this juicy gossip. Carmel pointed at the road, and her friend shook her head in frustration. "I can't talk to the road!"

"You're not talking to the road, you're talking to me. We just happen to be side by side, not facing each other," Carmel said through gritted teeth. "What's the problem with the money?"

"Wilson was in the middle of signing it over to his church when he died," Rhonda replied. "So the money is in limbo until it's all straightened out."

"Are they going to fight about it in court, do you think?"

Rhonda shook her head. "I can't see that happening," she said. "Besides, without Wilson here to hold the members together, the church will probably dissolve and die a natural death."

"Unlike his own," Carmel mused, glancing down at Snellen's Field and giving an involuntary shiver. "Where's Vivienne going, back to her home in the States?"

"Funny that," Rhonda replied.

"Road."

"Oh, fine. But she mentioned going to South America," Rhonda said. "Brazil, I believe. I asked her what on earth the attraction is for her there, and she said she just wanted to be free."

"Boulder!" Carmel exclaimed as she stamped her foot down on her non-existent passenger brake pedal and twisted her imaginary steering wheel to the left. After that, the thread of conversation was lost and they had arrived at their destination, at long last.

The black Mercedes pulled into Carmel's driveway with a groaning of springs and a cough. Jack would regret telling Rhonda to drive herself, for he was the one who would have to deal with any damage done to the vehicle. But that was not Carmel's concern at the moment. She stumbled out onto her path and up the steps of the veranda, getting out as soon as she could, in case Rhonda remembered she'd forgotten something and had to drive back to the store.

She waited at the top of the veranda for Rhonda to collect her parcels, brush her hair, and do whatever it was she needed to do. That was the worst driving Carmel had seen since——well——since the night this whole affair began when Vivienne's vehicle had almost knocked her off the road. Which was strange now she thought about it, because Franz was such a tidy person, and everything he did seemed well executed, even down to his tiny bow when he brought the coffee service in that day at Vivienne's. But that night, she remembered, they would have been headed to the shelter, and that would have been a highly emotional time for Vivienne. Franz would no doubt have been affected by this too. He was devoted to her, that had been obvious enough last night. Perhaps he was even a little in love with his employer?

"Right then, are we going in?"

The smell of the moose stew was like a warm Irish embrace to the senses. The kitchen glowed golden after the gathering gloom outside and laughter sounded over the music.

"What happened to you?" Bridget looked over as the two entered the kitchen. "You're as pale as old Cap'n Jem's ghost." That ghost was purported to haunt her house, the old pirate who had built the stone cottage and been hung on the ancient pine outside.

"It was rough," Carmel said shortly. "My car broke down. I didn't make it to the airport."

"I saved the day," Rhonda said as she breezed into the kitchen, unwinding the long scarf from her throat as she did so. A bottle of champagne appeared from within her deep designer bag. "Right, then. Who'll do the honours?"

Ian's eyes lit up at the sight. "I've always thought champagne would mix marvellously with Irish stew."

"Let's test it, shall we?"

"You might want to wait a bit," Carmel said. "If that bottle's anything like me, it's still feeling a little shaken from the ride."

"No need to be so dramatic," Rhonda tossed over her shoulder. "You made it back in one piece didn't you?"

"Barely," said Carmel under her breath, but she needn't have bothered for her reply was lost in the pop of the cork and subsequent squeals as Bridget and Rhonda looked for glasses to catch the champagne before it fizzed all over the floor.

A knocking at the front door sounded, and she left the three of them to clean up the mess. Darrow still hadn't quite cottoned on to the cove's lack of formality with regards to knocking at doors, and he stood outside patiently with the wind whipping snow around his bare head. His curls were laced with ice, but his brown eyes were warm as they looked on her.

"You came," Carmel said. It was a dumb thing to say, and right away she wished she could take it back. She had wanted to express more, something like how happy she was to see him, how his solid presence at her door lightened her mood, or how the sight of his slightly crooked face made her want to reach out and hug him. But, of course, she couldn't say any of those things.

He looked a trifle disconcerted. "I was invited, wasn't I?"

She gave a short laugh and opened the door wider. "Of course. Come in," she said. "Come in and join the party."

He handed her a gift bag holding a bottle of wine.

The others were already well into the champagne although she had not been gone two minutes.

"On Stephen's Day, On Stephen's Day, the wren and the robin came out to play." Ian was stirring the pot with one hand and his other held a glass, while he and Bridget sang the songs of his Irish childhood Christmases. Being a Ryan from St. Jude Without, Bridget had had a healthy dose of Irish traditions in her own childhood and so she knew all the words too.

"It's called Stephen's Day in Ireland, isn't it?" Rhonda queried. "What we know as Boxing Day."

"Yes," Ian replied. "While the English were packing up their leftovers for the poor, the Irish were out killing wrens, for some unknown reason."

"That's horrible," Rhonda objected and turned away, disgust on her face. "Oh, hello, Inspector Darrow."

Ian's back stiffened. Carmel had warned him the police officer was invited, and had made it quite clear that he was to drop any antagonism he might feel toward the man, at least for Christmas. She watched as he set his shoulders back and turned to greet the newcomer, a smile of welcome on his face. Her own shoulders relaxed with relief. It was all good, for now.

"The Scots tradition for Boxing Day is to be out buying their Christmas presents at the sales," Darrow said. "Nothing hurts more than to have bought something at full price and then to see it slashed down to half off not two days later."

The ice broken, he was handed a glass of champagne amid the laughter, and they all sat down to their early supper of hearty moose stew. Rhonda had found yet another bottle of champagne at the bottom of her bag and it continued to flow freely round the table. Even Darrow got into the swing of it, loosening up his tie. Carmel had quite forgotten the fast effect of champagne, how the bubbles went straight to the mind and caused the loveliest light-headed feeling.

"Oh," Carmel said, pushing away her bowl as she glanced at the clock on the wall. "It's 6 p.m. Anyone want to watch the news?" She had already shared the story of Josh with the others.

"The press release should be coming out about now, too," Darrow noted with a grin. There was little joy in police work these days, and a cop had to take his fun where he could find it.

They clustered around the small TV set on the kitchen counter. Carmel turned up the volume so they could all hear.

There was Josh in his full glory as the only presenter on the news. He wore a tie with brightly coloured Santas on it and a smile to match.

His script might have been written by his role model Gerald Smythe, he of the famous bow tie which had saved his life the previous summer. It was sensational and obvious, and Josh had almost but not quite mastered the art of eyebrow raising while following the scripted camera.

"The third murder of a cleric in Portugal Cove," he said as he described the scene lasciviously while the still shots he'd taken that afternoon thunderously displayed behind him. There was Sharran, a fallen heap at the bottom of the stairs, and Sid glowering down at her, his arms still outstretched as if caught in the act of pushing her. Carmel had to admit, they were good photos even if they were taken out of context. Too bad Josh hadn't hung around to find out the true story.

The young reporter was interrupted in mid-sentence by a techie who boldly walked across the camera's view and handed him a piece of white paper. Not wearing a microphone, his words were muffled, but Josh's weren't.

"What?" Josh stared at the paper as his eyes quickly scanned its contents. His face had turned pale with a touch of green around the edges. He turned to stare back at the camera like a rabbit in the headlights. Then suddenly, he drew himself up and, to the surprise of all in the kitchen, he saved what face he had left.

A large and professional smile etched itself across this visage. "Turns out this was not a murder––I repeat, not a murder. I'm happy to say that the United Church minister commonly known as Reverend Sharran is alive and well, and that the police have arrested a suspect in the murder of Father John." He glanced down at the paper again for a second, before looking up, his eyes like knives. "However, this begs the question: who killed the Mississippi Preacher Man, Reverend Wilson? The RNC have not fully addressed that issue yet." The screen quickly switched to a commercial.

It seemed that Inspector Darrow had made a new enemy among the media.

"Good save," Darrow murmured as Carmel turned the television off. "I wouldna ha' thought he had it in him."

"He brings up a good point," Rhonda said after she swallowed the last of her champagne and held her glass out for a refill. Ian upended the second bottle, making a play of squeezing the bottle to the last drop.

"That's the last of that," he said decisively, plonking it down on the table next to the other empty.

"Damn," the doctor said, staring at the single inch of champagne in her glass. "But as I was saying, who did kill Vivienne's husband?" She placed her elbows on the table and looked expectantly at Darrow, then Ian. "Experts, any opinion offered?"

"It's a man's crime," Ian began.

"But it was a woman who killed him," Carmel broke in, insisting on this fact for what felt like the fortieth time. "I saw her. A man couldn't move like that. And he must have thought it was his wife, as he was reaching out for her."

"Yet his wife was at the shelter when he was being killed," Bridget reminded them. "I was there, I held her hand. She was very upset."

Rhonda's glass was empty again already and she was busy attacking Darrow's contribution, wrestling with the foil wrapper before she realized it was a screw-top bottle. She looked doubtfully at the bottle before pouring.

"If it wasn't for the fact that Vivienne is a worse driver than I am," she said, "I would say Franzi is the only suspect." She laughed uproariously as the thought struck her.

All four of them stared at her.

"Why would you say that?" Carmel asked.

"Well, it's ..." Rhonda stopped as she looked around at the others. "Not as obvious as I would have thought, then." She staggered to her feet. "I think I may have drunk too much, too quickly. In the interest of preserving doctor/patient confidentiality, I'd best visit the little girl's room."

"Oh no you don't." Carmel pulled the doctor back down into her chair. "Are you saying Franz is a woman?"

"No," she replied indignantly, but then relented. "Well, technically, I guess. He's been having a bit of an issue with the change, but, legally, Franzi is male. He made that change before he moved to the States."

"Why didn't you bring this up before?" Carmel demanded of her.

"You mean you couldn't see?" Rhonda was crossing her legs tightly. "What, are you blind? Next you'll be saying that you don't know Vivienne wears a wig." She looked around the table at the open mouths. "Oh for God's sake, people! If I didn't have to pee so badly, I'd be falling on the ground with laughter." She pushed herself away from the table and swiftly ran through the hallway. They could hear her feet pounding up the stairs.

Chapter 34

C armel's and Darrow's eyes met across the table, the same thought flashing through both their minds.

"Franz is a woman," she said.

"The woman who killed Wilson," he replied.

"That's why the white gloves," she said. "He, she, wears them to hide her hands, a woman's hands."

"That's why there's no trace of him before he moved to the States," he said. "Franz did not exist."

"Vivienne drove herself to the shelter that night, that's why the driving was so erratic! Franz could never drive that badly, no matter how upset he was."

"He wore Vivienne's wig under the monk's robe." Ian was jumping into the fray.

"They planned this together," Darrow said, taking the logic to the next step.

Carmel gasped as she remembered something Rhonda had said on the drive over. "And they're flying to Brazil tonight. They're getting away!"

Darrow stood up so quickly, his chair crashed to the floor behind him. He was already reaching for his cellphone as he moved across the kitchen.

Carmel was right behind him and reached for her coat from the closet as he made his call for backup.

"They were home several hours ago," she said, thrusting her arms into her coat and slipping on her boots.

He quickly gave Vivienne's address over the phone and grabbed his own coat.

"You stay here," he ordered. "This is a matter for the police."

"Oh, no, you don't," she said. "I've come this far, I'm seeing it through." The battle of glares lasted a full second, but time was of the essence. They both turned to leave.

He started his car remotely as they ran down the veranda steps and he barked his orders. "My car, you drive."

He had parked, as always, for a quick getaway, a habit so long ingrained it was no longer a conscious decision. Carmel jumped into the driver's seat, disengaging the gears before he had even closed the passenger door. Set for forward motion, Carmel lurched as the car leaped toward the ditch, narrowly missing Bridget's picket fence.

"Darn it," she said as she got the car back onto the road and attempted to pick up speed but only succeeded in fits and starts. It was difficult when her feet wanted to push more pedals than were present. "No clutch. This is an automatic?"

"Of course it's an automatic," his voice began to rise. "It's a police car. Just drive, would you? I need to get there before they leave."

It wasn't easy, but if she remembered to keep her left foot firmly planted on the floor at all times it was doable and the car wouldn't cut out. She kept her right steadily on the gas, even when taking the twisty bends around the mountain. The entrance to Vivienne's driveway was right ahead. There was not yet any sign of the backup cars he'd ordered. Of course not—they would have to drive all the way in from the city, a good fifteen minutes away, and longer in this weather, especially with the added hazard of Christmas drunks on the road.

"What next, boss?" she asked slowing down slightly.

"Best drive right up," he said. "If the Land Rover's gone, we'll head out to the airport."

But the silver SUV was in the driveway, engine running and lights on. In the brightness reflected from the snow, she could see two figures standing by the side of it. As Darrow's car pulled up to the left side of the driveway and stopped, Vivienne and Franz were caught frozen in the headlights.

"Stay in the car. Leave the car on," he instructed in a low voice. "But get over to the passenger seat this time, will you?"

She shifted over as he cautiously got out, leaving the door between him and the would-be fugitives. A gun had appeared out of his coat pocket, the first time Carmel had ever seen one up close. It was black like a shadow in this light, only the glints off the metal showing its solidity.

"Vivienne Wilson, Franz Waldheim, stop where you are," he called. "You're both under arrest for the murder of Reverend Wilson. Cease and desist all movement, I have a gun."

Vivienne's small figure drew up angrily at those words. "I didn't kill Wilson," she cried. "It was Franzi." Her hair was short tonight, in a close cropped brunette wig that gave her face an elfin look, like a child's face. The sable coat fell open to reveal sparkling diamonds beneath. She pointed over at the other who was still standing by the opened tail with a suitcase in his hand.

In the glare of the headlights, they saw the defiance in the southern woman's face as she turned to her partner, and watched as it melted when she saw the look of betrayal on the other's face. "But I can't live without you," she said so softly that Carmel and Darrow almost couldn't hear. "You are my heart, my soul."

Without warning, Vivienne opened the passenger door. "Get in!" she screamed. "Get in now and come with me!"

"Don't move!" Darrow shouted to the wavering figure of Franz. The officer steadied his gun on the passenger door of the sedan as he aimed.

Vivienne jumped into the open door and threw herself over to the driver's side. The SUV gave a rock as she lurched it into drive. That made up Franzi's mind. He wouldn't let Vivienne leave without him. He dropped the suitcase in his hand without bothering to close the hatch, and in two quick bounds was up in the passenger's seat as the SUV reared into action. The door swung shut as the vehicle swerved toward Darrow's car, causing him to drop quickly and roll out of danger. By the time he could stand up, the red taillights were weaving drunkenly as the vehicle turned left to head into Portugal Cove and the airport beyond. There was no trouble to tell who was driving this time.

Darrow ran to the driver's side of his sedan and in no time the car was tearing off after the SUV. He drove with one hand and used the other for the two-way radio. "The suspects are heading into Portugal Cove," he said. "Send one car down Boulder Lane and the other down by the ferry terminal to head them off."

They watched as the SUV turned down the sharp lane to the ferry terminal and saw the flashing blue and red lights of a police car atop the facing hill at the ferry turnoff, just by the market. The coloured lights played with the warm orange of the cafe lights through the blowing snow to make a festive scene against the white snow covered hill. But quickly, Darrow plunged down the short lane and the lights were out of view.

Vivienne must also have seen the police car preparing to head her off. The lanes for the ferry lineup were empty at this time of night, leaving her a wide margin for an attempt to avoid the other, and it looked like she was going to make a run for it as the SUV swerved back and forth on the ice at the bottom of the hill. But at the last minute the silver vehicle took a right turn.

"Where's she going?" Darrow muttered. "There's nothing down there but sheds and the fisherman's wharf."

But Vivienne's right hand swerve got sharper and kept going, and it was soon clear the SUV was headed for the ferry wharf itself. Carmel caught a glimpse of Franz's frightened face as he scrabbled at the door as if to jump out. But this was a high-end vehicle with all the safety features, nothing but the best for Vivienne, the rich man's daughter. The doors could not be opened when the SUV was in drive, so Franzi was not getting off before the ride was through.

"No!" Carmel cried as she realized Vivienne's intention. The short wharf was bound by high wooden trestles on either side, but the site for the ferry landing at the end of the pier was not. She could either stop or just keep going, those were the only choices.

The large silver vehicle seemed to hesitate at the same time, as if it realized its mistake too late. But Vivienne revved up the engine again and nothing impeded the SUV as it flew toward the empty space at the end. It sailed noiselessly into the cold blackened waters of the tickle, white caplets in its wake as it moved through the water as if Vivienne was aiming for Bell Island. But even the force of her determination was not enough to keep the heavy vehicle afloat, and Darrow and Carmel could only watch as it slowly sank below the waves.

He stopped the car and called on the radio for the cold-water dive team, but there was little hope in his voice. Carmel got out of the car and, wrapping her coat tightly around her against the sharp wind on the wharf, gazed down to where she'd last seen the SUV. She'd seen a show once, it was Rick Mercer doing his crazy stunts, and that show had been about how to get out of a sinking vehicle before you drowned. He'd shown how, if you were quick thinking, you could unhook your seatbelt and use the force of your legs to kick out the nearest window, thus freeing yourself from the confines that would otherwise be a metal coffin. Franzi probably hadn't watched that show, or maybe the bulletproof glass in the SUV had resisted his efforts.

She didn't realize she was shivering until she felt Darrow's warm arm around her, but she couldn't let him lead her back to the car. "No," she said into his shoulder, still not taking her eyes off the spot where the SUV had disappeared. "We can't leave, I've got to keep watch," she said. "They might escape, they have to get out, they can't just die in there …"

Darrow knew the difference, but waited by her side all the same.

This was no time for divers to be out in those deep treacherous waters, but out they went anyway with the possibility––no matter how remote––of lives to be saved. The fact that one of the lives was that of a murderer, and the other that of the one who spurred him on, made no difference to the would-be rescuers. The ocean hadn't had time to bury the large vehicle and claim it for its own, so it was soon winched out of the waters. Carmel turned away as it emerged from the depths. The windows were wet with the salted sea water icing around the edges but the tinted glass thankfully prevented their view inside to the already bloating white faces which stared vacantly out.

There were no survivors.

Chapter 35

"Try it now," Billy the biker said from under the hood. Carmel turned the key and the engine reluctantly returned to life, still coughing in fits and starts. "That'll do you till you get to the garage down the road." Joe's Garage was one of the last independents still standing, the rundown clapboard structure housing two bays which were always busy, with a continual line of vehicles in various states of disrepair awaiting Joe's magic touch. Billy slammed the hood down, the late afternoon sunrays reflecting off his mirrored glasses. "Just leave it in his lot with the keys in the glove compartment."

Carmel was appalled. "What? Leave the car unlocked with the keys inside? You trust the yahoos around here? I don't."

He put his hands on his hips and rolled his eyes. "Like, you think someone would steal this heap?" he asked in his deep voice. "Hello, it's a fifteen-year-old car. If a car's in Joe's lot, that means it's on its last legs and isn't worth the bother."

When he put it like that, she had to agree. A thief would be doing her a favour. After she had it parked at Joe's, she climbed into the passenger seat of the lime green Lada which was far older than her own vehicle and was kept together largely through duct tape and Billy's own will. The springs were long gone, if they had ever existed. They sputtered back to Sid's bar, where Carmel took her leave of the biker.

One bright spot marked the days following the Boxing Day nightmare. Ian had been playing with her fancy new phone late one night and had it configured so that she could receive her emails on it. She'd had the phone since before she'd left for St. Kitts, but hadn't yet had the inclination to use it to its full capacity, just for calls and text messages. Now that it had been done for her, Carmel was still thrilled with this technology, checking the phone every time it alerted her of new post-Christmas sales from her favourite stores.

Yeah, she had to admit, life was back to what passed for normal in this cove. The ponies ran through the field down below, scraping at the light covering of snow to reach the grass underneath. Her wrist was feeling much better, likewise her cold was gone. Ian had given her the rent cheque, or at least most of what he owed, although he was spending most of his time at Bridget's. He had also given her the keys to his car for her use while hers was out of commission. She hadn't heard any more from Ruscan, or whoever was sending those emails, and that was okay, too. The less mystery the better, and she didn't want to reopen that wound. She'd also made the decision not to go back to the shelter and didn't feel guilty about it. Life was good.

Chapter 36

Inspector Darrow lifted his head from the sheet of loose leaf before him, leaned back away and gave a stretch. Anyone looking into the glass window of his office might think he was working late, finishing one of the numerous reports awaiting his attention. They would usually be right, but today his mind was on other things. He gave a small self-conscious smile at the drawing before him as he placed the pen down next to it and studied it further. A simple line drawing of Carmel looking off into the distance, sitting in the cafe's booth on Boxing Day afternoon with a ray of sun breaking through and highlighting her wind-tousled curls.

It was dusk out already, and not even 5 p.m. He watched the last of the reflected sun creep over the Southside Hills across the harbour. The cubicles outside his open door were largely silent, only a few bodies working still. It was New Year's Eve, after all.

His smile deepened as he looked upon his work again and realized he would give it to her. She would be tickled. Perhaps he couldn't put his feelings for her into words, it was too soon for that, but she would look at her image as seen through his eyes, and she would know.

If he was going to do it, he should just do it. Darrow loosened his tie and removed the phone from the inner pocket of his suit jacket. He pressed the button to call. He hadn't had the chance to tell Carmel he had her on speed-dial, too.

·····•••····

Darrow leaned across the formica-topped table, the fluorescent lights overhead marking each silver strand on his dark unruly head. "Thanks for coming at such short notice," he said, unsure as to where to start. He'd been a workaholic for too long, and his social skills were rusty when it came to things outside of his work. Or maybe they'd always been bad, and that's why he buried himself in the job.

He smiled at the woman across from him. He could forgive her impulsivity in sharing the information with Ian, for she had meant it with a good heart and besides, it was an integral part of her personality. A personality which he had found himself warming to since he met her last August. She was able to be satisfied with the simple things in life; she hadn't balked at a last minute New Year's date at a fish-and-chip shop.

Carmel smiled back with a rueful look. "It's not like I had anything planned. Well, except for sharing leftover pizza with the cat and going next door for a beer," she said. "And watching the guys light fireworks on the road after they got good and drunk."

A pained expression crossed his face. "There's a law against combining incendiaries and alcohol."

"Not in St. Jude Without, there's not," she said.

The waitress laid paper placemats and large laminated menus in front of them. Not that anyone ever really needed menus here at Ches's Fish and Chips, but they were in the dining room of this establishment and it was somewhat more upscale from the takeout counter in the next room. The smell of hot fries that lingered outside was pungent here, mixed with malt vinegar and fried fish. It was deep-fried heaven, actually.

"It's nice to be meeting you without being surrounded by murder," he observed.

The smile left her face. "It was horrible, wasn't it?" She thought for a moment. "Ian said there were three basic reasons for murder."

"A bit of a simplification," he replied.

"Wilson's was a murder committed for love," she said. "Franz loved Vivienne for all those years, right?"

He considered this and nodded. "Franz was the so-called lesbian love affair of Vivienne's youth. Before he began the transition into becoming male. But I have to disagree with you. The real reason for this murder was money," he said. "Remember, Vivienne was the brains behind it, and she controlled Franz. He acted out of love, yes, but she was in it only to prevent her father's money from being given away."

"That's what Wilson was talking about that day on the War Memorial," she said. "He must have found out about Vivienne and Franz; he was quite horrified by it all. He was going to sign all the money over to the church."

"It appears that way," Darrow agreed. "But all three actors are dead now, so we'll never know."

"She almost got away with it," Carmel said. "But I wonder why they chose Brazil? Why not Europe, or her home?"

"No extradition treaty with Brazil," he replied. "It was all well-planned out, every step of the way. She must have been delighted when Father John was murdered in the same way, for she knew it would muddy the waters even further."

As they ate, he thought about the drawing of Carmel in his briefcase. He'd told few people about his artistry for he'd learned early on in the then still male-dominated police force of Glasgow that this interest could make other cops uncomfortable. Anything to do with the arts had been considered suspiciously feminine. This reticence was a habit he carried even in this more enlightened age, but he looked forward to sharing it with Carmel.

They were almost finished their feed of fried fish when Carmel's phone gave another seductive ping. She had laid it casually on the table next to her plate, and couldn't help but glance over to see who was contacting her. She'd always hated when others did this, it was so rude for them to take their attention from the company they were with, but she understood the obsession now. Just a quick glance, she promised in the half-second space after the notification sounded, to satisfy herself that it wasn't a contract offer or an emergency from a friend or a fantastic last minute deal on a cruise.

The word "Luba" in the subject line stood out. She didn't want to check it but she knew she would. She had to. Only one person had ever called her Luba. It was a Ukranian endearment.

Luba, told you I'd return. Naughty you for leaving me! Have tracked you down. Meet at the Tower at 9 p.m.

It was Ruscan, resurrected from wherever he had been for the past year and a half, from whoever he had been. All awareness of the restaurant around her subsided. She could hear only the pounding of her heart in her ears. She'd thought she was over him, but she might have been wrong.

The Tower. Did he mean Signal Hill? He'd found her, so of course that must be what he meant. She quickly glanced at the time. 8:35.

Darrow, by now having lost his reticence, had removed his suit jacket and his lips were moving. The sounds reached her ears but her brain didn't have room for them. He was reaching into his briefcase to remove a single piece of paper.

The nerve of Ruscan, to just reappear without an apology, as if she'd still be waiting for him. As if he hadn't broken her heart and wrung it out to dry. And his lighthearted tone in the email—it sounded as if he wasn't even wounded. The bastard.

"What did you say?" Darrow asked. She looked up to see Darrow looking at her, paper outstretched toward her, an unreadable expression on his face.

"Sorry," she replied. "Sorry, not you." She glanced back at the email to see if there was anything she'd missed. Like an explanation of Ruscan's whereabouts for the past year. All the worry, all of the hours spent trolling the web for a mention of him and watching the European news for a hint of his trail, all that suddenly lifted from her and she knew only one thing. She had to go. Whether to embrace him or throw him off the cliffs to the ocean rocks far below, she wasn't sure, but nevertheless it had to be done. "I'm really sorry," she repeated to Darrow, and she meant it. "But a... an old friend is in town, and I have to go see him. God knows, it might be my only chance before he disappears again."

The man's face melted into neutral. "Of course," he said as the paper slowly crumpled beneath his hands. "You need to go. Catch your friend."

"Thanks for the meal," she said belatedly as she stood and struggled back into her winter coat. She felt in the pockets for Ian's car keys. "It's been great to catch up with you again." She turned to go, then looked back, conscious this was inadequate. "Call me, okay?"

He watched through the plate glass window as she hurried into the night, then took himself out the door, leaving behind the drawing now shredded into a hundred tiny pieces.

The end

·····•·••···

The story of Carmel, Darrow and St. Jude Without continues in Book 3, The Iron Dog, available as Ebook, Paper Back, Large Print and Audio, direct from the author at LizGraham.ca or through your favorite retailer!

Thank you for purchasing this book. If you would like a personally signed book plate, feel visit LizGraham.ca to order!

MORE BOOKS BY LIZ (E M) GRAHAM:

WITCH KIN CHRONICLES (E M GRAHAM)
·An Ignorant Witch, Book 1
·An Arrogant Witch, Book 2
·An Errant Witch, Book 3
·An Obstinate Witch, Book 4
·An Enigmatic Witch, Book 5
·An Embittered Witch, Book 6

CARMEL MCALISTAIR MYSTERIES (LIZ GRAHAM)
·The Cut Throat
·The Garrote
·The Iron Dog
·St. Jude Undone

OTHERS (LIZ GRAHAM)
·An Imperfect Death (The Unlikely Heroine)
·The Auction (An Unlikely Short Story)
·A Northern Romance
·Man from La Manche

All books are available in Ebook, PaperBack, Large Print and Audio formats from LizGraham.ca or through your favorite retailer.